MY
FAVORITE
PHANTOM

MY FAVORITE PHANTOM

Karen Kelley

BRAVA

KENSINGTON PUBLISHING CORP.
http://www.kensingtonbooks.com

BRAVA BOOKS are published by

Kensington Publishing Corp.
850 Third Avenue
New York, NY 10022

All Kensington titles, imprints, and distributed lines are available at special quantity discounts for bulk purchases for sales promotion, premiums, fund-raising, educational, or institutional use.

Special book excerpts or customized printings can also be created to fit specific needs. For details, write or phone the office of the Kensington Special Sales Manager: Attn.: Special Sales Department. Kensington Publishing Corp., 850 Third Avenue, New York, NY 10022. Phone: 1-800-221-2647.

Brava and the B logo Reg. U.S. Pat. & TM Off.

ISBN-13: 978-0-7582-2572-6
ISBN-10: 0-7582-2572-5

First Kensington Trade Paperback Printing: January 2009
10 9 8 7 6 5 4 3 2 1

Printed in the United States of America

Chapter 1

The old Victorian house was haunted.

And how did Kaci Melton know it was haunted? Because nothing had gone right all week—make that all month. It only stood to reason there would be a ghost lurking inside.

Besides, the place just had that creepy, haunted look about it. Dark, gloomy, and forbidding. The three main ingredients for a house with a ghost.

The porch was wide and wrapped around the house and had all the doodads you'd expect in a Queen Anne Victorian. The large, projecting bay windows, towers, and turrets. Not to mention the decorative finials, spindles, and brackets.

At least the color was subdued shades of brown. In the face of all the elaborate swirls and the fancy trim, the beige and coffee colors toned things down somewhat. But then you had the dark, gloomy, and forbidding look to deal with.

All she had to do was step on the gas pedal of her little blue compact and get the hell away from here as fast as she could drive. All the spooky movies she'd ever watched told her to do just that.

But she couldn't run away because she didn't have a choice. Come to think about it, the people in the movies never had a choice, either.

She was doomed.

No choice whatsoever. She had to help her father out of

this mess. She swallowed past the lump in her throat, put the car in park, and turned off the engine. Her hands trembled as she gripped the steering wheel. She wished she knew a calming mantra that would give her the courage to face her fears.

Unfortunately, she didn't.

"Okay, let's get this over with," she mumbled as she opened her car door and got out, eyeing the place with more than a touch of apprehension as she went to the trunk to get some of her things.

Why do I always have to be the one to clean up my father's messes?

Easy answer. She was an only child and her father had no one else. She sighed, knowing he meant well—most of the time.

She dragged a suitcase out of the trunk, then a satchel, shifting the strap on her shoulder so the weight was a little more balanced.

Knowing she'd be spending the next week or so here with some old dude made her queasy. Not because of the stuffy history professor. She could handle an old codger. A ghost was an entirely different matter.

Every step she took, she repeated the only mantra she did know: "I ain't afraid of no ghosts, I ain't afraid of no ghosts . . ."

It didn't seem to be working. It hadn't in *Ghost Busters*, either. She was terrified of ghosts, and she had a feeling they knew it.

A black cat jumped from the bushes and ran across her path. She jerked to a stop. Her heart pounded inside her chest. What the hell was this? Pick on Kaci day?

Stop being such a wimp!

She really hated her voice of reason. Why couldn't it tell her just once to turn around and run for her life? But no, the voice always wanted her to be courageous. *Pffft,* like that would ever happen.

She dragged her suitcase up the steps, cringing at each thump. Thumping noises were not good, either.

After setting her suitcase on the porch, she slipped the strap from her shoulder and set the satchel down as well. Her stomach rumbled. Even her gut was trying to tell her this wasn't a good idea.

She was here now; she might as well see this through. She tugged her baseball cap a little lower on her forehead and rang the bell.

"Act one. Here goes nothin'," she muttered. "You are tough, and you don't take crap off anyone," she said under her breath. *Become the part.* She rolled her shoulders, then tilted her head to the right, then the left.

She was ready. Good thing, too, as footsteps approached. She fervently hoped they were of the human variety—the alive human variety. As in the stodgy-professor-who-lived-here variety.

The door opened, and she looked at the man standing in front of her. Stared, actually. She snapped her mouth closed when she realized it was hanging open and that she probably looked like an imbecile. But this was no stodgy professor—not by a long shot.

He needed a shave, and his hair was tousled, as though he'd just gotten out of bed. Oh, that brought delicious images to mind. Her body tingled to awareness as her gaze moved down his sexy bod.

The white T-shirt he wore stretched nice and taut across his chest, and his jeans rode low on his hips. Her gaze dropped lower. And he was barefoot.

She quickly looked at the numbers beside the front door. Right address. But the man before her couldn't possibly be a history professor. She never had that kind of luck. This man was probably a student or a relative or something.

"I'm here to see Professor Peyton Cache," she told him.

He gave her the once-over. She felt a little insulted. She'd looked at him way longer, practically drooling, while he'd given her only a cursory glance. Damn, she should've put on a little lipstick or something, not worn the dumb cap and the baggy shirt and equally baggy sweatpants. She'd been trying to look the part so she'd be taken seriously, not girly.

"May I help you?" he asked.

"I believe I'm the one who is supposed to help you." That should make him take notice.

His eyebrows drew together in a vee. "Help me with what? Did the dean send you over? Are you a student?"

Or not.

"You called us—" she began, but he interrupted her.

"Listen, I'm expecting . . . someone. I'll talk to the dean later and we can get this straightened out. I told him I didn't need an assistant. I'm really busy, so if you'll excuse me." He shut the door.

Now, that was rude. She leaned forward and peered through the etched glass. He had a nice walk as he padded away from her. Her gaze dropped. A very nice . . . walk.

But she hadn't come here to be dismissed as a college student. Her father needed the money this job would bring. She rapped her knuckles on the door, then straightened when he turned around. His frown changed to a look of irritation as he marched back to the door and opened it.

"I told you . . ."

"Do you want me to get rid of your ghost or not?" she asked, crossing her arms in front of her. "I mean, it's no skin off my nose, buddy. I just thought I'd mention that I'm not one of your preppie college students before I turn around and leave."

"You're the ghost exterminator?" His eyes widened in disbelief.

No, but she wasn't about to tell him the truth.

She cocked an eyebrow. "Yeah, you got a problem with that?"

Okay, that had sounded good. Very tough. As though she

belonged to the mob and was ready to take out anything that got in her way—including a pesky ghost. She only wished she had some gum to chew. Chewing gum would've been a great prop.

His gaze skimmed over her again; then he arched an eyebrow as though he found her lacking. She squared her shoulders and glared at him. If not for her father, she would be so out of here.

"What happened to the man I spoke with?" he asked. "The owner? I thought he'd be the one coming out."

"The boss is busy. Name's Kaci. I work for him." Let him sink his teeth into that. It was her or nothing. But then, she didn't want him to send her away, either. That certainly wouldn't help her father. She softened her tone. "He's working another case."

Hiding, actually. From Guido. Her father owed him money. This job would pay off the two-bit thug, and then they could get on with their lives. She only had to do a little . . . acting and convince the hunk in front of her that she could get rid of his ghost.

She hated being dishonest. But she'd hate it even more if her father was given a pair of concrete boots and dumped over the side of a boat. Not that she really thought that would happen—they'd been in a drought for almost two years.

And besides, she did know how to get rid of ghosts if worse came to worst. They just scared the hell out of her.

Usually, she stayed in the background of her father's business. Way in the background, as in the back of the office buried in paperwork. So, she wasn't being that dishonest. She just had to convince the man in front of her that she was damn good at exterminating ghosts.

And she could get rid of it—probably.

Time for act two.

She lazily looked around the porch, then back at him. "You want me to get rid of the ghost or not?" she asked in a bored tone.

Pushing him to make a decision might not be a good idea, but she had a feeling bringing the ghost back to the forefront of their conversation and reminding him of his problem wouldn't hurt.

Maybe she should've taken up acting. She'd almost had the lead in the school play her senior year, but her father had been a little behind on the rent, and they'd moved.

The professor looked as though he was thinking it over.

She picked up her suitcase and satchel. "Call me if you change your mind."

Please stop me, she silently prayed as she headed down the steps.

"No, wait."

Relief washed over her. Now it was time for the grand finale. She smiled to herself as she started back up the steps. She would've been damn good in the lead, too.

"It's not like I have much choice since Ghost Be Gone was the only ghost exterminator listed in the Yellow Pages," he said as he opened the door a little wider and stepped back so she could enter.

Yeah, she knew they were the only game in town. It was like being the only plumber, except they didn't get the call volume for ghost exterminating that plumbers got for fixing leaky pipes, or the money.

She tightened her hold on the suitcase, adjusted the shoulder strap on the satchel, and then went inside, feeling really good. The professor was desperate.

As soon as she stepped inside, her ego did a downward spiral. She was here to get rid of a ghost, and she didn't like them any more than she had ten minutes ago.

The interior was just as dark and gloomy as the exterior. She didn't like dark and gloomy. And there was a slight musty smell. Her father had told her the professor had recently bought the house. That could account for the dank odor.

But she doubted it.

A ghost could cause certain aromas, too. Sweet and pleasant if it was a happy spirit or, she swallowed hard, musty if it wasn't.

Her palms began to sweat, almost causing her to drop the suitcase. Her stomach churned. She wanted to turn around, tell him there'd been a big mistake, and leave. She could almost feel the energy emanating from the spirit. She was almost certain it wasn't going to go softly toward the light.

"Is that your equipment?" he asked.

"Clothes," she mumbled as she glanced up the shadowed staircase. Where were all the lights in this house?

"Clothes?" he asked.

She looked at him then. Damn, he was a hottie. He was the only good thing that had happened to her all week. She had a weakness for men with deep blue eyes and thick dark hair and . . . actually, now that she thought about it, she had a weakness for hotties, and he was certainly that.

Concentrate! It would not do to let her guard down while there was a ghost in the house—if that was the case, and she was almost certain it was, even though she didn't have concrete proof yet.

"Yes, my clothes are in the suitcase," she answered him.

"As in, you'll be staying here?"

At least until the coast was clear to return home. Her father was working on a haunting in another state—where he'd be safe—for now, and hopefully, he'd also bring some money in from that job.

She cocked an eyebrow. "What? You thought I carried a can of ghost spray? A couple of squirts and no more ghost?" Her accent sounded good. Very New Jerseyish, and less like her slow, Texas drawl.

He frowned. Even that looked sexy as hell. Man, she was in so much trouble already. A ghost, a sexy hunk—she hoped there were no meteors traveling to Earth right now.

"Actually, I figured you'd hang garlic from the rafters or something," he said, sarcasm dripping from his words.

Oh, that was really snarky. Very well done. "Garlic only works on vampires," she told him.

"No," he began. "I didn't think you'd get rid of the spirit that easily. But I didn't think you'd have to stay the night."

The professor didn't look convinced that she needed to remain at the house. Time for more acting. Acting sounded so much better than telling herself she was flat out lying to the man.

She opened her satchel and brought out a cheap little meter, holding it high as she turned in a circle. When she faced the stairs, she pushed a button so the meter made a buzzing noise.

It was fake, of course, but it always seemed to reassure people more if you had a lot of gadgets.

"I should be so lucky that it only takes one night," she said as she dropped the meter back in her satchel.

"The dinner I'm hosting is in less than two weeks. The ghost has to be eliminated by then," he told her. "I don't want anyone getting hurt or scared to death."

"Then you'd better show me to my room so I can get settled in."

He frowned, and for a second or two, she thought this might be the end of her stay.

"Upstairs," he finally said.

Apparently, she was the lesser of two evils. She wasn't sure she liked the idea that she rated barely above a pesky ghost.

Peyton closed the door behind him, leaving Kaci to get settled into the guest room. His eyes narrowed as he stood there for a moment and digested everything that had happened. Kaci hadn't looked like a ghost hunter. At least, what he thought one should look like.

He was pretty certain she was a female, but with a name like Kaci, she could be male or female. It was hard to tell when she wore baggy sweats and that baseball cap pulled low on her forehead.

And she'd talked as though she were part of the mob or

something. This was Texas. Did they have mafia in this state? He didn't think so. Maybe she wasn't from here.

He scraped his hair back with his fingers.

What the hell was he doing? Calling a ghost exterminator hadn't been a good idea. If the dean or any of the faculty got wind of it, they'd think he was crazy.

Not that he cared much what people thought about him as long as he got to teach, but there was some grant money up for grabs, and he could use it for his research. He seriously doubted he would get it if people thought he'd lost his mind.

Hell, maybe he had.

In the beginning, he'd figured all the odd things that were happening had to be college pranks. He was new to the area. He'd thought it might be some kind of initiation or something. But it hadn't stopped, and when he'd questioned a couple of the students, they'd looked at him as though he'd lost his mind.

No, there was a ghost.

Personally, he'd never really believed in ghosts. Then he'd bought the Victorian. Now he believed.

He'd move if all his money weren't tied up in this place. Besides, the fact was he refused to let something dead scare him away. Calling Ghost Be Gone was a last-ditch effort to lead a normal life.

Except he was running out of time.

Whatever was happening—haunting, poltergeist—it had to stop in less than two weeks. That was when he was hosting the faculty dinner. The dean would be there.

Not that the ghost had done any real damage—yet. So far, only his underwear had sprouted wings and flown through the house, but would the ghost get tired of silly pranks? What would go flying through the air next? The dean? Yeah, right, that would help his cause—not.

He went downstairs. But when he paused on the bottom step and looked behind him, he saw the green mist beginning to form. His stomach churned. There was little that had ever bothered him, but he had to admit, the ghost did exactly that, and then some.

The mist moved to the right, then the left. Slow, deliberate movements.

It was taunting him. Damn it, this was his house! It might have been the ghost's at one time, but that time was gone. "Just wait, buddy, your time here is just about over," he muttered.

The mist slowly faded, but the chill remained. Damned creepy. Okay, he'd try Kaci for a few days and see if the ghost would leave.

He went into the kitchen and grabbed a soda out of the fridge, then continued straight out the backdoor, sitting in one of the patio chairs. His safe place on the property. The ghost hadn't bothered him out here—yet.

Kaci had looked tough enough to whip any ghost.

Had it been an act? The company hadn't come with references. How did you check out a place like that? He couldn't very well call around asking people if they knew anything about Ghost Be Gone.

Hell, they could be shysters for all he knew. A big waste of his money and time. Except they hadn't asked for money up front. So maybe they were on the level.

He pulled the tab on the can of soda, then took a swallow, letting the cool liquid slide down his throat. A gentle breeze whispered through the oak that stood tall and proud at the edge of the patio.

He glanced around at the low bushes and the deep green of the grass. This was one of the reasons he wanted the house. The terra-cotta patio offered relaxation at the end of a long day. And just like the first time he saw it, some of his tenseness began to ease, and he could feel himself relaxing.

He just needed to get rid of his unwanted guest.

That handheld thing Kaci had waved around the room looked real enough, and it buzzed. Apparently, it had detected the ghost. Not that he needed to be told there was one in the house. It had only confirmed what he already knew.

Equipment aside, from what he'd seen of Kaci, the exterminator didn't look that old. How much experience did one need to get rid of a ghost?

He shifted in his chair.

Now that he thought about it, he was pretty sure she was a female. From what little he'd seen, that is. Her face was too smooth to have ever been touched by a razor. He frowned. He wasn't sure he liked the idea of a woman living here with him. It could present problems he wasn't prepared to deal with—nor did he want to. She'd be under his feet, getting in his way, bothering him . . .

Hell, he knew the real reason he didn't want her in the house: he had a weakness for women. Always had. His siblings had teased him unmercifully, calling him Don Juan—more so now that he was teaching that other class.

Kaci hadn't looked as if she would be that hard to resist, though. Not when she wore baggy clothes and that cap. He snorted. It hadn't been that long since he'd gone on a date. Okay, he was safe. No worries.

"I just wanted to let you know I'll be coming in and out of the house as I bring my equipment in," a voice spoke behind him, softer than before but still with a slight edge.

"Good. The sooner you can rid me of my problem, the better." He set his soda can on the table and stood, turning around to face her.

His mouth dropped open. No, no, no! What happened to the baggy clothes and the baseball cap pulled down low, and she hadn't looked like this and . . . Damn it!

He waved his arm in front of him. "You changed." Where were her other clothes? The ones that made her safe. Hell, the ones that made *him* safe.

She wore short shorts that showed off long, wrap-around-his-waist-and-pull-him-in-closer legs, and a little blue tank top that stretched across her full breasts. And no more baseball cap. Now her long, beautiful blond hair tumbled over her shoulders.

She glanced down, then shrugged. "I'm cold-natured in the mornings. By afternoon, I get hot. I'll start getting my equipment." She turned and left the patio.

His glanced dropped to her sweet little ass. His mouth started to water.

By afternoon she got hot? Was that what she'd said? That was the understatement of the year. He wasn't sure what was going to be worse, the ghost or keeping his hands off the sexy exterminator.

Damn, he hadn't bargained for this. It seemed the hole he was getting precariously closer to falling inside just kept getting deeper and deeper.

Damn, she'd had a really nice twist in her walk, though.

No, he would not seduce Kaci. She was off limits—at least until she got rid of the ghost. But his mouth was already starting to water.

When his cell phone rang, he pulled it out of his pocket and flipped it open. He glanced at the number. His older brother. Great. He frowned. Things just got better and better.

"Hello."

"Hey, Peyton. How's it going? Has your ghost exterminator arrived?"

Peyton heard the unmistakable laughter in his brother's voice. Why had he even told Joe about his ghost? "Yeah, she's here."

"She?" The humor immediately vanished.

"Yeah."

"Get rid of her. You know how you are with women. It'll be the same as the last town."

He shook his head. "The last town, as you like to refer to it, was nothing more than a young woman who was infatuated with her professor. Nothing happened. I only left because I wanted to teach this other class as well as my history class and the dean offered me that opportunity. Have a little faith. Besides, I do have a ghost, and she can get rid of it."

"She stalked you." His sigh came over the phone lines. "A woman to you is like someone on a diet crashing into a candy store. You know you can't change. At least tell me she's ugly."

Okay, he could do that. "She's ugly." He wasn't lying or anything. Just telling Joe what he'd asked to be told. "I can't get rid of her until the ghost is gone."

"Please, just be careful."

"I'm always careful." Joe was acting as though he had a disease or something. Hell, maybe he did, but he really enjoyed a woman's company.

"If you need anything, I'm only a phone call away."

"Yeah, thanks, bro." He closed the phone, then slipped it into his pocket as he walked toward the front door.

Man, he should've told Joe not to tell his other brother or his sister. If they got wind there was a woman living with him, even if it was business, he'd never hear the last of it.

Could he help it if he loved women? It wouldn't matter if Kaci had been old or young. There was just something about women that he loved. All women.

The baggy sweats and cap had made her safer, though. Sort of.

But he would stay on guard around her. Just as soon as he helped her carry in the rest of her things. A slow grin curved his lips. She was damned sexy.

For just a moment, he closed his eyes and lost himself in the fantasy of her body pressed against his. Her naked body. His hands caressing her.

He quickly shook off the image.

Damn it, he was not going to sleep with her.

He wasn't.

Chapter 2

Not good. Kaci had sent Peyton into shock. She hadn't meant to—okay, maybe she had a little. When his mouth dropped open, she'd had her moment of victory.

Oh, yeah! And it had been so sweet.

Now let him think she looked frumpy. And he had. He'd taken one look, then dismissed her. Not worthy of his attention.

She hated when people did that.

And he was such a hottie! Definitely drool worthy.

Guilt swept over her. Okay, maybe she hadn't played fair when she'd intentionally dressed down before arriving at his home. But then, he was supposed to be an old dude, not a young hunk.

Professors were not supposed to look like Peyton. They should have gray hair, at least at the temples. And maybe a potbelly. A bulging stomach would've fit her mental picture of a professor.

That's all she had, too. She didn't know any professors, having never gone to college. Her high school teachers had all been old and acted as though they made a habit of sucking on lemons. Except maybe a couple that were kind of cool and saved her from detesting school.

But as far as the others went . . .

She'd had one algebra teacher who wore a constant dark

scowl and always pointed at his students with his great big fingers. He'd had fat lips, and one eyebrow was always raised as though his students weren't worthy to even look upon his greatness—which she tried not to do. He scared the crap out of her, and everyone else, for that matter.

Having Peyton look at her as though she were a hottie was sweet, though. He'd think twice before judging a book by its cover or a woman by the clothes she wore.

She smiled as she trotted down the steps, then across the sidewalk to where she'd parked her car. Her smiled drooped as she took a real good look at it.

Her car was an eyesore. There was no getting around the fact that the only things holding it together were rust, dents, and a whole lot of duct tape. Someday she planned to trade it in. But someday hadn't gotten here yet. Besides, it was faithful—most of the time.

She unlocked the trunk. It screamed like a banshee when she opened it. She really needed to oil it again. Damned embarrassing. She began to haul out the rest of her stuff. She had three cases in varying sizes and one more bag. Before she could grab the heaviest, strong hands brushed hers away.

"Let me get that," Peyton said.

"This is what you're paying me for," she said.

He turned to look at her, which put their faces only inches apart, and she got the full effect of the most beautiful blue eyes and dark thick lashes that she'd ever seen on a man. It should be a crime a man could look this sexy.

She sighed, enjoying the warmth of his breath caressing her cheek. How fantastic would it be to wake up beside him every morning? He could caress her with his heated breath or anything else. Peyton still hadn't shaved. She imagined his stubble would scrape, chafing her tender skin.

Damned if she wouldn't mind seeing just how much damage he could do.

"But if you get a hernia, you might sue me," he said as he grabbed the case and hauled it out. "Nice car, by the way."

"It runs." She was the only one allowed to talk about her car.

"Really?"

"Yes, really." She stepped back and straightened. So much for thinking there might be a little chemistry going on between them.

"It reminds me of my first car." He laughed. "I drove it until there wasn't anything left of it. Looked like crap, but it got me where I wanted to go—most of the time."

Okay, so maybe he wasn't making fun of her car in the way she'd thought.

"What's all this, anyway?" he asked. "And that thing you used before. The one that buzzed. What was that?"

"A GeoMag module. It measures flux density."

At least, it had until it broke and her father replaced it with the dollar store buzzer. It was a piece of equipment her father said they didn't really need.

But Peyton looked as though he wanted to know more, so she elaborated. "It picks up changes in the geomagnetic field." When he still looked confused, she continued. "Where ghosts hang out." At least that wasn't a lie.

He nodded. "And you detected paranormal activity."

A shiver ran down her spine. She glanced at the old Victorian, saw a slight shifting of shadow to light, and knew a cloud hadn't gone in front of the sun.

"Yes, you have a ghost."

"But you'll get rid of it with all this equipment. Right?"

"I hope so," she muttered, then in a stronger voice, "If not, you don't have to pay anything."

That was her father's policy, and he always stuck by it. She wished he was as conscientious about paying his debts. A weird set of values, but basically, he was a good man. And he did try. She'd give him that.

He shifted the case and grabbed another one, but stopped before he pulled it out of the trunk and looked at her. He was frowning again. She should mention that caused wrinkles, but he looked so good when his forehead puckered. Almost like a pirate about to ravage her. One could only hope.

"Why doesn't not having to pay if you can't get rid of my ghost make me feel better?" he asked.

Yep, damned cute. She wondered if he had a girlfriend. Probably. Most of the hotties she came in contact with were taken. Either that or he had something major wrong with him.

"Are you seeing anyone?" she blurted.

Damn, she wanted to bite her tongue, but it was too late. Sometimes she amazed herself with the stuff that came out of her mouth, which came from spending too much time alone.

She was here to do a job. That should be the only thing on her mind. Except now he'd probably tell her to hit the road. But he didn't. In fact, one side of his mouth turned up in a lazy smile.

"No, want to apply for that position as well?" he said with a lazy drawl.

Her body sizzled with the heat he stirred inside her. God, he had the cutest twinkle in his eyes. The man was absolutely irresistible.

"Do all professors look like you?" she asked, instead of answering.

"Do you always ask a lot of questions?"

The ice she was walking on was getting awfully thin. She grabbed the other satchel and the lightest of the bags, then started toward the house. "Pretty much." She stopped and looked over her shoulder, giving him what she hoped was a saucy look. She was so bad. "Does it bother you?"

He slammed the trunk closed and started up the sidewalk. "There's a lot about you that bothers me."

They were flirting. And it felt fantastic! When was the last time she'd flirted with anyone? High school? No, it hadn't been that long ago. But it had been a long time since it'd been this fun.

Which was crazy, of course. The ghost should be the only

thing panting and moaning. *Think job!* She couldn't let her guard down.

But she wasn't ready to end the teasing banter between them. "Should I lock my door tonight?" she asked.

"For your protection or mine?"

Oh, definitely his. Just the thought of him in her bed made her body tingle to awareness. As she reached the front door, it slammed shut, saving her from answering. The wind? She stopped, glancing around. Not a leaf stirred.

"It does that a lot," Peyton told her. "Even when there's no breeze whatsoever." He looked up at the trees as if to confirm what he'd just told her.

She swallowed hard. The ghost. That was all it could have been. Fear washed over her. Not only did Peyton have a ghost, but it was apparently a jealous one. Ghosts did that sometimes. Attached themselves to a human, then didn't want anyone encroaching on their territory.

She could handle this. For her father, she reminded herself.

Except her feet didn't get the message. They wouldn't budge. Not even one tiny baby step. It was as though someone had poured quick-drying glue on the soles of her shoes.

"You okay?" Peyton asked as he went around her and opened the door. He laughed. "Don't tell me you're afraid of ghosts. You're an exterminator."

She looked at him. He waited for an answer. She smiled, hoping it didn't come off sickly. "*Pffft*, of course I'm not afraid of ghosts. I mean, I am a ghost hunter." She waltzed past him and inside the house, so glad her feet finally decided to move.

She'd sounded good, too. Her voice had been strong and didn't betray a bit of the abject terror she'd felt.

Her father was so going to pay for getting her into this fix. If Peyton discovered she was afraid of ghosts, he'd probably kick her out on her butt—no matter how cute he thought it was. And from the looks he'd been giving her, she knew he liked what he saw. At all costs, she could not let him know she was scared to death.

"Where do you want this stuff?" he asked.

Be professional, she told herself. It was the only way she was going to pull this off. "In what room do you notice the most activity?"

"My study. I practically live in that room."

"Television? Radio?"

"And a computer if you need it."

She nodded. "Do you have trouble with any of your electronics?"

"Yeah, I thought it was the wiring or something. It's an old house."

"Paranormal events can cause electrical disturbances." It was nice to know she'd picked up a lot of information from her father over the years. The next time she talked to him, she'd tell him that she'd been paying attention.

Peyton nodded, and led the way to the other room. The study wasn't quite as dark and dreary as the rest of the house. The walls were a cheerful butter color. White curtains with yellow trim hung over the windows. She set the cases down.

"Very pretty," she said.

"It's about the only room I've completely finished. The other rooms I've only started on."

"It has a very calm feeling. Probably why the ghost likes it." She opened one of the cases and brought out the machine.

"What does this equipment do?" he asked, nodding toward the machine she was putting together.

"Each instrument has a different task. This one will let me know whether there's any paranormal activity or not."

One thing she could say for her dad, most of what he had was state-of-the-art—except for the little buzzer from the dollar store. He'd probably replace that once he was out of debt to Guido.

She'd tried to fix it, but it was beyond repair. She might not be the greatest with the books, but she was damned good when it came to fixing things.

She looked around the room. It was pretty with long, flow-ing sheer curtains—almost feminine. "Why did you buy the Vic?" she asked when she looked back at him.

"I'm a history professor." He shrugged. "The Victorian time period is interesting."

Damn, why hadn't she picked up on it sooner? He didn't have a girlfriend. He liked an age where men wore frilly stuff on their shirts and buckles on their shoes. His study was—pretty, and a little on the froufrou side. The professor was gay.

It wouldn't be the first time a gay man had flirted with her, then laughed his butt off when he had her to the point of dragging him to her apartment and into her bed. That's what Rob had done. He couldn't stop laughing. It had been a sick joke, and she'd fallen for it. Never again.

This had been a close call. She'd been having all these sexual thoughts. Hell, Peyton didn't like her ass; he liked her short shorts.

"I can almost see the wheels turning inside your head. Do you have something against history or that particular era?" he asked.

She might have his number, but she certainly didn't want to offend him at this point in time. Money was an issue here. "No, of course not," she told him.

It was a shame. Peyton didn't have a girlfriend, but she'd bet her last dollar he had a boyfriend. What a waste for the female population.

Not that she'd thought there might be a chance of getting up close and personal while she was here. She was on the job, so to speak. It had been an awfully long time since a man held her close, and she'd enjoyed the feel of his strong arms around her.

The last guy she'd met might as well have had "loser" tattooed and flashing on his forehead. He'd dressed nice enough, but she just hadn't been able to get past the fact he snorted when he laughed.

Even that wouldn't have bothered her so much except his

nose turned up a little, add that his nostrils also flared when he snorted, and his cheeks were kind of pink. She might even have gotten around all that if he hadn't groped her under the table on their first date. When she'd called him a pig, she'd meant it.

That was the last time she'd been on a blind date. Maybe she'd try that Internet place that matched people up. The bar scene wasn't her thing. And she didn't want to meet a nice guy in church.

No, she was looking for a bad boy. A guy in a leather jacket and riding a motorcycle.

It had been a fantasy of hers since Erik Bonner had walked into class her freshman year. She'd wanted to eat him alive right then and there.

Damn, he'd been scrumptious. Dark hair that was a little too long, and a little scruffy, but wearing a sexy leather jacket and a pair of tight, low-riding jeans.

When he'd turned and looked at everyone, there'd been a collective sigh from the girls in the room. His gaze had lingered when it landed on her; then he'd winked.

Well, actually, he'd been flirting with Sandy Carlson, who sat right in front of her. Not that she blamed Erik. Sandy had been stacked and she wore tight sweaters in case someone didn't notice. Tight sweaters and short skirts.

Kaci, on the other hand, had been flat as a pancake, wore braces, and pretty much went unnoticed by everyone, including the teachers. Which wasn't a bad thing since the math teacher had scared the hell out of her.

And maybe it had been a good thing Erik hadn't noticed her. Six months later Sandy was knocked up. Did she not listen in sex ed? Duh, condom.

Peyton cleared his throat as he sat in the chair, drawing her attention back to him. Very unnerving having him watching while she set up her equipment. It didn't help knowing he was probably more interested in what she was doing rather than being in her company because he might get lucky.

"What do you like to do when you're not getting rid of ghosts?" he suddenly asked.

A lame attempt at conversation? Did he not know that he didn't have to play host? Okay, she'd bite.

What did she like to do? She thought about it as she went back to work and rolled out the cords, making sure they wouldn't be a hazard.

"You do have interests, don't you?"

"Of course I do." She looked up, frowning. He was being a smart-ass now. "I read a lot."

"What do you read?"

"Romances mostly."

"Romances?"

She really hated the condescension in his voice. Just a trace, but it was there. She stopped what she was doing to look at him. "So, let me get this straight, your interests consist of an age that was full of frippery, and you own a house with fancy scroll work, but you're going to judge me because I like relationship books?" She raised an eyebrow.

"Not judge. Only surprised."

Darn, she'd jumped to the wrong conclusion. She'd just thought . . . that was what she got for thinking. It got her into trouble all the time.

She stood and went to another case and opened it. "Why would you be surprised?" she asked as she looked inside.

"You don't strike me as the type who would enjoy romances."

"And what type am I?" She didn't think she liked the turn of the conversation, but she was interested in knowing what he thought about her. How did she come off?

"No-nonsense. You're all business." He leaned back in his chair and stared at her.

For a gay man, he had a way of looking at her as though he would like more than a platonic relationship. Had she misjudged and labeled him wrong?

No, it was much safer to think of him as off limits in that area.

"I'm working," she told him. "I believe in doing a job right." She glanced around at all the stuff she'd laid out. "And if you want me to get rid of your ghost, then I suggest you let me do my job."

"You're right." He gathered some papers and stood. "I'll leave you to your work."

She frowned as she watched him walk out of the room. He didn't have to take her so literally. She'd enjoyed the company. She was so used to being alone that someone to talk to had been nice. Peyton had seemed genuinely interested in what she was doing.

Was she all business? He'd said she was. She stooped to insert a multiplug into one of the outlets, then sat back on her heels. She thought back to the last few years working in her father's business, mainly in the back room trying to keep his books straight, which was an almost impossible feat, and when she wasn't doing that, she was working on broken equipment.

She didn't have a lot of friends that she went out with. It was hard for her to get close to people. Probably because of years of moving around. She missed having friends.

She stood, looking at the machines. Why was she even doing this? She walked to the window, looking out at the semibusy street, and her old rusty car parked at the curb.

If she tried something else, she would have to step out into the unknown, and that frightened her almost as much as ghosts.

She leaned her head against the glass pane. Maybe someday she would take that first step and reach for what she really wanted in life.

If she ever figured out what that was.

She sighed and turned.

Cold enveloped her. Fingers of death caressing her skin.

She gasped, taking a step back. It almost felt as though the life were being sucked right out of her. She plopped down on the window seat. The feeling was gone in an instant, leaving her trembling from head to foot.

Oh, God, she'd almost wet her pants. The faint sound of mocking laughter echoed through the room. The ghost. Being scared half to death was so not good.

"You think it's funny now, but just wait," she muttered, not at all brave, but it made her feel a hell of a lot better to sound courageous. She really hated a ghost who got its kicks from terrifying people.

"Did you hear that?" Peyton rushed in, coming to a stop in the middle of the room and looking around as though trying to see if anything appeared out of the ordinary.

"Hear what?" she managed to ask.

If he saw her shaking hands, he'd probably guess that she and the ghost had crossed paths, then wonder why she was scared silly. She was the ghost hunter, after all. She couldn't let him see her fear. She would get through this. At least, she hoped she would.

"Laughter," he said. "I thought I heard someone laughing. I could've sworn . . ."

"I told myself a joke I'd never heard before," she said as she came to her feet and moved to the computer.

"Are you okay? You look a little pale."

"Perfectly fine. Why wouldn't I be?"

He shook his head. "Sorry to bother you."

"No problem." She smiled. "By the way, where's the bathroom located on this floor?"

"Second door on the right. Just past the dining room."

"Thanks." She scooted past him and walked as casually as her shaking body would let her, going straight to the bathroom. She hadn't even been here an hour and she'd already been scared out of her skull. Not good at all.

She was so going to kill her father for sticking her with this job, and getting into debt with that two-bit hood Guido. Really, who would borrow money from someone with a name like

Guido? He might as well have worn a T-shirt that said, "You don't pay, I dump you over the side of a boat wearing concrete boots." It didn't take a genius to figure out the guy was bad news.

Her father never looked at what the end result could be. He never planned ahead. And she always got caught in the middle. Never failed.

But Peyton was an unexpected bonus. A very sexy bonus even though he was gay. Shoot, that just made him safe. And looking never hurt anyone.

She squirted soap on her hands. The tropical fragrance rose to her nose. She inhaled the soothing aroma and imagined the two of them alone on an island, soaking up the sun and each other.

An icy chill suddenly washed over her. Okay, enough daydreaming. She dried her hands and quickly exited the bathroom.

She had a ghost to get rid of!

Just as soon as the queasy feeling was gone.

Chapter 3

Peyton watched as Kaci left the room. She was acting funny. Not like he'd expect a ghost hunter to act. He leaned against his desk, staring at the door. What was it about her that bothered him? She came across as tough, edgy, but a ghost hunter would need all those strengths. That couldn't be what bothered him.

The phone on his desk rang. Damn, he hoped it wasn't another sibling. Pete wasn't too bad, but Becca was a different story altogether. She'd decorated the study for him. Kind of frilly. But it was growing on him—sort of. That, and he wouldn't hurt her feelings for anything.

He turned and picked up the phone. "Hello."

"Peyton, Daniel here."

He frowned. His day had just gotten darker. Daniel was okay if one wasn't around him for long periods of time. He took himself too literally. That, and he had all the trappings of what he thought it took to be a professor: pipe, except he never smoked it, a fedora, and a scarf that hung down on either side of his long, black tweed coat. And he had just a trace of a bad English accent. Someone told Peyton that Daniel was originally from Ohio and had never even been to England.

Whatever rocked his boat.

"Hello, Daniel. What can I do for you?"

"I wanted to inform you that I'll be bringing a guest to the dinner party. Will that be an imposition?" His words were stiff, nasally, and very proper.

Daniel had a girlfriend? Peyton tried to picture Daniel with a woman, but the visual just wouldn't quite form. It would be interesting to meet this other person.

"Of course not," he told him. "Bring whomever you like. A girlfriend?" He had to know. Curiosity would kill him if he didn't.

"A colleague who's visiting."

Of course. Should've known.

He looked around the room at all the equipment and said a silent prayer that Kaci would be able to get rid of the ghost by then.

"No problem," he said.

"Very well, old chap, looking forward to the get-together."

He just bet Daniel was since he was after that grant money, too.

They spoke for a few more minutes, then said good-bye. Daniel was a fake. Peyton had gotten his number after talking to him for less than ten minutes. So far, he'd managed to be civil, but just barely. The guy was like a mosquito that wouldn't die.

"Oh, you're still in here," Kaci said as she returned.

He looked up, his eyes narrowed as he studied her. That's what wasn't meshing. There was something about Kaci that didn't quite ring true. Fake. She was a bit like Daniel. Yeah, something wasn't exactly right.

"What?" she asked.

He shook his head.

It was worth exploring—later. There was a lot about Kaci he'd like to explore. Like her luscious lips, her sensuous body . . .

"You're staring. Is something the matter?"

"No, nothing." He started toward the door, but turned before walking out. "I have a meeting, then classes this afternoon. Help yourself to any food in the house."

She clasped her hands together. "Thanks."

She acted nervous. Or was he starting to imagine something that wasn't there?

He left the room. The ghost had put him on edge. He was starting to doubt everyone around him. That wasn't good. Kaci would get rid of the apparition, and his life would return to normal. It had to.

He walked up the steps, glancing around as he did. The ghost loved to jump out at him. It was getting bolder. But Peyton made it to his room without mishap. He took a quick shower, shaved, then dressed.

As he walked past the study on his way out, he could hear Kaci talking to herself. She mumbled, so he couldn't quite make out her words. She was a very odd woman. Odd and extremely unnerving.

He wasn't sure how it was going to work out with the two of them staying in the same house. Maybe the ghost would be gone by the time he returned.

Kaci heard the front door close and glanced out the window. Peyton strode past. She stepped closer, her heart beating a little faster. He wore a leather jacket, and jeans. A black leather jacket. And low-riding jeans. Just like the jacket Erik Bonner had worn in high school. Her mouth watered now just as it had back then.

She didn't breathe easier until he disappeared inside the garage; then she slumped to the window seat. What was it about black leather that turned her on so much? Maybe she had a dormant fantasy to be a dominatrix.

A roar drew her attention back to the garage. She shook her head. The garage door slowly rose. No, this just wasn't fair—not fair at all.

Peyton pulled out of the garage on a badass motorcycle.

She took in the sleek, low contours of the black bike and chrome mufflers. A fully restored Indian motorcycle. Parts alone for the bike were hard to come by, and yet, he owned one. Her gaze stayed glued to the window as he roared down the street.

Okay, now she really was drooling.

God, he was the embodiment of James Dean, a young Marlon Brando, Johnny Depp, Justin Timberlake—okay, maybe not Justin. Definitely James Dean, though.

She pressed her nose to the glass, watching until he turned the corner and was out of sight. Then she slowly melted back down to the cushioned seat, grabbing one of the pink embroidered pillows and hugging it close.

What had she done to deserve this? History professors weren't supposed to be hunks or drive badass motorcycles or wear sexy black leather jackets.

Nor should they be gay!

Well, she hadn't exactly established that fact. He hadn't flirted as though he were gay. She leaned back against the pillows on the window seat and looked thoughtfully out the glass panes.

Maybe he was straight. Oh, the possibilities that swirled inside her head. Her body tingled to awareness. Until she glanced down at the pretty pink pillow with "Home Is Where The Heart Is" embroidered in red thread. Yeah, right.

The phone rang, cutting into her heated thoughts. She uncurled herself from the window seat and hurried over to answer it.

"Hello."

Silence.

"Helloooo?"

"I'm terribly sorry. I seem to have dialed the wrong number," an English sort of sounding voice said. "I was trying to reach Peyton Cache again. Forgot to tell the old chap something."

The accent was awful. She thought about mentioning that

fact, but it was no skin off her nose if he wanted to pretend to be English. People should just be themselves. She cringed. Ouch, that hit a little too close to home. As though she weren't trying to pretend to be a full-time ghost hunter.

"He's not here," she told him instead.

Silence.

This guy was really spaced out. Drugs?

"I didn't know there was a female staying at his home. I apologize if I sounded shocked."

Shocked? Great. Peyton was gay. Why else would this guy be stunned there was a female in Peyton's house. Oh, Lord, what if they were in a relationship?

"He just hired me to clean his house. I certainly don't live here." She really doubted Peyton would want her to tell anyone she was a ghost exterminator. People were funny about that.

Was that a relieved sigh?

"Of course. I should've guessed."

He didn't sound apologetic, and what the hell had he meant when he'd said he should've guessed? Unless Peyton was gay.

"You said he's not there? Is that correct?"

This guy was a real flake. "Correct, and I really need to get back to work since he's paying me by the hour."

"Certainly. I'll catch him at the university." He hung up without even a good-bye.

Humph. He'd treated her as though she were the hired help. Well, technically, that's what she'd told him she was, so she couldn't really fault him for that, except he didn't have to be condescending about it.

She set the phone back in the cradle and leaned against the desk. Apparently, her first assumption was right about Peyton, though. What a waste—for her, that is. She didn't have the right to judge anyone for his sexual preference.

She glanced around the room, feeling the isolation that always seemed to be with her. She was all alone again. Something rattled outside the door. A shiver of apprehension ran down her spine.

Alone, except for the ghost.

"You could make this easy on the both of us and just leave," she said. Silence. Not that she thought the ghost would agree, then leave. Her life had never been easy. Why would she think it would change now?

The hours moved slowly after she got everything set up. With time on her hands, she began to worry. Was this a prankish spirit or an evil spirit? It was unlikely that it was a bad spirit, but there was always that possibility. Evil spirits were rare and didn't interact with humans that often. Those spirits had never been human.

The other spirits were the ones trapped on Earth for one reason or another. Maybe guilt kept them here. Sometimes they didn't know they were dead. For whatever reason, she usually let her father deal with them. Ghosts were not her cup of tea. She didn't even like tea.

But she did believe in keeping her promise, and she'd told her father that she'd help him out—again.

She glanced at her watch. Three o'clock. Goose bumps popped up on her arms as a cold chill swept over her. Most spirits were quiet during the day. They didn't get wound up until the evening hours, usually after six, and then they would stop in the wee hours of the morning.

Except this one had come before the usual time. The spirit's way of warning her that she was the interloper.

Not good.

Now that she thought about it, Guido wasn't that bad of a person. He probably wouldn't do anything to her father except rattle his cage a little.

But she couldn't be certain.

Okay, so she was pretty much stuck here. And she had a few hours to check out the rest of the house. If something happened and she had to make a quick escape, she wanted to make sure the door she opened led away from the house and not inside a broom closet where she might become trapped.

She went down the hallway and into the large kitchen. This room certainly hadn't been renovated. Tall, dark cabinets reached almost to the ceiling. The only new additions were the refrigerator and stove.

You could tell a lot about a person by what was in their refrigerator. Besides the fact that she was hungry. She opened the door. Well stocked. It either meant he didn't want to make many trips to the grocery store or he had a very healthy appetite. It could mean he had a lot of company, too.

It was a good thing Peyton had offered to feed her. She didn't have much of a choice since she had only five dollars to her name. She reached inside the refrigerator and pulled out the chocolate milk—a man after her own heart. And it wasn't expired. Glory days were here again!

She was addicted to chocolate milk. Just couldn't get enough of the stuff. She poured a glass, then returned the carton and closed the door.

The pantry yielded peanut butter and jelly and a loaf of fresh bread. All her favorite food groups. Who could ask for anything more?

She cleaned up after she finished eating, then set about checking out the rest of the house. There wasn't much else downstairs besides the parlor, the kitchen, the dining room and Peyton's study, and thankfully, the bathroom.

The parlor was nice with a big fireplace. She could envision herself and Peyton curled up on the sofa on a cold winter's night.

She sighed.

It didn't matter that he was gay. She was entitled to a fantasy or two. And her fantasies were really, really good. She closed her eyes and mentally slipped the black leather coat on Peyton. No shirt, just the open coat and low-riding jeans.

Oh, yeah, that's what she was talking about.

She sighed. It was so not going to happen.

Back to work.

Upstairs yielded what looked to be another guest room, and Peyton's room. She furtively glanced around the hallway before slipping inside his room. All clear. What had she expected? That Peyton would catch her sneaking into his bedroom? There wasn't any danger of getting caught. She'd hear the motorcycle when it pulled up.

The room was masculine—thank goodness. She'd been afraid it would have pink frilly stuff everywhere. Tassels hanging from fringe-trimmed light shades and what have you. Nope, she didn't want an image of Peyton sleeping amongst pink frills.

Thankfully, she didn't have to. The walls were beige and the bedding a chocolate color without even one fringed pillow. It definitely looked like a man's room.

She ran her hand across the dresser. Clean. No dust. That didn't make him gay because he liked cleanliness. She went to the far side of the bed where a picture sat, her heart sank when she picked it up, and she plopped down on the edge of the bed.

Okay, the evidence was building against him. He stood with a man, and the man had his arm around Peyton. It could be a relative. She brought the picture closer to her face and squinted as she stared harder but couldn't see a resemblance. The man in the picture was blond, and he had the look of a man deeply in love.

Darn. She wasn't going to get laid while she was here. She might as well face facts.

Back to business. She returned the picture to the end table and stood, straightening the covers before she left the room. She'd hate if he returned and found an indentation of her butt on his bed.

As she stepped into the hall, she looked around. Something bothered her. There had been a set of windows above the second floor. There was an attic somewhere. Not that she wanted to go up there, but knowing each room was part of the job.

There was a door at the end of the hall. She glanced at her watch, despite the fact that this ghost didn't seem to have a set timetable. It was still early, though.

Kaci drew in a slow, steady breath as she continued to stare at the door without moving from her spot.

What was the worst that the ghost could do?

It could scare her to death, that's what. Then Peyton would have a real mess on his hands. Two ghosts and a dead body. Let him try to clean that up before his faculty dinner. And her father would still be in the fix he was in now because she really doubted Peyton would pay him for a botched job.

She could do this. She could. Just as soon as she forced her feet to move forward.

One step . . . two . . . A few more and she was standing in front of the door.

Made it.

Her hands shook as she turned the knob. Darn, it was unlocked.

Dark stairs led up into the attic. A short trek, that's all. She could do this. Just in case, she looked behind her. Nothing. Tentatively, she took a cautious step, then another, and another until she was standing in the attic.

Other than a few boxes, the small room was bare. Okay, she came, she saw—maybe not conquered, but close enough.

Now she was outta there! She turned and rushed down the steps, slamming the door shut behind her, then turned to face the hallway.

And screamed at the top of her lungs!

Chapter 4

Peyton jumped back a step as Kaci's scream hammered his eardrums. Damn, the woman had a set of pipes!

He grabbed her shoulders. "Kaci, it's me."

She took a deep breath, then exhaled. Her body trembled all the way to her feet, but he couldn't help thinking how soft her skin was or how it felt to touch her.

He took a deep breath and inhaled her fragrance. This was wrong. How the hell was he going to keep his distance when she drove him to distraction with her sexy curves? Man, she had really nice curves.

She pulled out of his arms before he could get too comfortable holding her. He was left with nothing but air and empty fantasies.

Her eyebrows veed. "Of course it's you," she sputtered. "I can see that now. Do you always go around scaring people like that?"

He raised an eyebrow. "I scared you?"

"No, I just screamed for the hell of it." She slapped her hands on her hips. "What do you think?"

Damn, she was cute, adorable, and all he could think about was what it would be like to pick her up and carry her to his bedroom. But he didn't . . . couldn't. He'd promised himself that their relationship would stay professional.

He focused on the only thing that should be happening in

his house—getting rid of the ghost. "I didn't think ghost hunters were afraid of anything," he remarked.

That should put things back in perspective. Besides, he wanted to know why she'd been so scared. She *was* a ghost hunter. He wouldn't think she'd scare easily.

She raised her chin defiantly and glared at him. "You're solid," she said. "A ghost isn't. You could've been a burglar for all I knew."

Her behavior was suspicious, but she had a point. "I'll call out the next time," he said.

"Good."

"Is the ghost still here?" he asked, looking around.

" 'Fraid so. I have all my equipment set up, though." She glanced at her watch. "When do you notice most of the activity?"

"In the evenings, late at night. Sometimes early morning."

She nodded.

"You don't seem surprised by the times. Do ghosts have certain hours they like to haunt?" Now he was being sarcastic. But the thought of a ghost punching a time clock was a little much.

"As a matter of fact, they do." She looked around. "Since most of the activity happens downstairs, maybe that's where I should go."

Not waiting for him to agree or disagree, she swept past and headed in the direction of the stairs. Okay, so maybe they did punch an invisible time clock. How the hell was he supposed to know?

He followed. Man, she had a nice walk, though.

She headed for the study, going inside. He was right on her heels, but he came to a stop when he saw the room's transformation. It didn't look the same, but he had to say, she'd kept the cords and what have you out of the way. At least he wouldn't be tripping over anything. Still, he couldn't help but think it was all a little fake looking.

"Tell me again what this is supposed to do?" he asked, touching one of the machines.

"It measures the amount of energy the spirit generates."

"And why is that important?"

She came over to stand beside him. The device resembled a graph that measured earthquakes. She pushed a button and the machine spit out paper. She studied it for a minute before turning to look at him.

"I have to know the strength of the spirit we're dealing with. An older spirit will be harder to remove."

He waved his arm. "Then you what?"

She cocked an eyebrow. "I zap it if the spray doesn't work."

He crossed his arms and leaned against his desk—and waited. She stared right back, but it lasted less than a minute.

"There's more to it than just zapping a ghost. The first step is to see exactly what I'm dealing with. When I do, I'll know how better to eliminate it, but yes, I have a zapper."

"I didn't mean to imply that it was that easy. I was just curious."

Her smile was slow. "Why? You thinking about starting up your own ghost-busting business? Do I need to be afraid of the competition?"

His gaze slowly swept over her. He liked what he saw. Her curves were in all the right places. When he met her eyes, he saw the flare of desire there.

"Yeah, maybe you should be a little afraid," he said, knowing she knew he wasn't talking about anything remotely close to being business related.

Why'd Kaci have to be so blasted tempting?

She drew in a deep breath, then moved away from him, turning some dials on another machine. "I need to set up some more things before it gets much later."

Running away? Yeah, he thought she was, and maybe it was for the best. But Kaci put on a good front. All tough and sarcastic. Peyton had a feeling there were a lot more layers that she kept hidden.

"I grabbed some steaks on the way home," he said, deciding he should probably leave her alone, no matter how tempting she was to him. "Tell me you're not a vegetarian."

She looked at him then and smiled. "Not even remotely. I love meat—the thicker the better." As soon as the words were out of her mouth, a rosy hue crept up her cheeks.

"I'll fire up the grill."

But as he left, he was smiling. Yeah, there was a lot more he wanted to find out about Kaci.

Oh, Lord, had she just told him she liked meat? Then added the "thicker the better"? Damn. She couldn't have said steak? Anything but meat. Did he think she wanted him rather than food? They'd been flirting. That was a no-brainer. Which made what she'd said even worse.

Peyton was so not gay. He couldn't be.

She shook her head and went back to adjusting dials and taking readings until the tantalizing aroma of steak on a grill wafted into the room.

She closed her eyes and inhaled. The PB and J had worn off a long time ago, and her rumbling stomach quickly reminded her she needed heartier sustenance if she was going to remain sharp around Peyton.

She took one last quick look around. She couldn't do anything more until the ghost decided to make an appearance. Besides, she rather liked the stimulating conversations she'd been having with Peyton.

As she left the room, she knew she was treading in deep waters. It wasn't good to mix business with pleasure. But it had been so long since a man had made her feel this nice.

Her heart thumped loudly in her chest as she walked into the kitchen.

She saw him through the windows, on the tiled patio, poking at the steaks on the grill with a large fork. He was a handsome man. Comfortable in his own skin. Some people weren't. They were self-conscious about who they were. They made small flaws out to be huge gaping wounds that they had to hide. They didn't realize everyone had them.

But Peyton wasn't like that. He seemed cool about who he was. Very relaxed.

He looked up, saw her, and smiled. She returned it as she walked to the French doors and joined him outside.

"The smell got to you, didn't it?" he asked with a twinkle in his eyes.

"How could I resist?"

"I love cooking," he told her.

She bit her bottom lip. Just because he loved to cook, that didn't mean he was gay. Lots of men cooked, and grilling was manly. Damn, the next thing she knew, she'd be picking a flower and plucking off the petals one at a time. Is he gay? Is he not gay? Is he . . .

He rested the fork on a holder and held up a glass and a bottle of Merlot. She nodded. One glass wouldn't hurt.

When he handed it to her, she took a drink. "It's good."

"My brother's vineyard. He's quite proud of the wines he makes."

She took another drink, savoring the taste. "And so he should be." She looked around. Saw that he had put a salad on the table with the place settings. "Is there something I need to help with?"

He shook his head. "The rest is just heat and eat. Make yourself comfortable at the table."

"Do you always cook for people you hire?"

"Only the ones who will get rid of a pesky ghost."

She hoped she could get rid of the ghost.

He joined her at the table, pulling out the chair and sitting across from her. The steaks sizzled on the grill, the aroma drifting over to them. Silence surrounded them except for an occasional bird chirping. It was comfortable. Maybe too comfortable.

"Do you have other siblings?" she asked, breaking the silence.

"Two brothers, both older, and a little sister. And you?"

She shook her head. "An only child. It's been just me and my father for as long as I can remember."

"He's the owner of the company?"

She hadn't seen that one coming. He was good, she'd give him that. "Yeah, he owns Ghost Be Gone. He was tied up on another job, so I took this one." She hurriedly changed the subject before he could probe any deeper into her life. "Do you enjoy being a professor?"

He took a drink, and she wondered if he was going to answer her. It was as though he knew she was turning the conversation away from her. He might appear laid back and casual, but she'd better stay on guard.

"I do. I enjoy showing students another time, another place. Making it come to life for them."

"And you teach them about Victorian times."

He shrugged. "That's one time period I teach. I think it's interesting the Victorians would tamp down their sexual drive and perceive it as evil. Sex is a natural part of living. Like breathing and eating. Sex should be something that's enjoyed and savored."

His gaze slowly caressed her. Her nipples tightened. It was all she could do to take a breath. Was he talking about them? It felt as though he was. Hinting?

"It's fascinating that a society would condemn sex yet have an overabundance of prostitutes," he continued.

She shifted in her chair. "That's . . . uh . . . interesting."

He stood. Her hands gripped the arms of the chair. She held her breath, but he only turned and walked away.

"How do you like your meat?"

She opened her mouth, but no words came out. He turned and looked at her.

"Rare? Well-done?"

The grill, you idiot! "Medium-well," she managed to say without making too much of a fool out of herself.

No, he'd only been having a discussion about history—which was what he did for a living. He hadn't meant anything by what he'd said, and he certainly wasn't inviting her into his bed—was he?

The heat from the grill seemed to reach out and caress her with its fiery touch. Or maybe it was the images that she was having of her and Peyton in bed together. It had been so damn long since she'd had sex—good sex, that is.

Now that she thought about it, she was positive he hadn't meant anything by his discussion of Victorian times. He'd only been stating facts. The Victorian age had been very anti-sex. Even she knew that much about the time period, but maybe they should stick to business while there was a ghost in the house.

He carried over a platter with the steaks, then went back for a foil packet. When he opened it, the strong aroma of garlic wafted up to her.

She cocked an eyebrow. "I told you garlic won't get rid of a ghost."

He smiled. "Garlic bread."

Their conversation of a moment ago might never have occurred. The tension eased, and she started to relax a little. It had just been a conversation that she'd taken the wrong way. Nothing more.

Before he sat down, he refilled their glasses.

"Tell me about your ghost," she said as she cut into her meat. "The more I know, the better I'll be able to figure it out."

"Your father didn't tell you anything?"

"Some." She chewed, then swallowed. "This is good."

"I know."

When she looked at him, there was laughter in his eyes.

"I'm not very modest. I know when something is good or

not. Why pretend otherwise. I think if more people were honest, the world would be a much better place to live."

Great. So what would he think if he knew she was a big fake? Not much probably.

"The ghost?" she prodded, not even wanting to get into a discussion about people who lied, even though she had a perfectly good reason for doing so.

"At first, I thought it was college kids pulling a prank."

"What changed your mind?"

"The mist. I walked into it once." He set his fork on the table and leaned back in his chair, crossing his arms in front of him. He seemed to lose himself in the memory. "It wasn't like anything I've ever felt before. Cold, clammy—it felt like death."

Man, could she relate or what? "That happened to me once. Took me a week to feel warm again."

He sat forward. "Exactly. That's when I knew it wasn't a prank and that I might be in serious trouble. So I called your father's company."

The first time it happened to her, she'd taken a hot bath at least three times a day for a week. She'd thought she would turn into a prune before she ever felt warm again. A shiver swept over her as she remembered. She reached for her glass and took a drink.

"But you can get rid of the ghost, right?" he asked. "You're a professional."

She almost choked. She swallowed hard and set the glass back on the table. "*Pffft,* of course I can get rid of it. I'm a ghost hunter."

"Yeah, right." He didn't sound convinced.

"Have there been any other occurrences?" As long as he talked about the ghost, she was fairly safe. And she probably could get rid of it—eventually.

"Articles of my clothing will sometimes fly through the house."

She raised an eyebrow. "More specific."

"My briefs."

Kaci laughed. She couldn't help it.

He frowned. "I don't see anything funny about it. So far I haven't had any guests over when it happens, but that's not to say it won't."

"No, it's not at all funny, but it brings the ghost out of the demon realm and puts it into an area of mischievousness. Believe me, that's a lot better than a demon. You don't want to mess with one of them. Bad news all the way. Only the very best can get rid of one of them."

"I should be grateful, then. Funny, but at the moment, I don't feel very thankful."

He didn't look it, either. "You would if you'd ever crossed a demon's path." Just the thought made her look over her shoulder.

"And you have?"

She shook her head. "No, but I've heard stories from people who have. They're bad—real bad."

"But you're sure that all I have is a ghost."

"Yeah." She watched as Peyton visibly relaxed. "Well, pretty sure."

He straightened. "How sure is that?"

She was trying to be as truthful as possible. She didn't want to lie about everything. "You could have a demon pretending to be a ghost to lure you closer."

"Then what?" His face lost a little of its color.

This probably wasn't a good time to ask if he'd ever seen *The Exorcist*. "I think what you have is only your average, run-of-the-mill ghost."

"No, you said before that you were pretty sure that's what I had. Pretty sure is a lot stronger than just thinking that's what I have."

"I'll know more tomorrow morning." Maybe. She hoped she would.

He opened his mouth, then snapped it closed. "Good." He stood and began to gather their plates.

"There's nothing to be scared about. Most of the time ghosts can't hurt you."

He paused in taking away her plate. "Most of the time? What's that supposed to mean? What, ninety percent of the time people don't get hurt? But what if this ghost falls in the ten percent range that does hurt people?"

She thought about what he was asking. There was a percentage of ghosts that were strong enough to cause humans to hurt themselves. She couldn't very well deny that.

She sighed when she looked at him again. "I guess if you fall in that range, then you're just shit out of luck if I can't get rid of it."

He frowned at her.

Okay, she shouldn't have been that truthful.

Chapter 5

Peyton closed the door of his bedroom. What had Kaci meant when she'd told him that he'd be shit out of luck? He didn't like the sound of that, but when he'd questioned her further, she'd brushed him off and told him she really had to get back to work.

She was right. Kaci was here to do a job.

He heard the guest room door open, then close. Softly, but he heard it. The door had a distinctive squeak that no amount of oil had fixed. So where was she going?

He went to his door and opened it. She was just passing by. She jumped, hugging the blanket and pillow close to her. For a moment, she closed her eyes. When she opened them again, she glared at him.

"Do you have this thing about scaring people or what?" she asked.

He looked pointedly at the pillow and blanket and ignored her question. Instead, he asked one of his own. "Something wrong with the guest room?"

"Most ghost activity happens at night, when humans are more vulnerable. I need to be with my equipment to monitor it and see if I can figure out what I'm dealing with."

He didn't like the idea of her being down there by herself. "Want me to come with you?"

She looked as though she might say yes.

"No," she said. "I work better alone."

"You don't sound that convincing."

She arched an eyebrow. "This isn't my first rodeo, cowboy. I know what I'm doing."

Man, she was touchy. "I didn't say you didn't. I was only offering you some company."

"Oh." She hugged the pillow closer. "I'll probably doze most of the time unless something starts happening. I really do work better alone."

"If you need anything, you know where I am."

"Thanks, but I'm sure I'll be fine."

He nodded before going back inside his room and closing the door. Kaci wanted to call out to him to come back, not to leave, but she didn't. She was the ghost exterminator, and she could do this.

Or not.

No, she could get rid of the wandering spirit. She had all the knowledge. Her father had taught her well, even though she'd never used her skills. At least, not alone. In the early days, she'd gone with her father a few times. She only had to get rid of her fear and she'd be fine. She snorted. That wasn't likely to happen anytime soon.

She'd once read a book when she was a teenager that said she should meditate about her problems, and the solutions would come to her. The book had said she needed to embrace her fears. The next time her father had dragged her on a ghost hunt, she'd attempted just that.

It hadn't worked.

She'd opened her arms wide and told the spirit she wasn't afraid. That she wanted to make friends and envelop its essence.

The ghost had taken her literally and settled inside her like a block of ice. The one that had left her chilled to the bone for days. She hadn't told the ghost it could take up residence. Yuck, she'd felt clammy and cold for a week. Not good. She'd just as soon not embrace her fears again. No, she'd much rather run away from them.

Now, Peyton, she would gladly embrace. And a whole lot more if he'd let her. He was definitely scrumptious, and she didn't even want to think about him upstairs in his bed. Did he wear pajamas? Oh, she didn't even want to go there.

She went inside the study, leaving the door open. Just in case she had to scream, she wanted Peyton to hear her. Not that he could do a whole lot—besides fire her butt and possibly sue her father for misrepresentation.

Life could get complicated sometimes.

She tossed her pillow and blanket on the window seat and went to her instruments, frowning when she saw there was some activity—right now. The spirit was in the room with her. She quickly reminded herself the bathroom was just down the hall. She might be needing it.

You aren't afraid of ghosts. You are strong. You are tough, smart, and nothing will get the better of you.

She trembled because she was chilled. Yeah, right. Who was she trying to fool? It was only her and the ghost in here, and she was scared shitless.

Deep breath. What should she do? Talk to the spirit. Yeah, she remembered her father telling her sometimes you could convince ghosts to cross over. To go away.

She held her ground and looked around the room. "Why are you haunting this house?" Why had she spoken in a low voice? This wasn't the movies. She rolled her eyes.

Nothing.

Sometimes a ghost would communicate by raising the spikes on the graph. She watched the graph, but the spikes continued at a low level. The ghost knew something was going on, and it wasn't about to fall for any of her tricks.

Smart ghost.

She turned the bright overhead light off, leaving one small lamp glowing in a corner of the room. The stage was set.

Almost.

She'd been working on something when Guido started getting testy and wanting the money her father owed him. Her invention would knock the paranormal world on its ear.

The zapper!

Sometimes she amazed herself.

Her ghost zapper worked similar to a flashlight with built-in jets of heat and prisms to reflect light at angles. Ghosts hated light and heat. That was one reason most séances were held at night. Well, that, and shysters could fake stuff better in the dark than they could in the light of day.

She went to the one case that was still closed, running her hand lightly over the zipper before tugging it open. The zapper wasn't fancy. She'd made it from scrap parts. It resembled a gun. A very big gun.

Her father had seen her working on it once and told her it looked like something out of *Mad Max*. If it would get the job done, she'd use a garden rake.

There was only one minor glitch. It hadn't been tested. That could be a bit of a problem. She hadn't had time to see exactly what it would do, until now. It wasn't her most thought out strategy, using something that hadn't been checked out, but right now it was all she had.

She brought it out of the case, stroking her hand down the gleaming finish. Sweet. She took it with her to the window seat, making herself comfortable, and waited.

And waited.

And waited.

She glanced at her watch. After midnight and the machines weren't even humming. No ghost. Apparently, it had left the room.

She yawned, wishing she hadn't drunk the wine. She was so sleepy she could barely keep her eyes open. She stifled another yawn and snuggled down deeper into the downy softness of the pillow. She would close her eyes for a few minutes. A power nap, that's all.

Damn, she was so . . . so . . . sleepy. . . .

Peyton walked toward her. He was wearing his leather coat and jeans. She sighed. And no shirt. God, he was delicious looking.

He couldn't sleep?

But why would he be wearing his coat—not that Kaci minded. Maybe she was asleep. Oh, that wasn't good.

He stopped in front of her and slowly removed his coat, letting it drop to the floor, then hooked his thumbs into his jeans. His oiled body glistened, begging her to touch, to run her hands over his rock-hard, six-pack abs.

She needed to wake up. She needed . . .

He tugged the metal button through the buttonhole of his jeans.

Or not.

She rolled to her back, her breathing ragged. "Kiss me," she mumbled.

Peyton grinned, but his face changed, became distorted. In the next instant, she was looking into the grotesque face of the spirit. Ectoplasm dripped from its teeth. Gooey, slimy gunk plopping near her face.

She immediately came awake and fumbled for the gun, then whirled it around, aimed, and fired.

There was a pop and a crack.

The ghost laughed.

She didn't blame it. The gun sounded like a kid's toy. She fired again and again. The spirit loomed in front of her, claws bared and coming toward her.

"Screw this!"

She tossed the gun and made a beeline for the stairs. The spirit was right behind her. She'd go into her room and lock the door. There she'd be safe. Maybe.

But when she got to her room and turned the handle, the door wouldn't budge. She whirled around. The ghost was there, right in front of her. The most hideous thing she'd ever seen. She opened her mouth to scream, but nothing came out.

"Go away," she finally managed to squeak and ran to Peyton's room, slamming the door behind her and executing a flying leap that would've earned her a gold medal in gymnastics. She landed with a plop on Peyton's bed, quickly scooted beneath the covers, and threw her arms around him.

"What the . . ." His words slurred together from sleep.

"The ghost is out there," she whispered. "Shhh . . ." She pressed closer and realized he slept nude. She was too frightened to be embarrassed . . . or leave the safety of his bed or the heat of his body.

"Isn't that what you wanted? To draw the ghost out, then zap it into oblivion?" His words were thick with sleep.

She stilled.

"That is what you wanted?" he prodded, seeming to come more awake. At least, his words were getting easier to understand . . . unfortunately.

It was time to lie . . . act. "Yes, of course. I . . . uh . . . dozed off, and when the spirit showed itself, I was startled."

"This is more than startled. You're trembling."

He started to move away, but she clung tighter. She couldn't help it.

"Please, can I stay in here tonight?"

Silence.

God, she was such a wimp.

"If you stay, we won't be sleeping."

She drew in a breath. "You're not gay, then."

"Why would you think that?"

"You like the Victorian time period so much that you bought this house—and we both know that was an era of frippery and frills—some guy named Daniel called and was surprised you had a female in your house, and there's a picture on your bedside table of you and a man. He has his arm around your shoulders, and he looks very much in love. And you have to admit the study is kind of feminine."

"I bought this house because I couldn't afford a castle—I like the Crusades, too. Daniel is another professor, and a snoop. He probably hoped you would give him a juicy piece of gossip. The picture on my bedside table is my brother the day before his wedding, and his fiancée was taking the picture. My sister, Becca, decorated the study, and I didn't have the heart to tell her it was a little over the top for me."

Darn. She'd missed all the way around.

"You're scared of ghosts, aren't you?" he asked.

She frowned. "Just a little." Actually, she wasn't nearly as frightened as she'd been a few minutes ago. Peyton made her feel safe. Not that she thought he could protect her from the ghost, but it helped having someone to be scared with.

Except the ghost hadn't followed her inside his bedroom. It had probably drained all its energy scaring the hell out of her.

"This is more than being a little afraid of ghosts."

She bit her bottom lip. "Okay, they scare me a lot, but that doesn't mean I can't get rid of the spirit. I'm experienced. Really, I am."

"And how do you propose to go about that when you're trembling so much the bed is shaking?"

She frowned at him again. Not that he could see as dark as the room was, but it made her feel better. "The ghost took me by surprise. I won't let it get the upper hand again. Anyway, it's your fault."

"My fault? How do you figure that?"

"The wine. When I dozed off, the ghost weaved its way into my dream. That's when we're the most vulnerable, you know. When we're asleep." God, she was rambling uncontrollably.

"I didn't open your mouth and pour the wine down your throat."

He had a point. "True, but you shouldn't have refilled my glass."

He didn't say anything. Not that she was paying that much attention to the conversation. The guy was naked beneath the covers. Her mind had wandered to other things. Things she probably shouldn't be thinking.

"Are you staying or not?" he asked. He lightly ran a finger down the side of her face.

She closed her eyes, enjoying the heat from his touch. The ghost had made her feel cold, but Peyton was warming her up nicely.

"There's chemistry between us," he continued. "You know it as well as I. Kaci, I want to make love with you."

That was now obvious. Oh, what the hell. They both wanted the same thing. She'd been daydreaming about it since—this morning? Gads, this was a first. She'd never gone to bed with someone the same day they met.

She glanced at the clock and the illuminated numbers. Technically, it was the second day. Did that make her not quite a slut?

He kissed her. She jumped, even though it was only a gentle brushing of his lips against hers.

"I've wanted you since the moment I laid eyes on you," he continued.

"I doubt that. You barely looked at me when you opened the door."

"You're right. I wasn't sure if you were a young man or a woman because of those baggy sweats you wore. And you talked liked something out of a mafia movie. Why did you talk like that?"

She smiled, taking his words as a compliment to her acting abilities. "I was acting tough so you wouldn't tell me to get lost. Admit it, if I'd been dressed like I was when I came downstairs, you wouldn't have let me through the front door, let alone to get rid of a ghost."

"I probably would've dragged you inside—then ravished you," he admitted.

Now, that had interesting possibilities. "Are you going to ravish me now?" Her words were soft and sultry, and there was no way he could mistake that she wanted him.

"Yeah, I think I am."

"What about the ghost? Aren't you a little bit worried?"

"It usually has a burst of energy and then goes away for a while," he said. "I think we'll have the room to ourselves."

"A young spirit. Its powers don't last long. That's good to know."

And good because her body throbbed with need. She rather liked the idea of being ravished. He ran his hand up and down her arm. Oh, yeah, she was warming up nicely. She leaned closer to where she thought his mouth was and pressed her lips against his, closing her eyes as delicious sensations swept over her.

He returned her kiss, deepening it further, his tongue lightly caressing hers, while his free hand slid beneath her shirt and massaged her back.

Oh, yeah, this was what she needed. She'd think about the repercussions later. She'd probably have lots of time when he fired her. But right now, she was going to enjoy the sensations he created.

And the ones she wanted him to feel.

She scooted closer, running her hand over his back, taking it a little farther downward each time until she ran her hand over his butt, then up his thigh. He jerked in response to her touch.

"Do you like that?" she whispered close to his ear, then flicked the lobe with her tongue.

"You know I do," he growled.

Her smile was self-satisfied until his hand snaked under her top and cupped her bare breast. She'd changed to her sweats before going downstairs and hadn't bothered to wear a bra, so he had easy access. She gasped when he lightly tugged on her nipple with his thumb and forefinger. Hot sensations swirled all the way down to her belly.

"And do you like that?" he asked.

She couldn't say anything. Her pleasure center was on delicious overload.

Until he stopped.

"No, don't . . ."

"What? Don't do this?" He lightly squeezed her nipple again at the same time he tugged on it.

She wet her lips. It was hard to breathe.

"No, don't stop touching me."

"But I wanted to kiss your breasts, take each one into my mouth." He kissed her neck, then ran his tongue down to her shoulder.

"Yes," she barely managed to get out.

He adjusted his position, leaving her wanting so much, till he pushed on her shoulders, moving her to her back and tugging her shirt over her head. Then there was a click, and the bedside light came on, casting a warm glow over the room, and Kaci.

She covered her breasts, even though he didn't seem a bit shy. Not that he should be. He was definitely built—she cleared her throat—well. Very well.

It didn't matter. She'd always made love with the light off. It seemed to work better if she didn't have to look the guy in the eye.

"Why did you cover yourself?" he asked.

Telling him she was shy sounded laughable at this point in time. They were about to make love, and they were practically strangers. But she was shy with the light on.

"I . . . uh . . . don't usually make love with the light on," she stammered, feeling like a virgin, but it certainly wasn't her first time.

"I want to see you." His eyes filled with passion. "I want to see every inch of you. When you came in the kitchen in those short shorts and that tank top, you nearly drove me crazy. Since then, I've wanted to see what lay beneath . . ."

Oh, God, the way he said that almost made her have an orgasm. This was going to be so good.

He took her hands. She hesitated only briefly, letting him pull them away.

"Absolutely beautiful. You're perfect."

She wasn't, but the way he looked at her, he made her feel perfect. "You're pretty hot yourself." Her gaze dropped. She stared at his magnificent erection, her mouth watering.

When she looked back up, he had a knowing grin on his face. She hadn't just said that, had she? She hadn't just ogled his dick, had she? Yes, she had. Why couldn't she think before she spoke? Or looked?

When he lightly ran the back of his fingers over one breast, then the other, she stopped thinking. She didn't even care when he tugged off her sweats.

Thank goodness she'd washed clothes the day before she'd locked up the office and taken off. She'd been down to her scrungy underwear. The ones that bagged in the butt and were so thin you could read a paper through them. But she had, and right now she wore her pretty pink bikini panties— correction, while she'd been lost in thought, he'd slid them down her legs, too.

She kicked them off.

"You really are magnificent," he murmured.

He scooted back up, sitting on his knees beside her. She knew the heat she felt right now was from embarrassment, no matter how brave an act she tried to put on.

When he dragged his fingers downward, she closed her eyes, and coherent thought immediately fled. Suddenly, she wasn't as concerned the light was on as she had been a moment ago.

Her breathing became ragged as he tangled his fingers in her curls, massaging her clit. "Oh, yes." She arched her back and reached out, grabbing him.

He grunted with pain.

Her passion was gone as fast as if she'd blown out a flickering match when she realized she'd grabbed his erection as though it were some kind of love handle.

She slowly sank down into the bed, opening her eyes. "I'm so sorry." She released him. "Did I hurt you when I grabbed your . . . uh . . . when I grabbed you?"

Peyton grimaced. "No, I think the pain came when you squeezed."

She rolled to her side, burying her face in her hands. "Maybe it would be better if I went back to the guest room." Putting up with the ghost would be so much easier than embarrassing herself further.

"Not on your life, ghost hunter."

"Now you're making fun of me." But she'd heard laughter in his voice. Laughter might be a good sign.

He nuzzled her neck just before he lay beside her, spoon-fashion, his erection nudging her. She sighed with relief. Good, she hadn't damaged him. Kaci scooted to her back, wanting more, but determined to slow down a little and not act like a sex-starved nymphomaniac.

"You're sure I didn't hurt you?"

"Oh, yeah, I'm sure." He wrapped his arms around her and pulled her against him.

Good, because her body was starting to warm up nicely once again.

Chapter 6

Peyton wasn't hurting nearly as much as he would've been if she'd scurried back to the guest room. As she pressed her body closer, he was glad she'd stayed. If she hadn't, he didn't think any amount of cold water would've relieved him.

Who could blame him for making love to Kaci? They both wanted the same thing, and no one would get hurt. They were only going to enjoy each other tonight. That was all.

She moved her hands over him, cupping his butt as she flung her leg across his hip, and nudged herself against him. A moan escaped from between his lips, and all thoughts of what could've happened fled as other, more sensual thoughts filled his mind.

He squeezed one hand between their bodies and fondled her breast. She gasped, stretching her head back and giving him even more access to her luscious body. He lowered his head, unable to resist tasting her a second longer.

He swirled his tongue around the taut nipple before sucking it inside his mouth. Her fingers tangled in his hair, pulling him closer. This was sweet, so damn sweet.

He pushed her to her back again. She didn't resist. His lips found hers. He kissed her, his tongue probing the inside of her mouth, sparring with hers.

In one swift motion that took him completely off guard,

she shoved against his shoulder. He wondered briefly, painfully, if she'd changed her mind, but as soon as she straddled him and looked at him much like a cat would look at a juicy treat, he knew their night had only just begun.

He lay there wondering what Kaci would do next now that she had control. He rather enjoyed the idea of being at her mercy. Especially when she fit herself perfectly on top of his erection. He sucked in a deep breath when she lightly wiggled against him.

"Do you like that?" she asked.

"Yeah." Peyton chuckled. "A lot." Why wouldn't he? He was looking right at her curls, and the fleshy part of her sex peeked out at him. Yeah, he really liked the position she'd put him in.

When he looked up at her, she grinned back, and he marveled again just how damn sexy she looked. Even more now that she was completely naked. Her high-pointed breasts were full and fit his hands perfectly. She had a small waist. Her hips nicely rounded.

His gaze dropped lower, but before he had much time to once more admire what was between her legs, she leaned forward, brushing her breasts lightly across his chest. He closed his eyes and let the sensations she created wash over him.

"Incredible."

"Umm, yes, it is," she murmured.

She licked him, flicking her tongue over his nipples. He arched his back, grabbing her ass and keeping her anchored against him.

"This is good," she breathed.

"Hang on," he told her as he scooted backward until he rested against the cushioned headboard of his bed.

"Much better."

She frowned. "I don't know about that. I was having a lot of fun where I was."

"Yes, but I couldn't quite reach your perfect breasts. I wanted to massage them and taste them some more."

She bit her bottom lip, her eyes half closing. Peyton could almost see the waves of heat coming off her body. He wondered if she knew just how close to an orgasm she was.

But he wasn't ready for their play to be over yet. There was a lot more he wanted to do to her body, a lot more he wanted to make her feel. He'd been dreaming about this ever since she'd trotted downstairs in those short shorts and that tank top.

"Peyton," she said, her words reflecting the ache she felt right now.

"What? This?" He cupped her breasts, rubbing his thumbs over the nipples, then squeezing them.

"Yes. That."

"Not shy anymore?"

She shook her head.

"Sex should be something each person can enjoy to the fullest," he said as he continued to massage. "Some people, even now, think the word 'sex' shouldn't even be mentioned. They pretend it doesn't exist. They wouldn't dream of having sex with the light on. But don't you see how much more pleasurable it is? I love looking at a woman in the throes of passion. It increases my own desire."

She nodded, but didn't speak.

"I want to see every inch of your body." He moved one hand over her rib cage, past her waist, and slid the back of his fingers across her abdomen, always moving downward.

Did she realize she'd wiggled her ass when his fingers dipped lower, almost touching her sex, but not quite. Her breathing was coming out in tiny little puffs. He didn't think Kaci realized she was unconsciously begging him to touch lower. To do whatever he wanted to her. Whatever it took to take her body higher and higher.

She whimpered when he brought his fingers close to her mound, but still didn't touch. Before this night was over, he'd have her doing more than whimper. He wanted her whimpering and crying out in ecstasy.

He flicked a finger over her clit. She leaned back, placing her hands on his thighs. He feasted his gaze on her sex. Man, he didn't know how much longer he could last. His body had started to tremble from the effort it took to hold back.

Her sex was right there in front of him, and he had to do more than touch. He quickly scooted down in the bed again until he was half lying, half sitting. Her ass ended up on his chest—right where he wanted it. He only had to bring her a little closer. He nudged her bottom until her sex was only inches from his face.

Then he blew across her soft, silky curls. She gasped and moved closer.

"I want to lick you," he said. "I want to suck you inside my mouth and taste you."

She moaned, and stretched her body closer. He swirled his tongue around her clit. She tasted hot and musky. He couldn't get enough of her.

She cried out, her body rocking against his mouth. "Yes! Oh, God, that feels so damn good!"

He grabbed her ass and pulled her in tighter, sucking harder. Her legs were opened wide. He held her with one hand but slipped the other between her legs and inserted a finger inside her. God, she was so damn wet. He moved his finger deeper, feeling the heat of her body as it seemed to wrap around him. For a second, he didn't move as he thought about how it would feel to bury himself deep inside her with her moist heat surrounding him.

He grit his teeth. Not yet. It was still too soon. He pulled his finger out, then moved it back inside, increasing the tempo. Her body rocked harder. Her breathing grew more ragged. She whimpered as her body tightened.

"I'm . . . I'm . . ." She screamed out as her orgasm trembled over her.

Kaci began to collapse. He eased her body down to the bed. He stood, pulling a condom out of his bedside drawer and quickly sliding it on. Sweat broke out on his forehead. Just touching himself increased the ache inside him. But when he looked at Kaci lying on the bed, her legs spread open, he couldn't move. He could only stare. She was truly beautiful.

She opened her eyes; her cheeks turned a rosy hue. She started to bring her legs together, but Peyton grabbed her ankles and opened them wider.

"I love looking at you—all of you. Please . . ." He wanted her in the worst way.

She nodded.

One hell of a woman. He started at her ankles, massaging her feet.

"That feels good." She stretched like a cat, practically purring.

He didn't say anything, only moved farther up, continuing to massage. The backs of her knees, then trailing his fingers up and down the insides of her thighs. She wiggled her bottom ever so slightly. He watched her facial expression closely, knowing she was getting turned on again.

Knowing how to take a woman higher and higher until she reached the ultimate orgasm was the ultimate high.

And Kaci was getting close.

"Does that feel good?" he asked.

She nodded.

"No, I want to hear you say it."

She opened her eyes, her expression a little surprised.

He chuckled. "It's not an ego trip. I like to know you enjoy what I'm doing—if something feels better, tell me. Besides, talking about sex while experiencing it is a major turn-on, don't you think?"

"I've never talked about it," she admitted. "I've always just done it."

He shook his head. Her sexual education had been sorely lacking. "You mean, if I said I want to kiss you . . ." He moved his fingers lightly over her clit. Her body jerked. "Right here again. That I want to suck you inside my mouth and run my tongue over your sex, that wouldn't make you hot? It wouldn't make your body ache?"

She whimpered. "Yes."

He moved between her legs and lowered his head. "Good, because that's exactly what I'm going to do." He gave her a brief kiss on her clit before sucking her inside his mouth. Damn, she was sweet.

She arched her back and grabbed his head. He didn't want her to come this time, though. He only wanted her hot and bothered.

When he straightened, she groaned.

"I'm just getting started, sweetheart." He slid deep inside her body. She opened her eyes and looked at him.

"I'm sorry," she mumbled.

He paused. Oh, God, not now. Please don't let her stop me now. "Why are you sorry?"

"Because I doubt I can give you as much pleasure as you've just given me. At least, not this time."

He sighed with relief. "You already have, and it's only going to get better."

He pulled out, then plunged back inside but kept his movements slow and easy, even though it cost him every ounce of restraint that he had left inside him. He wanted to pump hard and fast, but he wanted to build the heat until it felt as though they'd both burst into flames.

She wrapped her legs around his waist, shifting so he would have better, deeper access. "Feels good," she said, moving to his rhythm.

"I want you to experience more," he said.

Her eyes widened. "Believe me, what I've already had was more than I've ever had."

He shook his head.

Her eyes widened.

"I loved the way your breasts felt in my hands." He glanced down at her tits. The nipples were still hard. "And licking your sex, drawing you into my mouth, really turned me on. I like the way you taste."

Her body jerked. She wiggled just a little.

"What are you doing?" she asked.

"Talking sex. Remember? I'm going to continue sliding in and out of your body all the time I'm telling you how great it was to suck on your sex, to run my tongue up and down your hot clit."

She gasped. "But . . . but . . ."

"What? Why shouldn't I tell you how much I enjoyed sucking on you? Or the way it felt to squeeze your ass and draw you even closer to my mouth—to my tongue. Or that just talking about it makes me want to suck on you again." He felt the tremble run through her body.

Kaci began to pant, her breathing ragged. "Oh, damn." She met each thrust, except now there was an urgency to her movements.

Peyton couldn't hold back any longer. He drove inside her faster and faster. He closed his eyes as the fire began to build hotter and hotter inside him. He vaguely heard Kaci moan but he was too lost in what was happening to his own body.

He cried out, teetering on the edge before plunging over. He drove deep inside her one last time, and with another cry, he came harder than he'd ever come before, and it was incredible. His body shook and trembled.

And then he was falling back to Earth.

He took a couple of deep breaths and forced himself to slide off Kaci's glistening body. For a moment, he lay beside her, then opened his eyes and looked at her.

"That was incredible," he said.

"I had two orgasms, and I screamed out with both of them. I've never screamed out. Hell, I've never had two orgasms in one night." She spoke with amazement in her voice. "God, that was great. Fantastic. Damn, I feel as though I've run a marathon and come out the winner."

Yeah, he pretty much felt the same way. It surprised him. He hadn't expected that.

"I haven't had sex like that since—hell, I don't remember the last time it was that good."

Probably because he hadn't been with a woman in months, what with the move to a new town, a new job.

"Kind of scary, isn't it?" she asked.

"Yeah."

"How come you know so much about how to please a woman?" she mumbled close to his ear.

If he told her, she'd either be pissed or she'd laugh in his face. He decided not to take the chance. "It's not hard to please a woman when she's pretty terrific herself."

She snuggled closer to him. "Ahhh, that's sweet. Not a bit of truth to it, but sweet just the same."

He automatically pulled her in a little tighter, caressing her shoulder as he stared at the ceiling. She didn't give herself enough credit. Kaci was pretty amazing.

But on the heels of that thought came the truth of the matter. Damn it, the lady was a fake.

The one thing he couldn't abide was someone trying to take advantage of him. So why was she snuggled next to him? Why had he made love to her? The second one was easier to answer—what would any red-blooded man do when a woman jumped into his bed and pressed her supple body against his? Especially if he was half asleep.

As soon as he'd figured out he wasn't having a great dream, and that she really was in his bed, he'd realized she wasn't wearing a bra and her full breasts were pushing against his arm. Maybe if he hadn't been sound asleep when she joined him, things might not have progressed as far as they had.

Not that he was complaining.

But she had, and they had, and he had no idea where that left him. She was afraid of ghosts. She'd lied to him. And now he had another problem.

He had to fire Kaci and hire someone who could get rid of the ghost.

Chapter 7

"We have a problem," Peyton said the next morning when Kaci joined him in the kitchen.

She frowned, not liking the tone of his voice. "Don't tell me, you're pregnant. Damn, I knew I shouldn't have gotten on top."

"That's not funny."

She'd thought it was pretty good for first thing in the morning after having the daylights scared out of her, then mind-blowing sex.

She hadn't even had a cup of coffee yet. So yeah, she thought it was a pretty good quip.

Speaking of which, the coffee smelled great. She glanced around, spotted the pot, and aimed herself in that direction.

"Coffee first," she told him, reaching into the cabinet where she'd seen the cups yesterday, and brought one out. As she poured a cup of coffee, she glanced at the cup—Galveston. She loved the coast.

Yeah, Kaci, do whatever it takes to keep your mind off the problem Peyton mentioned.

She added powdered creamer and sugar, knowing that thinking about something as mundane as whether Peyton enjoyed the beach as much as she did was easier than thinking about the problem he'd mentioned.

Who could blame her? Facing the problem held a lot less

desirability. She didn't want to think about it at all. She had a feeling she knew exactly what problem he was going to want to discuss. Then she would have to convince him she could get rid of his ghost. It was just too damn early in the morning to think about anything.

God, now she was even babbling to herself.

Coffee. She wasn't any good to anyone until she'd fueled up with caffeine. She brought the cup to her nose and inhaled. The aroma was to die for.

Then she turned around and saw the grim expression on Peyton's face. It was going to be worse than she'd imagined. But before she could take a seat at the table, the doorbell rang.

Peyton stood, then went to the hall. She stayed where she was but heard his mumbled curse. He hurried back to the kitchen.

"It's Daniel." He looked at her, his expression turning darker. "He always bums me out of a cup of coffee. If he sees you, it'll be all over campus."

"Are you ashamed of me?" She didn't think she liked his attitude.

"It's not that. I've heard the dean is a little stodgy, and I'm new. There's grant money up for grabs that Daniel and I both need and want." His gaze skimmed over her, leaving a trail of heat in its path. "But, sweetheart, I'd never be ashamed of you."

She sucked in a deep breath. Alrighty. She quickly cleared her mind. Okay, she could relate to needing money to get a job done right.

But if Daniel walked into the kitchen and saw her . . . She gripped the cup, knowing full well what she looked like, even though she'd dressed before coming downstairs. She still had the look of a woman who'd just crawled out of bed after a night of hot sex.

"We can fix this. I'll hide," she volunteered.

He frowned. "It isn't right."

"Do you want the grant money or not?"

"Yes."

"Then where?" She glanced around. She certainly couldn't fit into one of the cabinets. "The closet." She didn't wait for him to say anything, but headed right toward it and opened the door.

Just before dipping inside, she raised her eyebrows at him. "Go let him in. If you keep him waiting, he'll start to think you have something to hide."

"Okay, okay."

Not good. The broom closet had shelves and a trash can, but she might be able to squeeze herself around everything. She wiggled inside, bending at the waist at the same time she pulled the door closed. She heard Peyton say something about getting rid of Daniel as fast as he could; then his footsteps were going away from her.

That's when she realized just how uncomfortable she was. She felt like a pretzel.

And she still held her coffee. Oh, well. She attempted a drink, but managed to burn the tip of her nose in the process. This was so not fair. Here she had a perfectly good cup of coffee, the aroma tantalizing her senses, and she couldn't even get one measly drink.

She tried to shift her body into a more comfortable position until she heard more than one set of footsteps approaching the kitchen. She kept as still as she could, practically holding her breath, which wasn't that much of a problem since the smell from the trash can had started to blend with the aroma of her coffee.

"I still can't understand why you bought this house when you could have gotten a newer one," Daniel said. "But I guess this one was cheaper."

Now, wasn't he just hoity-toity.

"Newer homes don't have a history," Peyton responded.

Good comeback, but he'd failed to mention they didn't have a ghost, either.

She heard them moving around; a cabinet opened, then

closed. She assumed Daniel was getting himself a cup of coffee. Great. Maybe he would drink it really fast and not be a sipper. Her father was a sipper. It took him forever to drink his coffee.

"I know you haven't been here long," Daniel began, "but I think you'll enjoy life at the university. The faculty have quite a few get-togethers. We're almost like an extended family."

After talking to him briefly on the phone, she had a feeling if he were a relative of hers, she'd probably disown him.

There was silence for a moment.

"Of course, with that comes a price," Daniel continued. "There are certain standards that need to be met."

Oh, brother, was this guy for real? She'd run up against so-called standards before. They were a bunch of BS. Rules used to control people. Cliques. She'd hated them.

Mainly because she'd never made it into one. They'd moved too often for her to make friends. Not that she'd ever have wanted to be in a clique. Too snooty for her. She'd been perfectly happy by herself.

"What standards?" Peyton didn't sound as though he was too thrilled, either.

Okay, maybe he'd raised a notch in her book. She grinned, liking the idea of him raising a notch. He'd certainly risen more than a notch last night.

"No different than what anyone in polite society would consider to be morally ethical and proper for the faculty of our esteemed university . . ."

Kaci tuned him out. Her back was starting to ache. Hiding in the closet had seemed to be a good idea at the time. She tried to shift just a little. If she could just move a bit to the right.

Coffee sloshed over the rim of her cup.

It was still hot.

She jerked her hand, dropping the cup when more coffee became a geyser and poured over the side. The cup hit the rubber top of the trash can with a dull thunk.

"What was that?" Daniel asked.

"Rats?" Peyton suggested.

Oh, God, Daniel was going to open the door and see her. He'd go straight to the dean, and Daniel would get the grant money instead of Peyton. Peyton might even get fired from his job. It would be all her fault.

Panic set in.

Her gaze quickly scanned the small closet. She could make everything right. Maybe. At least she hoped she could. She grabbed the broom and opened the door, quickly slipping out as she pushed the door closed behind her.

"All clean in the basement, govna." She looked around, pretending to be startled when her gaze landed on Daniel. Poor Peyton looked as if he was about to stroke out, but she wasn't sure if it was from holding back his laughter or how she must look. He should be grateful she was saving his ass.

"This is . . . uh . . ." he began, a smile quivering around his lips but not quite breaking through.

"Ah didn't know you had company, sir," she said before he could say more. She wiped her palm on the back of her capri's, then stuck her hand toward Daniel, who immediately cringed away from her. She planted it on her hip. "Ah clean for the prof. Real good at me job, too, if you be needin' a cleanin' woman, govna."

"That leads to the basement?" Daniel asked with a deepening frown.

"That it does. Clean as a whistle, too, now that I've had a go at it."

Daniel still didn't look convinced. "You don't sound like the woman I spoke with yesterday."

"That must've been me sister."

His brow furrowed into even deeper grooves, and she realized her mistake.

"Our parents divorced," she quickly clarified. "Ah was raised by our mum in England, and she lived with our father." And it was a good thing she'd watched *The Parent Trap* again last month.

"Oh."

Just oh? Hey, she was doing a pretty darn good job acting. Maybe it was time to shake things up a bit.

"Ah noticed you had a bit of an English accent, too, govna. What part are you from? Ah have to say, it's good to me ears to hear one of me countrymen, God Save the Queen."

"Yes, I'm sure it is." He dismissed her as beneath him with just one look before turning back to Peyton. "Thanks for the coffee, old chap. I have a class in a bit and must be on my way." He cast a disparaging glance in her direction before setting his cup down and heading toward the hall.

"Don't forget, govna, if you be wantin' a fine woman to clean your 'ouse, I'm available." She grinned when she saw his back stiffen.

Peyton frowned at her, but she could see the unmistakable twinkle in his eyes just before he hurried after Daniel to see him out.

She was so good. She'd known his accent was as fake as hers. People usually ran in the opposite direction when they were confronted with their lies. Daniel was no different. He wanted to play the English earl. That was fine by her, but she hated when people tried to put others down just so they could feel better about themselves.

Kaci went to the sink and washed her face and hands. The closet had made her feel grungy. With eyes closed, she felt around for the towel, but it wasn't where she'd thought she'd last seen it. She reached out, her hand coming into contact with a hard chest. She jumped, jerking her hand away, then realized it had been Peyton.

"Towel," she said and reached out again.

He had a really nice chest, and her body reacted to what she'd blindly encountered. Before she could get all hot and bothered, he took her hand and placed the towel in it. She wiped her face, then her hands, before tossing the towel on the counter.

"Your shirt's wet," she commented when she looked at him.

He glanced down at the wet imprint of her hand. "Ya think?"

She arched an eyebrow. "I saved your ass. You should be thanking me."

"You're the one who's gotten it in trouble."

"Your attitude sucks."

He pulled her into his arms and kissed her. She was not a piece of meat he could manhandle! She was not . . .

God, he was a great kisser. And when he pulled her tighter to him, she felt his need. She pressed even closer, loving the way his need connected with hers. It was stirring all kinds of sensations inside her, and if she kept rubbing against him, then she might . . .

He moved away, leaving her feeling empty and unfulfilled, and unsatisfied. He didn't look as if he was too happy, either.

"Why did you pull away? It was just starting to get interesting."

He glanced at his watch. "Because I have a class in an hour."

"And your point is?" He was the one who'd kissed her, not the other way around. He'd gotten her feeling all sexy and ready to jump his bones. She wanted satisfaction. Hell, she'd settle for a quickie. Quickies were nice. They could do a longie tonight.

"We have to get some things settled before I leave," he interrupted her thoughts.

Oh, there was the problem again. She'd hoped he'd forgotten about it. "Like what?" she hedged.

He leaned against the sink, crossing his arms in front of him. "Like the fact you're afraid of ghosts. I thought I'd hired a professional."

That was so not nice of him. She turned, going to the window, taking a calming breath, then facing him again. "You did. Just because I'm nervous around ghosts, it doesn't mean I can't get rid of one."

He didn't say a word. She knew the game. He was letting her do the talking, hoping she'd dig a hole she couldn't get out of. It wouldn't work.

"My father raised me in this business. I know almost as much as he does about exterminating ghosts."

"You actually go with him on ghost hunts?"

He had her there. Still, she refused to back down. "I used to. I still help him map out his plan of action, and I work on any of the equipment that breaks down."

"But you don't actually go with him."

She raised her chin. "I can do the job; besides, do you know any other ghost hunters in the area? You don't, and the reason I know this is because my father has the only company within five hundred miles. It's me or nobody."

He walked toward her, stopping when there was only a foot between them. He studied her face. She kept her expression impassive, not giving an inch.

"I think you're a pretty good actress."

Her heart began to pound. If he kicked her out, she had nowhere to go. Maybe he would let her continue to park her car in front of his house. Her gas tank was a hair away from being on empty. Five dollars wouldn't even get her around the block, and that was all the money she had.

How long did it take to starve to death? Maybe he'd feel sorry for her and toss her a PB and J occasionally. When she thought about it, feeding her would be the smart thing to do. He certainly wouldn't want a rotting corpse sitting in her car at the curb.

"But you're right," he continued.

She took a deep breath. A reprieve? She could see he was thinking it over.

"There aren't any other exterminators in the area," he finally agreed. "So it looks as though I have to trust you."

She slowly let her breath out.

"But I need to see some progress."

Progress? What was she supposed to do, get rid of part of the ghost? Exterminate the thing's head. Oh, yeah, that would definitely be a relief to have only a headless ghost stalking him. He'd really appreciate that. But she decided agreeing was the best policy at this point.

"Sure, and I swear I can get rid of it."

He nodded, but he still didn't look convinced.

"I have a class," he said.

"You already mentioned that." That was the reason they weren't making wild passionate love on the floor right now.

He went to a tablet of paper and jotted something down. "This is my cell phone number. Call if you need me."

"Okay."

His forehead puckered. "You'll be all right?"

"I'll be fine."

"Good."

There was an awkward silence; then he turned and left the room. A few minutes later she heard the front door open and close. A few more minutes passed, and she heard the roar of his motorcycle.

A tremble went up and down her spine. She'd ask if he would take her on a ride, but it would be just her luck that Daniel would stop by. It might be kind of hard to explain why Peyton was taking the cleaning woman for a ride on his motorcycle.

She sighed. Her timing had always been a little off. She went to the coffeepot and felt the glass—barely warm. She still hadn't had a cup of coffee yet.

"I'm not about to face the empty house, the ghost, or anything else until I've had at least two cups of coffee inside me," she mumbled.

There was a thumping noise upstairs as if to tell her she would never be ready, no matter how much coffee she drank.

God, she really, really hated ghosts.

After the second cup, she felt better prepared to face the

day if not the ghost. She went to the study, but stopped at the doorway.

Oh, this wasn't good. Her gaze slowly scanned the room. Apparently, Peyton hadn't looked inside before he left. The study was in shambles, and there were black spots all over the walls that the heat from her zapper had made. She wondered what he would think about yellow with black poka dots.

Not good.

She stepped closer, running her hand over one burned area the size of a plate. Well, now she knew what her zapper would do. If she ever made contact, no more ghost. But what would Peyton's house look like when she finished the job?

Nope, he wasn't going to like this at all.

Still, she couldn't stop the little niggling of pride that swept through her. She'd invented a ghost zapper all by herself.

Damn, she was good.

Chapter 8

Peyton didn't like the idea of leaving Kaci alone at his house. She was afraid of ghosts, damn it. How the hell had he gotten so unlucky as to hire a ghost hunter who was afraid of ghosts?

Kaci had told him she was only a little nervous. Get real! A person didn't shake like a leaf when they were only a little nervous. And now she was all alone. Just her and that . . . thing.

But he had a class that he had to teach if he wanted to keep his job. He scraped his fingers through his hair. She'd insisted she could take care of herself, and she probably could if she didn't fall asleep. He had a feeling she would stay alert from now on.

So where was the problem?

If he were being honest with himself, the ghost wasn't the only reason he hadn't wanted to leave. When she'd pressed against him, he'd almost come unglued.

Damn it, he shouldn't have kissed her, but she'd looked at him with all that sassiness, and her lips were so full and pouty, practically begging him to kiss them.

But had it been worth it?

He closed his eyes and drew in a deep breath.

Damn right, it had so been worth it, and then some. She'd tasted sweet and hot and full of spice. When he'd rubbed against her, she'd pressed closer. Kaci was a woman made for making love to on a lazy summer day or in front of a roaring fire in the cold of winter. Hell, she was just made for making love.

Damn, now he had a killer hard-on.

He quickly ducked into the nearest men's room and went to the sink, leaning the palms of his hands on the porcelain. He had to quit thinking about Kaci. For Pete's sake, he'd just met her. She was there to do a job and that was all. A lot was riding on this dinner, and he couldn't blow it by having a ghost scare the hell out of everyone.

"Here you are, old chap. I was wondering what had happened to you. I haven't seen you since this morning. I thought maybe you might have been . . . detained at home."

Peyton frowned as Daniel joined him at the sink and began washing his hands.

"Speaking of this morning," Daniel continued. "I'm not sure I would trust that cleaning woman you've hired. I mean, she acted quite strange."

"She came with references," he lied.

Daniel reached for a towel and began drying his hands. "In that case, I'm sure there's nothing to worry about." He sighed deeply. "She did seem rather odd, don't you think?"

She'd seemed odd? Daniel needed to have his eyes checked. Even though she'd been acting as though she were his cleaning lady, she still looked hot to him. Was Daniel trying to glean more information?

Their gazes met, and he saw the calculating look in Daniel's eyes. Maybe they hadn't fooled him. Peyton knew damn well that Daniel would do whatever it took to get the grant money. Not because he needed it, but because he wanted the prestige of everyone knowing he was the one chosen to have it.

He decided to take a page from Kaci's book and turn the tables on him. "Odd? I didn't notice anything except her accent, but then I'm not from England, never even been there. Since you were . . . what? Born there? I suppose you would know more about that. What part of England are you from, by the way?"

Daniel cleared his throat. "The northern part." He looked at his watch. "I'd love to continue this discussion, old chap, but I have a class." He hurried out of the bathroom.

"No, you don't have *any* class, old chap," he mumbled as he headed toward the door. The only good thing that had come from his talk with Daniel was the fact he no longer had a killer hard-on.

Kaci picked up the ringing phone and cautiously put it to her ear. She hoped it wasn't Daniel, but just in case . . .

" 'Ello, govna, you've reached Peyton Cache's residence, but he be out for a bit. I'm 'is cleanin' lady.' "

"Kaci?" her father asked.

She exhaled. "Dad, hi! I thought you might be someone else." She took the cordless to the other room and sat down on the sofa, curling her feet beneath her.

"So you're staying at the professor's house. Good, good. You should be safe there."

She raised an eyebrow and wondered what his definition of safe was. "Except for the ghost, you mean." And the fact that she'd made love with Peyton, but she wouldn't mention that part. She didn't even want to think about it while on the phone with her father.

He cleared his throat. "Well, yes, there is the ghost, but nothing you can't handle. You were trained by the best." He laughed.

"The ghost is smart."

"Not a demon, though. If you even suspect it's a demon, I want you out of there. I won't have you getting hurt."

She smiled wryly. That was her dad. Always trying to keep his little girl safe, but always putting her in harm's way. She still loved him. Probably because he really did try, and probably because neither one of them had anyone else.

"I don't think it's a demon. I think it's just mischievous. I'm just not sure exactly how to go about getting rid of it."

"Remember what I've taught you. The more ammunition you have, the better prepared you'll be."

She grimaced at his choice of words. "I think I've already used enough ammunition."

"The ghost zapper?" he guessed. "What happened?"

"I think it'll work, but the sights are off. Peyton's study looks as though it was in a war zone. Black burned patches everywhere."

"But at least you know it works."

"Well, I'm not positive, but I'm pretty sure."

"Good enough."

"How are you doing?" she asked.

"Fair. Pesky ghosts, for sure. I think there's a whole family of them living here, and it's crowded. Might take me a while to get rid of them."

He wouldn't be joining her anytime soon, then. She could really use his knowledge.

"You'll be fine, little missy."

She smiled at his use of her nickname. "Of course I will. Like you said, I was taught by the best."

"See what you can find out about earlier occupants. Always work backward to discover who the ghost is." He cleared his throat. "But be careful. Guido is still out there somewhere, too."

"I'll be careful. Promise."

They talked a few more minutes, then hung up.

Her dad might have made a lot of mistakes, but she'd always known he loved her. She sighed, looking toward the study. It really did look bad in there. Maybe Peyton had some yellow paint that she could use to repair the damage.

But later. Right now, she was going to take her father's advice and work backward. See what she could discover about the previous owner.

After making sure the study door was firmly closed, and

praying that Peyton wouldn't come home before she did and look inside, she grabbed her keys and went to her car, remembering the other car she'd noticed in the garage when Peyton had pulled out.

Please let luck finally be on her side, she silently prayed as she started her car. Kaci slowly backed up, then pulled into Peyton's garage, parking beside the small convertible. Of course he'd have a little red convertible. Someday she'd have what she wanted, too.

But right now what she needed was gas. She nibbled her bottom lip as she got out of her car. She wasn't really stealing, only borrowing a few gallons. It didn't count if you were only borrowing. Then why did she feel guilty?

She opened her trunk and took out a piece of garden hose. Both ends were cut. Then she grabbed a jug and the funnel.

She said another quick prayer as she opened his gas tank, then twisted the gas cap. Thank goodness he didn't have one that locked. She slid the hose down inside, then sucked on the other end before ramming the hose into the funnel. Gas began to pour into the jug. When it was almost full, she raised the jug in the air to stop the flow.

She really shouldn't even know how to siphon gas out of a car. It made her feel like such a criminal. But if he wanted her to get rid of the ghost, then she needed to do a little research, and a hair over empty wouldn't get her around the block, let alone to the places she needed to go.

Thirty minutes later, Kaci figured that should be enough, she hoped. She had no idea how many gallons that was. But when she got into her car and started it up, she was afraid it might've been a little too much. Sure her tank was small, but it was now three-quarters full. Maybe Peyton wouldn't notice he had less gas.

She drove to the abstract of title office first and parked in back. No sense letting Guido know she was still in the area, and she had a feeling he would recognize her car. That was the last thing she needed.

Once inside, it wasn't hard to smile and flirt with the young clerk until she had the information on the last four owners of Peyton's house. He even told her about a young boy who had supposedly died there, although he couldn't remember when, but he'd also heard the place was haunted.

Hmm, she wondered why they hadn't called Ghost Be Gone. Some people would rather move and pass on their problem to the next owner. Oh, well.

Next, she went to the library. She knew the librarian well. Sue kept her supplied in romance books, but getting information out of her was like pulling teeth. She had a feeling she'd be here for a while.

"Sue, I know the last four owners, and I know the place has a ghost. I only need to find out who is doing the haunting, but I want to be as discreet as possible. The owner doesn't want the information to get out."

Sue frowned, then sighed dramatically. She was an older woman who had a flare for the dramatic. Kaci had always felt it was because the woman was surrounded by fiction.

And she'd been right; today wasn't proving to be any easier. "Please, I really need this information." Sheesh, you'd think she'd asked for state secrets or something.

"I suppose it won't hurt to tell you what I know, since you are doing a service of sorts. I've met the young man, by the way. Quite nice." Her smile was dreamy.

Kaci stopped herself just short of shaking her head in exasperation. Sue was at least thirty years Kaci's senior, but then she supposed if it made Sue feel good to have Peyton flirt with her, then no harm, no foul.

"He's very nice," Kaci commented.

Sue studied her for a moment. "How nice?"

"This is business."

"He's single, you know."

"I know."

Oh, Lord, what had she gotten herself into now? Why did some people think everyone should have a partner?

She cleared her throat. "Can you tell me if anyone died in the house?" Better to redirect her back to why Kaci was here.

Sue frowned thoughtfully. "I don't recall how the story goes. It was so long ago, and I'm sure people have added and taken away a lot. I think it happened in the early nineteen hundreds, I believe."

Kaci glanced at her list, looking at the oldest one. "The Stone family?"

"Yes, I think that was it. I'll pull up the old newspapers if you have the year."

Kaci gave it to her, following her to the back. Once she had her set up to scan the films, Sue left. An hour passed, and Kaci's eyelids were starting to droop when she ran across something. An article about the loss of Eric and Agatha Stone's nineteen-year-old son, Edward, to consumption.

Interesting. She drummed her fingers on the table.

Of course he didn't want to leave the house, even now that he was dead. He'd probably been forced to stay inside in case someone should suspect he had TB, in which case he'd be sent to live the rest of his life in a sanitarium.

She glanced at the grainy picture of the young man and felt a moment of pity.

Edward Stone, what could you have been if given the chance?

Just as quickly, she pushed the thought aside. There was no room in this business for pity. She had a job to do, and that was rid Peyton of the spirit.

She thanked Sue on the way out and went to her car. There wasn't much traffic on the street, so her vehicle stood out like a sore thumb. She kept checking the rearview mirror to make sure she wasn't being followed. She even circled the block twice. Finally, she pulled her car back into the garage. Just to be on the safe side.

Not only did she have Guido to worry about, but in case Daniel stopped by again, too. He would get suspicious if her car was always parked in front of Peyton's house.

As soon as she stepped inside the house, she noticed the

musty smell had gotten worse. "I know you're here," Kaci said as she walked down the hall and slipped inside the study. The machines were going crazy. That, and the house was freezing. Cold chills were popping up all over her.

A fog appeared in the corner. Deep green, it lingered for a moment, then slowly dissipated. Her zapper wasn't near enough to reach. Great. It would've been nice to tell Peyton his ghost was gone. Then he'd change his tune. She would've made him grovel at her feet.

She had a feeling he would've groveled very well. She closed her eyes and, for a moment, remembered how he'd massaged her feet, then her ankles. Moving to her knees, then thighs then . . .

She really needed to stay focused.

And now she felt a little remorseful that she had to zap the ghost. What if getting zapped hurt? This ghost used to be a nineteen-year-old young man. He'd had no life to really speak about.

"Edward," she spoke softly.

The green mist appeared again. "I know you were sick a long time. It must've been hard living here, not being able to do what other men your age could do. I understand. I've been alone most of my life, too."

She reached a hand toward the mist as she eased forward.

"It's okay to go toward the light. You have relatives waiting for you on the other side. It will be so much better for you than staying here."

She opened her palm in supplication. Tears of sadness welled in her eyes.

Frrrtttt!

A big glop of ectoplasm plopped in her hand. *Ewwww!* Maniacal laughter followed.

"That was so not funny, Edward."

Maybe the next time she would zap his ghostly ass and not feel a bit of remorse.

Chapter 9

Kaci went to the bathroom and washed her hands. *Bleh!* Ectoplasm was like one giant ball of . . . No, she didn't even want to think about it.

Cold washed over her. She shivered.

Still, as she dried her hands, she couldn't stop thinking what it must've been like for a man so young to be trapped in his own home. No friends, no going to parties, no . . .

Damn it, she had to stop feeling sorry for Edward. He was causing all kinds of havoc, and it was her job to get rid of him. She would not turn soft now.

Why the hell didn't Edward just go toward the blasted light? Not that she was positive there was even a light. It wasn't as though she'd ever seen it, except in movies. But if so many people knew about the light, then it had to be there, right? She didn't like to think this was all there'd ever be.

She was a Christian and all, but sometimes she wasn't quite sure about things. She'd never really trusted in anyone but herself, and even that was on shaky ground most of the time. It was kind of hard to have faith in something she was only semipositive about.

Did that doom her to hell? Probably.

When she went back to the study, the machines had stopped buzzing. The chill had left the room, and she was pretty sure so had Edward.

Had he walked toward the light?

Yeah, right, like her life had ever been that easy. Nope, the spirit had only gone for a little while. She had a feeling it would be back full force the next time. God, it gave her the willies knowing there was a dead person living in the house.

She swallowed past the lump in her throat.

When the front door creaked open, she jumped, then hurried into the hallway. Peyton. The sunlight beaming through the doorway cast him in silhouette.

For a very brief second, she'd thought maybe the ghost was actually moving toward the light. Okay, maybe not exactly the kind of light it was supposed to enter, but whatever worked—right?

"I was afraid the ghost might have scared you off," he said.

She planted her hands on her hips and raised a haughty eyebrow. "I told you that I'm a ghost hunter."

"And that you're afraid of ghosts."

"That's beside the point."

"Has it appeared?" he asked, changing the subject.

"Yes, but I wasn't close enough to my zapper to do anything. It left a short time ago. I don't think it'll be back for a while."

"Then let's get out of here."

Kaci was tempted, but she didn't feel right about getting paid for a job that she wasn't doing.

"I insist."

"In that case, let's go." Okay, so he didn't really have to twist her arm or anything, and she did need to get out of the house after her confrontation with Edward. If for no other reason than to plot a new strategy now that she'd had more interaction with him.

They went out the front door. Her heart began to pound. Were they going to take the bike?

"I noticed you parked in the garage. Smart move."

"I thought Daniel might find it strange if every time he drove past your house, my car sat in front."

He walked past the motorcycle.

The convertible was sweet, too. At least she would be with Peyton, and that was a lot better than Edward the ghoul.

She scooted inside the car and closed the door before buckling her seat belt. Peyton got in on the driver's side. This was a really small car. They were almost shoulder-to-shoulder.

You cannot jump his bones here in the garage.

Tempting thought. She'd never made it in a garage before. When had she gotten so horny? Since Peyton had shown her how great making love with the right person could be. Damn, he had some good moves.

But right now they consisted of backing out of the garage and driveway. Oh, well.

"Where are we going?"

He glanced down at the gas gauge. "To a station. I'm almost on empty. I could've sworn I'd just filled up. Unless I have a leak somewhere. I thought I smelled gas inside the garage. Did you notice anything?"

"Me?" she squeaked. "Nope, I didn't notice anything."

His words effectively killed any desire she'd been feeling a few seconds ago. She kept her gaze fixed straight ahead. Next time she'd remember to borrow only three jugs of gas. If he ever found out that she'd taken his gas, she would absolutely freakin' die of embarrassment.

"Where did you say we were going? I mean after you buy gas."

"Someplace where we can talk. I don't like the idea that the ghost knows exactly what we're saying."

She nodded, and leaned against the back of the seat and watched the scenery pass by. Talk was good. Getting away from Edward, even better.

And this was nice. The top was down, the wind blowing through her hair. She loved the end of summer. The temperatures were still in the mid to upper eighties, but not so hot that a person could lose ten pounds of water weight just stepping out the front door.

It was good to get outside—healthy . . . or something. She should do it more often, rather than spending so much time in a back corner of her father's office.

Peyton pulled into the station and filled his car, paying at the pump. When he finished, he drove a little farther down the street, then turned in at one of the city parks.

It just so happened to be her favorite. Not that she should put any significance to the fact they both liked the same park. It was also the closest one to his house.

He parked the car. "Let's walk."

Sounded good to her. She got out and followed beside him.

"How long have you lived here?" he asked.

"Twenty questions? Didn't you ask my father anything?"

"But your father's not here."

He had a point. She strolled over to a tree and leaned against it. The park was nice, and there was a slight breeze to make it seem cooler. A fountain bubbled water from one level to the next. If they kept walking, there would be a small pond where koi would come right up to the edge and let you feed them.

"We moved here a couple of years ago," she said. It was the longest they'd ever stayed in one place. She was getting used to the town. That made her nervous. She realized falling in love with a town wasn't good.

"Before that where did you live?"

She focused on him again. "What does this conversation have to do with getting rid of your ghost?"

"Nothing. Maybe I just want to get to know you better."

She could've reminded him that he'd already done that last night, but decided to keep her naughty thoughts to herself.

She shrugged. "We moved a lot."

"It must've been hard on you."

Had he caught the trace of sadness in her voice? She was usually pretty good at hiding her emotions.

"It wasn't that bad. What about you?" she asked, turning the conversation away from herself . . . again.

"But we weren't talking about me. We were talking about you."

He put his hand on the tree above her head. His nearness made her body tingle.

"I think we'd better stick to talking about the ghost."

For a moment, she wondered if he was going to drop the twenty questions about her life history. He looked as though he'd like to probe a little deeper.

"Okay, we'll talk about the ghost," he finally said.

She breathed a sigh of relief. "What do you want to know?"

"Can you really get rid of it?"

She met his gaze head-on before pushing away from the tree and walking toward the pond. "If I can't get rid of it, no one can. I know you're worried about whether I can do the job or not, but you shouldn't be. My father trained me well."

"So, you'll what—zap the ghost with your zapper and it'll be gone?"

"Something like that. At least, that's the best case scenario."

"And the worst?"

"That I can't get rid of it." She stopped, and turned to look at him. "Have you ever thought about moving?"

His expression was grim. "I sank a lot of money into restoring the house. The ghost hasn't actually been anything more than a nuisance, but if it turns violent, then yeah, I've thought about moving."

"I went to the library today and found out a little about the previous owners."

"I was going to do that, but I haven't had time. Please tell me I'm not living in Lizzie Borden's house."

"Huh? No, Lizzie lived in Massachusetts."

"Good, I think. What did you discover?"

"It seems a couple of people from around town knew some things about the previous owners. The rest I found at the library, looking through newspapers on file. I was very discreet," she quickly added.

"And?"

"The first owners had a son, Edward, who died from TB when he was nineteen. From what I gathered, he stayed close to the house. He was probably too ill to socialize.

"I would imagine his parents were cautious since they usually put people with TB in sanitariums back then. They were treated like diseased outcasts. Patients condemned because they had an illness that didn't have a cure. Once they were sent there, they weren't expected to return."

"And so this Edward died at home."

"That's my guess. Of course, I'm not positive it's him, either."

"Who else could it be?"

"Possibly an interloper."

"A what?"

"A vagabond ghost. One who really doesn't have a home. It finds a house it likes or a person, and it attaches itself to them. Some will stay with the house or person until . . ."

"Until what?"

Too much information. Peyton's face had lost a little color. "Until I get rid of it for you."

"And if you don't?"

"How do you feel about houseguests?"

"That's not funny."

"I didn't intend it to be."

"But if it is this Edward, why didn't he just move on to the next realm?"

She shrugged. "Maybe he feels cheated because he was so sick in life."

"So he's going to make everyone miserable now that he's dead."

"Pretty much."

"You're a big comfort."

"Thank you. I try."

He leaned toward her. For a moment, she thought he might kiss her, but instead, he brushed a leaf from her hair, then stepped away, and the moment was gone.

When he started walking again, she had no choice except to follow.

Had he been about to kiss her?

Peyton could feel himself sweating. He'd come so close to kissing her. He needed to keep their relationship professional. Kaci needed to do her job, and he needed to stop lusting after her.

His life was getting complicated. He looked over his shoulder, reaching his hand toward her. She hesitated before taking his. Her hand felt warm and small inside his. So what if his life got complicated. He'd always enjoyed a challenge.

"Tell me about this ghost zapper," he said, more to hear her voice than anything. Now that she'd dropped the tough act, he liked her soft southern drawl. "Did your dad come up with it?"

He glanced her way and saw her frown.

"No, I did. Does that surprise you? I've always liked tinkering with things."

Now he'd offended her, and that was the last thing he wanted to do. "I bet you took apart your tricycle as a kid."

"Why would you think that?"

"Most kids who like to tinker with stuff took their tricycles apart as kids. Did you?"

She raised her chin. "I did, but I also put it back together."

"And this zapper works?"

Was she blushing?

"The sights are off a little."

He knew when someone was hedging, and right now, Kaci looked guilty. What exactly was she hiding from him? Did he want to know? He had a feeling he didn't, but he was afraid he would eventually.

They stopped at the pond, and a dozen or so fish came over when they approached. Some of the koi were ten inches long. They ranged in colors of deep gold, to gold with black spots, and white ones with gold spots. Their tails were like graceful, iridescent fans.

"They're beautiful," she whispered.

He wanted to tell her that he didn't think they'd shy away so she didn't need to whisper, but he had a feeling the softness of her words were more out of reverence to the beauty of the fish.

This was another side to Kaci. He'd seen her trembling in fear, her stubbornness. Her mafia act and her innovativeness when she'd come out of his broom closet pretending it was the door that led to a nonexistent basement. Her inventive side when she talked about her ghost zapper . . . and now this side. A very feminine side.

"Has anyone ever told you how beautiful you are?" Before she could answer, he continued, "That was a really bad line. I'm sure a lot of men have told you just how beautiful you are."

She cocked an eyebrow. He'd forgotten about the sassy side of her.

"You think a girl ever gets tired of hearing it?"

He grinned. The Jersey accent was back in full force. She was a consummate actress. That alone should make him keep his distance. Not start up something that he had a feeling could quickly get out of hand.

Ah, but she was so damn beautiful, and he just couldn't stop himself. If that made him crazy, then he guessed there were worse things in life.

"In that case, you're very beautiful." He brushed some loose strands of her hair behind her ear.

"Actually, I haven't dated that much." She started walking again. "I know we moved too fast last night. And we probably should take things a little slower and get to know each other a little better." She looked at him. "But no, no one has ever told me that I was pretty, except my father."

"Good."

She raised her eyebrows. "That's a good thing?"

"Yeah, I like knowing I'm the first one to tell you, and I don't mind taking time to get to know you before we go any further in our personal relationship."

She smiled, but just as suddenly, it was gone.

"Quick, kiss me!" She grabbed his forearms and pulled him toward her, planting her lips on his.

This was taking things slower? As he lost himself in the kiss, he wondered what exactly she meant by her definition of slower.

Chapter 10

Guido was in the park! What the hell was he doing here? Wannabe mobsters didn't go to parks.

Kaci ended the kiss, but pulled Peyton close so she could peek over his shoulder. Someone was walking toward Guido. A meeting, then. That's why he was here. Something illegal, more than likely.

"I like your version of taking things slower," Peyton said. His hands moved lower, caressing her back.

She closed her eyes and took a deep breath, but when she did, she inhaled his scent. She wasn't sure what aftershave he used, but it had a woodsy aroma that made her want to draw even closer.

"I'm sorry," she told him. "I just couldn't stand not kissing you when you were right here in front of me, tempting me."

It was actually the truth, and she had been thinking about kissing him. Then Guido showed up and scared the bejeebies out of her. She did the first thing that came to mind.

"I felt the same way," he said, nuzzling her neck.

She bit her bottom lip as she was caught up in the haze of sensual desire he created inside her. This was good. No, she had to keep an eye on Guido. She forced her eyes open.

Guido was about five-foot-six and built like a pit bull. He even snarled like one. He had the boxy shoulders, and what he didn't have in height, he made up for in muscle.

He always wore a suit, as though that would make him seem more important, and shoes you could almost see your reflection in. None of that was out of the ordinary. He liked dressing nice. No biggie.

But not only was the guy a major jerk, he had a comb over. Ten strands of hair spread out to cover the top of his bald spot. It didn't work. It reminded her of the sides of a tent flapping when the wind blew. Up and down, up and down.

There was something about the flapping hair that could mesmerize a person as it moved up and down in the wind. It had a hypnotic effect. She kept expecting Guido to say, "You're getting sleepy."

But right now she was very alert. Guido raised his hand, and she thought for a second he might bust the other man in the chops, but he only shook his fist in the air before spinning on his heel and marching off in the other direction. A few moments later, he was gone from sight, and she breathed a sigh of relief. Thank goodness he hadn't seen her. There for a minute, she'd thought he'd followed her.

"Why do I get the feeling this is one-sided?" Peyton asked as he stepped back and gazed into her eyes. "You seem more than a little preoccupied."

"I got sidetracked and was thinking about my next step in getting rid of your ghost?" Damn, she could've sounded a little more assertive than that. She was losing her touch.

"Now, why don't I believe you?"

He was sexy as hell even as he held the ax above her head. Okay, she needed to focus. The last thing she wanted was for Peyton to find out about Guido.

She stepped away from him and opened her hands in supplication. "And why wouldn't you believe me?" She widened her eyes innocently. "What do you see here in the park that could possibly distract me?"

He looked over his shoulder. The park was empty. The hour was growing late, and the few people who had been there had already left as the sun began its descent. Which was probably why Guido thought it was safe to meet here.

When he turned back around, he looked a little confused. "I guess I've been jumpy since the ghost first appeared." He sighed deeply. "I'm starting to question everything and everyone. I'm sorry."

Major guilt trip.

She should come clean. Tell him the truth. Confess everything: that he now had blotches of burned spots in his newly refurbished study, that she lusted after his motorcycle and his leather coat, that she'd siphoned his gas, and that Guido was looking for her father to do him bodily harm because dear old dad had foolishly borrowed money from the two-bit thug.

Yeah, right, like that would ever happen!

She looked Peyton in the eye. "You're forgiven."

Relief washed over Peyton. Man, how had he gotten so lucky? Here he was practically accusing her of doing . . . what? Hiding something? Yeah, that's exactly what he'd been doing. And there wasn't a soul in the park besides them.

And on top of that, she had come clean about being afraid of ghosts. Something she could've admitted to sooner, but better late than never.

No, Kaci had been up front pretty much most of the time, and right now she was looking at him as though she were trying to figure out what he could possibly be accusing her of this time, and forgiving him anyway.

She was the most sincere person he'd ever met. He pulled her into his arms and felt her sigh of relief.

"I know you'll be able to get rid of the ghost. I have no doubts."

He actually had a lot of doubts, but he'd at least give her the chance to prove herself. Besides, it wasn't as though he could get rid of the ghost himself. The least he could do would be to trust her capabilities.

"I'll do my best," she said.

"That's all I ask." He kissed the top of her head. She tilted her chin up and looked him in the eye. He didn't know what she'd been about to say as his eyes focused on her lips. Full, pouty lips. The kind that begged to be kissed.

He lowered his head. Maybe he wasn't ready to take it slow, either. What was it about this woman that pushed him over the edge?

He slid his hand under her shirt and unsnapped her bra, feeling a sense of urgency. He wanted to touch her breasts, fondle them.

She moaned when he moved his hand to the front and let the weight of her breast rest in his palm. She ended the kiss and laid her head against his shoulder, her breathing ragged.

"We can't. We're out in the open. Someone will see us."

"No, they won't. We could be any other couple who is standing close to each other looking at the fish. Besides, we can see if anyone approaches."

"I don't want to get arrested."

"I want to touch you." He moved his hand across the fullness of her breast and rolled her tight nipple between his thumb and forefinger.

"You win," she moaned.

"I already knew that."

"Ass."

"It feels good, though, doesn't it?"

"Are we doing the sex talk again?"

"Yeah. Does it feel good when I lightly squeeze your nipple? When I tug on it, applying just a little more pressure?" His actions followed his words.

"Yes, it feels better than good, and you know it." She wiggled closer to him.

"I want to see your breasts."

"Ain't gonna happen. Way too out in the open for that, but you can keep doing what you're doing."

"My caressing your breast would only get frustrating after a while. You'd want more."

"Then keep doing it until just before I get frustrated." She sighed.

He was already to the point of frustration. "I want to see your breasts."

"I've never been naked in a park. I'm not sure I want to start."

She moved away from him and looked nervously around, making sure her shirt was in place, as if there might be a crowd gathered around her staring, waiting to point their condemning fingers.

"I had you pegged wrong," he said.

Her gaze jerked back to him. "What exactly do you mean by that?"

He shrugged. "I thought you were this tough ghost hunter afraid of nothing, but then, I find you're afraid of ghosts. I think maybe it's all an act."

She frowned. "Because I won't take my clothes off in a public place. I'd say that was self-preservation and having a brain."

"You're afraid someone will see you." He let his gaze roam over her. "You're a coward, Kaci."

"A coward? Those are fighting words, mister," she drawled, her body stiffening.

God, he loved the way she drawled. And he loved when she got mad. And, yes, he'd provoked her anger. He waited to see what she'd do next. Anticipation built inside him.

She raised her chin, then looked around again as if she were scouting the area. His gaze followed hers. There was a stand of trees not far away, completely shadowed, even more so with the slowly sinking sun and the shroud of bushes.

"I'll show you afraid," she said and marched toward the trees. Just before slipping behind them, she looked back at him. "Are you afraid?" she taunted.

"Not in the least."

Horny, now, he was that. He hadn't actually thought she would take her clothes off in the park, even though it was doubtful they'd be caught.

When he stepped into the shroud of semidarkness, it took

a few seconds for his eyes to adjust. She stood in the middle of the small clearing. Slowly, she raised her hands and began unbuttoning her shirt. When the last button slipped through the buttonhole, she moved her shoulders, and her shirt slid gracefully down her arms. Her bra was already unfastened, so it quickly followed.

"You're beautiful," he breathed, his gaze lingering on her high-pointed breasts.

"So you've told me." She slipped out of her pants, letting them fall onto the top of the pile, and stood in front of him wearing only a pair of red bikini panties.

Sexy as hell.

The front of his pants tightened. He unbuttoned his shirt and tossed it on the pile. His jeans followed, then his briefs. They landed on top of the discarded clothes before he walked toward her.

When she reached to take off her panties, he stopped her. "No, I want to do it."

She leaned toward him slightly.

"But I won't use my hands," he said. "I'll use my teeth. Much more erotic, don't you think?"

She moaned.

He walked behind her. "God, you have the sweetest ass. It makes me so damn hard when I watch you walk in front of me. You don't know how many times I've wanted to reach out and cup those sweet cheeks and squeeze them."

He stepped closer, blowing softly against her shoulder blade. In the fading light, he could see her body tremble.

"How does it feel to be almost naked? To know that someone could discover our little place."

"Naughty, very naughty."

He stepped in front of her. "Naughty is good. That's one of the spices of life." He brushed his hands lightly over her breasts before cupping them in his hands. "I love the weight of your breasts in the palms of my hands. They're just right. Your nipples are hard little nubs—and oh, so sensitive."

"Are your nipples sensitive, too?" She flicked a fingernail over one. He jerked. "Umm, I see they are."

She leaned forward and licked her tongue across one nipple, scraping her teeth over the hard nub. Pleasure shot through him. He continued to massage her breasts while she continued to taste him, flicking her tongue back and forth across his nipples.

"That feels good," he told her.

"But I want to do more. I want to explore every inch of you." She spread out their clothes.

"You don't seem to mind being outside anymore."

She grinned when she looked at him and motioned for him to lie on top of the clothes.

"I feel free." She raised her arms above her head and stretched toward the sky. "I feel like a nymph in the woods. I've never felt like this before. I think I like it."

He lay down on the clothes, leaning back on one elbow as he watched her. Damn, he could just lie here and look at her for the rest of the day. "Remind me to take you outside more often."

She strutted over and planted her foot on his chest. Damn, why hadn't he gone ahead and removed her panties? If he had, he would have a very nice view right now. Still, what she was showing him looked pretty damn hot.

"It's my turn to taste," she said.

His dick throbbed. She was using his techniques on him, and had effectively turned the tables. Damn, she was good—real good.

She lowered her body down to his, straddling him, brushing her breasts against the hairs on his chest, her nipples grazing him, sending spasms of sensation down his body.

But she hadn't touched what needed her touch most of all, and it was killing him. He could feel the sweat beading his forehead.

"Are you in pain?" she asked.

He didn't buy her act of innocence, not for one second. "You know I am."

She lowered herself just until the silky material of her panties brushed across his dick.

He sucked in a deep breath. Sweet torture. Before he had time to enjoy what she was doing, she moved away. He groaned his frustration.

"Oh, you'll like this even better."

She slithered down his body, then took him into her mouth, sucking on only the tip of his penis. His body jerked upward, wanting her to take all of him. But instead, she licked slowly down his length, then back up.

"You taste wonderful. Just as I knew you would. I want to take all of you."

"Yes," he breathed. All coherent thought fled as she sucked him deep inside her mouth. Hot, wet heat surrounded him; then she began to gently suck while sensuously stroking him up and down.

Lights exploded behind his eyelids. He raised his hips. He didn't think it could get any better until she moved her hand to his balls and began to lightly squeeze.

He was dying. His heart raced, his body trembled. He couldn't take a deep breath. His vision clouded. Ah, it was such a sweet death.

His penis was swollen and throbbing with the need to fill her. He couldn't take any more. His whole body ached for release.

He slipped his hands beneath her arms and pulled her up next to him. "Let me catch my breath," he told her.

"I want you inside me," she said, gently biting his earlobe. "I want to feel you thrusting in and out, going deeper and deeper."

He'd created a monster with his sex talk. Now she'd turned the tables and was using it on him.

And it worked.

Very well.

He rolled her onto her back. The sun had set, so all he saw was a shadowy outline. God, he wanted to look at her, watch her as she spread her legs wide. He wanted to fold back the lips of her sex and see the fleshy part. He wanted to taste her.

Later, he'd do all that later. Right now, he wanted to be inside her. He slid her panties down and tossed them to the side.

"What happened to using your teeth?" she asked in a sultry, gloating voice.

"You're what happened. I'm so damned horny I feel as though I'll explode any second." He fumbled for his pants, which wasn't easy since he couldn't see, and she was lying on them. He finally managed to get a condom and slip it on. He tossed the pants away from him.

She actually had the nerve to laugh.

"Have you ever been spanked?" he asked.

She drew in a sharp breath. "No . . ."

"Maybe I'll show you sometime."

"I'm not so sure about that," she spoke hesitantly.

"You weren't sure about being naked in the park, either. Spanking can be very erotic if done right."

"And I bet you know exactly how to do it," she said, her words trembling.

"As a matter of fact, I do." Then he was entering her, breathing a sigh of relief as he sank down into her moist heat. "Damn, you're so tight."

"More," she whispered.

"More what." It was all he could do to hold back.

"I want you to fuck me," she said, but the words were spoken softly, seductively. They were like an erotic caress as her heated breath fanned across his naked flesh. "And maybe next time I'll let you spank me."

His body quivered at her words. He began to stroke her. Slowly at first. She brought her legs up, wrapping them around his waist. He sank deeper into the heat of her body.

For a moment, he didn't move. "This is nice."

She stretched her body, her breasts brushing his chest. "More," she breathed, tightening her inner muscles.

He sucked in a deep breath. "I didn't realize you were so greedy."

"Because no one has ever made love to me like you have. I think you're quickly becoming an addiction."

Addiction? His blood ran cold.

No, Kaci hadn't meant anything by her words. They were just two consenting adults sharing hot sex—nothing more. He was pretty sure she wasn't a stalker.

To prove it, he began to move inside her. Going deep, then pulling almost all the way out.

It was only sex.

God, she felt hot and wet. Her inner muscles contracted around him, giving him more pleasure.

It was only sex.

Her breathing grew ragged as she strained toward him. He pumped inside her faster and faster. Her body grew hotter and hotter. The fire inside him began to build until he thought they would both be engulfed in flames.

Her body tightened, and she grabbed his shoulders, her nails biting into his flesh. Seconds later, his orgasm swept over him, rocking his body with the force. Then he returned to Earth, to his surroundings.

He tried not to crush her with his weight, but she was like a soft welcoming pillow. He lay on top of her for a moment before rolling to the side.

It was just sex, he told himself.

"Thank you for giving me this," she said. "It was fantastic."

And he knew he felt the same way.

Oh, God, he was in deep shit. It wasn't just sex. It had been mind-blowing, incredible sex. The best he'd ever had. The kind that was going to be hard to forget. The kind it was going to be hard to walk away from.

And maybe he wouldn't. At least not for a while.

"It was wonderful, wasn't it?" she asked.

"Oh, yeah." In fact, he couldn't remember ever having sex this good. "I think I could stay out here all night making love to you."

Then he heard the voices.

Chapter 11

"Did you hear that?" Kaci frantically whispered. It had been so stupid to get naked and have sex in the wooded area of the very public park. What the hell had she been thinking? That she was a friggin' hippie?

No, that was the problem. She hadn't been thinking, only feeling Peyton's caresses. Now they were going to get caught and probably thrown in jail. She could see the headlines now:

LOVE NEST IN DOWNTOWN PARK!

Guido would see her picture and come looking for her. She didn't want to die. She was too young!

"All we have to do is dress and we'll be in the clear. Just stay calm," Peyton quietly told her.

Stay calm. The voices were getting closer. How the hell was she supposed to stay calm? She rolled away from him. Her damn slacks were beneath him. She tugged on them until they were free.

"Of course I'm calm," she spat out, keeping her voice low. "Why the hell wouldn't I be calm? Just because I'm bare-assed naked in the middle of a public park and someone is going to discover us. I'm sure that's a good enough reason for me not to be friggin' calm!"

She rammed one foot inside the leg.

"I can't find my pants," he whispered.

Good, now she heard panic in his voice. She shouldn't be the only one horrified by the situation.

"Well, find them!" Sheesh, it was his idea they get naked. He could've at least kept up with his clothes. Unless he wanted to play Adam and grab some leaves.

A visual formed before she could stop it.

She bit the insides of her cheeks to keep from laughing. Would there be enough leaves to cover him? Oh, Lord, that was naughty even for her.

The voices sounded louder. She really needed to stay focused.

"I don't know where they are," she said. "It's not like I have a flashlight or anything." She tugged her pants up. Except they weren't hers. Crap! "I have yours," she whispered. "Can you find mine?"

"Here they are." He flung his arm outward, smacking her up beside the face.

"Ow." Her eyes watered. She had to blink rapidly to clear them—not that she could see in the dark, anyway.

"Kaci, I'm sorry."

"Just put on your clothes. I'm okay." She wasn't. Her eye hurt. Man, he'd smacked her a good one. But at least she had her pants. "Where's my panties?" she asked.

"Give me a second."

She heard him shuffling around.

"I'm afraid they're a lost cause."

Damn, she'd really liked that pair. They were practically brand new. Red with a tiny rosette on each hip.

Think! God, she was moving in slow motion. After fastening her pants, she scooted back to the ground and began searching for her bra and shirt.

"Hey, Joey, did you hear that? Sounds like someone's over there in the bushes."

They froze. She could barely hear Peyton's breathing.

"I didn't hear nothin'. Hey, did you bring a lighter? I forgot to get my dad's."

"Yeah, I got it covered. Man, this is going to be so cool!"

There was a whistle, then a pop. The sky lit up into a shower of multicolored lights. There was another whistle, and another pop, and another sprinkling of lights across the night sky.

Yea, she spotted her shirt. She made a wild grab for it as the twinkling lights in the sky flickered out.

"Hey, get Big Bertha out. I want to see if it really does what it says it will."

She gave up locating her underclothes and quickly slipped her arms inside her top, then buttoned it up. Okay, now she could breathe a little easier.

"I don't think I want to find out what Big Bertha will do," Peyton said, keeping his voice low as he slipped his feet into his shoes.

"Me, either." She quickly tied her shoestrings. "Let's get the hell out of here."

A siren echoed through the trees. She froze. It sounded really close.

Any second she'd wake up from this nightmare.

Or not.

"We can slip out the back side of the park, then make our way to the car.

"Are you laughing?" she asked. She'd swear she heard the unmistakable sound of laughter in his voice. This situation was so not funny!

"Of course not," he denied.   .

No, she'd distinctly heard laughter in his voice. "This isn't funny. You have a hell of a lot more to lose than I do." He didn't, but she wasn't about to explain Guido to him. She'd save that for another day.

He grabbed her hand and pulled her against him. "But it was so worth it." He kissed her. A quick touching of their lips but it lit the flames of desire inside her. This man was so dangerous, but he made her feel so alive.

And he said she was worth it.

He ended the kiss and grabbed her hand, pulling her along behind him. They couldn't move fast because of the trees. There wasn't a lot of brush.

"You do know where you're going, right?"

"Sort of."

"Sort of?"

"Yeah." He stopped, and pointed toward the sky. "There's the north star. We're moving away from it, so we should be going south. When we're out of the woods, we'll cut back to the west, and that should take us to the parking area where we left the car."

His plan sounded good. It was a lot better than hers. Mainly because she didn't have one.

"I think that's the clearing. I can see the lights from the streetlight."

Good. She felt as though she'd been running for miles, even though she knew she hadn't. Too damn much time spent in the back office. She really needed to get more exercise. She would move it right up to the top of her to-do list.

He was right. The trees were thicker, but slivers of light were making it easier to see. They went around a really big tree and stepped into the clearing.

"Get your hands up!" voices yelled.

Kaci screamed, but thrust her hands in the air. She saw Peyton had done the same thing. She squeezed her eyes shut. If she was going to die, she didn't want to know it.

"Who are you?" a deep voice said.

"I'm Peyton Cache. I'm a professor at the college. We were on the other side of the park about to leave when we heard what we thought might be a gang of men, so we backtracked and came through the wooded area."

She opened her eyes and saw the two men standing beside patrol cars. Cops. She breathed a sigh of relief until she re-membered exactly what they had been doing.

"There must've been at least fifteen men," she elaborated. "Maybe even twenty. A badass gang." Thank God for her acting abilities. She'd had just the right amount of fear and innocence in her voice.

"You can put your hands down," the cop said. "Don't you think it's a little late to be in the park?"

"We were feeding the fish." They were feeding the fish? How lame was that? Okay, maybe that line wouldn't go over very well.

The officer's eyes narrowed. "You okay, miss?"

"Yeah, why wouldn't I be?"

"Looks like your eye is swelling."

"A limb hit me." She didn't have to mention it was one of Peyton's limbs.

The officer's radio crackled. "Hey, Jim, we got them. Two kids shooting fireworks."

She looked at Peyton, then at the cop. "Well, it had sounded like there were a lot more men. Voices carry really well at night and voices sound deeper."

"Yeah, sure." The officer sighed. "I suggest you two go home and try to remember you're not teenagers anymore."

She opened her mouth to retort, but Peyton grabbed her hand. "Yes, sir, and thank you, officer."

He hurried them away before she said anything more. She'd seen the smirk on the officer's face and knew exactly what he'd thought. His being right was beside the point.

It wasn't that far to the car. As soon as she got in, she turned to Peyton. His shoulders were shaking.

"It wasn't funny."

He pulled her into his arms. His lips were warm against hers. She melted, any anger dying a quick death. When he ended the kiss, she felt like a limp dishrag.

"I haven't had this much fun in years," he said.

"If this is your idea of a good time, I'd hate to see what happens when you have a bad time."

"You had fun, admit it."

"No."

"You did."

"No, I didn't."

"Not even a little?"

She fastened her seat belt and crossed her arms in front of her. "Maybe a little," she said, but kept her gaze straight ahead. She refused to look at him because she was pretty sure he'd be wearing a knowing smirk.

"I'm sorry I smacked you."

"It was an accident." Her eye was still sore, though.

"Your eye looks like it might be bruising. We should probably put some ice on it when we get back to my house."

"Yeah, sure."

The next few minutes were quiet as he started the car and backed out of the parking lot.

"I think the cop had started to believe us," she finally said. She hated to think he might have guessed what they'd been doing.

"He didn't buy our story for a second."

Was he questioning her acting abilities? She looked across the dim interior of the car. "Why do you say that?"

"Because you buttoned your shirt up crooked and there's a twig in your hair and your lips look kiss swollen."

She reached up. He was right. There was a twig in her hair. She wiggled it out. And he was also right about her shirt being crooked.

"Do you think you might have mentioned this before now?" She could feel the heat rise up her face.

"The damage was already done. Besides, what does it matter if he knows what we were doing?"

"Oh, now you don't care what people think? Why not tell people you have a ghost, then?"

"There's a difference between someone knowing you gave in to your desires and someone thinking you're crazy."

He was right. She'd run up against a lot of prejudice because her father had a ghost-hunting business. She could still remember the sting of the taunts when she was going to school. Which was probably why she'd kept to herself.

Peyton pulled into the driveway, but left the car outside the garage. She assumed so he could park his bike inside. They got out, and she waited for him to do just that.

She told herself it was because he had the key to unlock the front door, but even if the house hadn't been locked, she still didn't want to go in by herself.

She was such a coward.

Kaci followed him up the steps, stopping at the door. He unlocked it, and they went inside, flipping on a light. She breathed a sigh of relief when she saw everything looked the same.

"I just need to get some papers out of my study," he said.

She could feel the color drain from her face. "No!"

He stopped, hand on the doorknob. "No?"

If he saw the burned patches, she didn't think he'd be happy.

"The ghost. Uh, it upsets the balance of the magnetic fields when too many people go in and out of the room where . . . uh . . . most of the ghost's energy is centralized." She drew in a deep breath.

"Really?" His expression was skeptical.

She nodded. "Oh, yeah. It could screw everything up. Throw me off at least a week, and you did say that dinner was coming up pretty soon."

He let go of the door. She kept her face impassive. She could tell he was thinking it over. He finally nodded, accepting her lies—no, her acting. She didn't lie. This was for his own good. If he walked inside the study and saw the burned areas on the wall, he'd probably freak out. That wouldn't do either one of them any good.

"I can get the papers for you."

"Top shelf on the desk. The whole stack."

She nodded. He stood there. She squeezed around him and opened the door mere inches, then slipped inside. Just before she closed the door, she looked at him. "Magnetic field," she whispered, then clicked the latch.

She leaned against the door, closing her eyes and taking a cleansing breath. Except it wasn't cleansing. It was rancid.

Bleh! She opened her eyes as she flipped on the light switch, then looked around.

Oh, yuck!

Ectoplasm dripped from her machines. Gooey greenish ectoplasm. Great big globs.

She slapped a hand over her mouth and forced herself to swallow. She'd get the papers and get the hell out of there. Later, she'd clean up the mess.

Damn, she really hated ghosts.

Kaci tiptoed over to the desk, careful not to step in any green globs.

"You okay?" Peyton called out.

"Fine. I'm getting the papers right now. I just have to be careful about not . . . disturbing the magnetic field."

She clamped her lips together, then reached up and got the papers. Peyton was a lot of fun, and he had all the moves down pat when he made love, but he was kind of gullible. Not that she would expect him to be anything less when it came to the machines and getting rid of ghosts. If he'd known how to do it, he wouldn't have called her.

She took one last look at the room and was glad he did believe her. He wouldn't like what he saw if he got a glimpse of this mess.

She cut off the light and eased out of the room, making sure he wouldn't see anything. She thrust the papers at him.

He wrinkled his nose. "What's that smell?"

She just barely stopped herself from raising her arms and sniffing. "What smell?"

He frowned. "I think it's coming from the study."

"Ghost farts," she automatically replied, then felt her face getting warm. "I mean, that's what my father calls it. It's just the odor of the ghost."

"I knew the house could smell a little . . . rough at times. Kind of musty, but ghost . . ."

"Farts," she supplied when he seemed to have a little trouble saying the word.

"Okay." He appeared to think that over for a moment. "What about spray . . ."

She shook her head. "Won't work. It's kind of like the boys' locker room in high school. I was on the decorating committee one year. No amount of spray could get rid of that odor."

It was the one time she'd attempted to join in and volunteered to help decorate for homecoming. Big mistake! Her nose burned when she remembered the smell. Kind of like rotten food that had been sitting in the heat for about two days. She shuddered.

"But it'll go away when you get rid of the ghost, right?"

"*Pffft,* yeah."

"Good." He sighed with relief.

"It won't linger more than a month . . . or two."

His expression turned a little green. "What about the faculty dinner?"

"That might cause a problem. Did you ever think of having it at one of the area restaurants?"

"No, you'll just have to think of something."

"Me?"

"You're the ghost guru. The one who can supposedly get rid of them."

That didn't mean she could get rid of the smell they left behind. Maybe she should tell him he might want to start ordering a lot of air freshener. Like maybe a couple of truckloads.

"I'll do my best," she said.

"I have to grade papers." He turned to go, but looked at her once more. "Don't forget to put some ice on that eye."

"Sure." She watched him leave. He'd seemed a little dazed and confused.

But damned sexy.

Chapter 12

Peyton could smell the ghost stink all the way to his bed-room. He shook his head. No, it wasn't that bad—at least not on the second floor.

What else would go wrong?

He paused outside his door, hand on the knob. Which re-minded him, why had Kaci been afraid he'd go inside the study? And she had been. It was written all over her face. He didn't really buy all that garbage about magnetic fields and central-ized energy levels—at least, he didn't buy into it one hundred percent.

Something was going on other than the ghost. Or maybe because of the ghost.

He opened the door to his bedroom and went inside, toss-ing the papers onto the desk that was in the corner. As he sat down, his mind wasn't on the papers he needed to grade. He leaned back in his chair, crossing his hands behind his head, and closed his eyes.

No, he knew where his mind was, on Kaci. He hadn't thought she'd strip down to bare skin right there in the park, even though she'd slipped between the trees to do so. Hell, he hadn't planned on stripping, either, but he'd been caught up in the moment . . . the fire of passion.

It was just about the sex—wasn't it? There wasn't any-thing else going on between them. Sure, he'd thought it was funny when Kaci had pretended to be his cleaning lady. He smiled. She did a pretty decent mobster imitation, too.

But was she pulling a fast one on him? It was something to think about.

Something banged downstairs. He wondered what she was doing. Maybe he should check on her. He started to get up, but sat back down at the last minute. No, she had a job to do, as did he. He leaned forward and began to read the first paper.

Kaci clamped her lips together and wiped the last of the ectoplasm off the machine. This was really gross. If she croaked and came back as a ghost, she was so not going to blow loogies all over the place.

"You know, this was pretty juvenile. Not to mention just plain sickening."

A green mist began to form in the corner.

This was her chance. She eased toward the zapper.

"Wouldn't you much rather walk toward the light," she said in a soft voice. If she could keep his attention, she might be able to zap his ass. "You have family waiting for you."

Edward seemed to reach toward her. She refused to stick her hand out this time and end up getting slimed. Besides, she was almost there. Only a couple more steps back . . .

Before Kaci could get the zapper, she heard what she thought was snickering laughter. Then Edward disappeared.

A cold shiver ran down her spine.

When she looked at the readings on her instruments, they had all but come to a complete stop. He was gone. So much for zapping him this time. She needed to call her father anyway.

She flipped her cell phone open and speed dialed his number. Then waited. And waited. Her father was getting to the point where he couldn't hear a thing. She ended the call and dialed again. He answered on the fourth ring.

"Hey, little missy, what's up?"

"Hi, Dad. I saw Guido today," she blurted out, then wanted to bite her tongue when he sucked in a deep breath. She should've led up to it.

"Are you okay? I want you to pack up your things and come up here where I'm staying. I'll tell them you're my reinforcement."

"It's okay, Dad. He didn't see me."

"You could've mentioned that fact sooner. I almost had a coronary."

"I'm sorry."

"Where'd you see him?"

"The park."

"Huh?"

For a moment, her mind blanked out, and all she could think about was her and Peyton making love. Not something that went with talking to her father on the phone.

"Peyton thought we needed to get out of the house to discuss the ghost without being overheard. While we were at the park, Guido showed up. He met some man. He looked really pissed. Guido, not the other man. The other man just looked scared out of his gourd."

"You're calling the professor by his first name?"

That was a slipup, but he'd zeroed in on it. "I would think you'd be more concerned with Guido since you're the one who owes him money."

"Don't try to change the subject."

She rolled her eyes. "Well, yeah, Peyton's not that much older than I am."

"I thought he was a lot older. He sounded older when I talked to him on the phone that first day. I'm not sure I like you living in the same house with him. He hasn't gotten fresh, has he?"

Now her father decides to act like a parent?

"He's been a gentleman. He's a history professor. Very stuffy, very formal. You know the type." How many lies could one tell before they were condemned to hell? It was for his own good. She certainly didn't want to send him into shock or anything.

"Sounds like the type you want to be careful around," he grumbled.

"I'm always careful." She made sure she always had protection. She wasn't about to end up like Sandy Carlson from high school. Nope, she would choose when she had a baby, and she wasn't ready for a child—someday, just not right now.

"Was the guy big?"

She opened her mouth, but no words came out.

"The one who met Guido?" he clarified.

He really had to stop changing the subject midstream or she'd be the one having a damn heart attack.

"He was a lot bigger compared to Guido. Big and ugly. Military haircut, square shoulders, beefy arms . . ."

"Benjamin."

"You know him?" She didn't think she liked the idea of her father associating with the likes of Guido, let alone this other man. "Who is he, Dad?"

"Benjamin works for Guido. A real intellectual giant. The guy couldn't pour water out of a boot with the instructions on the bottom. Likes to push people around. Guido was probably mad because Benjamin hasn't found me yet. All the more reason for you to come up here."

She didn't want to think about leaving Peyton just yet. Besides, she'd promised him she would try to get rid of his ghost.

"I can't, Dad. I have an obligation to at least try to get rid of the ghost."

There was a moment of silence.

"Then lay low," he warned.

"You know I will." She really did love her father a lot. "How's it going up there?"

"Wild."

She knew what that meant. More ghosts than even he liked to encounter. They spoke for a few more minutes, then ended the call.

She hadn't counted on Guido having a hit man. How much danger was she in? Guido had seen her a few times when he'd stopped by the office to collect money. Would he remember her? Did she want to take a chance he wouldn't?

There was only one thing to do; she'd stay in the house until the ghost was gone and she could join her father. She'd lay low. Be as inconspicuous as possible. *Pffft,* she could do that, no problem.

"Where did you say we were going?" Kaci asked. How the hell had she let Peyton talk her into letting him take her to dinner? She'd been good the last two days. She'd stayed close to her monitors, tested the zapper so the sights were right on target, and now she was ready to nudge Edward toward the light.

Except Edward hadn't come around. He'd made himself scarce. As if he knew something was up.

And she'd avoided Peyton. It had worked, too, sort of, a couple of days. Maybe he'd been trying to avoid her, too, because she hadn't seen much of him, either. At least, until he'd knocked on the study door and invited her to dinner.

"I thought I'd try a new Italian restaurant that just opened over on Fifth Street. If you don't like Italian, I was told they have other dishes to choose from."

"I like Italian."

"Great." He glanced her way, hand casually resting on the steering wheel, then he turned his attention back to the traffic.

One glance and he made her heart pound. She took a deep breath and cleared her mind. She would think of this as a business dinner.

He pulled into the parking lot, and they got out. The

restaurant was nice. The outside of the building reminded her of a painting from the Renaissance period with its stone façade and overhanging trees.

"It's beautiful," she told him.

"I thought you might like it."

They walked up the cobblestone path that led to the wooden front door. Inside there was a gurgling fountain and terra-cotta tiled floors. The walls were textured and gave the interior an old-world look. Whatever tension she'd been feeling immediately vanished as she let her surroundings envelop her.

"I feel as though I've stepped back in time," she said as a waiter approached, wearing dark clothes and a black velvet beret. The waitresses all wore full skirts and white blouses. On their heads were French hoods. "It's beautiful."

"I thought you might like it."

"And if I hadn't?"

"There's a Burger King down the road. If all else fails, no one can resist a juicy burger and onion rings."

"You had all your bases covered." She smiled.

The waiter led them to a table tucked away in one of the secluded alcoves. A candle flickered in a vase in the middle of the table. It all looked very romantic. Did he have ulterior motives?

She certainly hoped so.

"Your eye looks better. Not as bruised."

So that was his reason behind taking her out. He still felt guilty. "It was an accident. And you didn't have to take me out to make up for it."

"I'm not. I enjoy your company. And you've been scarce lately."

Not being around him had affected her, too. Forty-eight hours without feeling his arms pulling her close, his lips on hers, and making slow, sensuous love was too long. She was starting to get the shakes.

Or maybe it was just her body quivering with anticipation

because she had a feeling they both knew they wouldn't be sleeping alone tonight.

Time to get her mind off sex. If not, she might be tempted to jump him right here in the restaurant.

"The ghost has been quiet," she said. There, just thinking about Edward was enough to cool her ardor.

Peyton placed his hand on top of hers. "I don't want to talk about the . . . about Edward tonight."

"Aren't you worried he'll wait until your dinner party to show himself?"

"I hope he'll be gone by then, and I have no doubts you'll get rid of him before that."

She cocked an eyebrow. "No doubts?" She eased her hand from beneath his. He was causing sensations she wanted to ignore while there were people around them.

He shrugged. "Okay, maybe a few. But I'll worry about them later."

"Tell me about what you teach, since you don't want to talk about Edward," she said.

He straightened his silverware as though her question had thrown him off guard. Was there a problem? But when he looked up and smiled, she knew she must have been mistaken.

"I teach the political, social, and cultural history of different countries as well as this one. I try not to fill the students' heads with a lot of empty facts." He glanced around. "If you can show, rather than tell, I believe students will be more likely to remember."

"Like this restaurant."

"Sure. The architecture of the building is only a façade, but it depicts a period of time that once existed. If we're talking about the Renaissance period, I encourage them to go to Scarborough Faire."

"A field trip?"

"Why not?"

"I remember them from grade school."

"Exactly—you remember them."

She laughed. "Okay, I concede."

When he grinned, she had a feeling he'd known all along that he'd win. That's okay, she didn't mind if he won a few rounds now and then.

"I wished I would have had teachers like you," she said.

"Hot, sexy . . ."

She laughed. "Be careful, I'm not wearing my high-top boots, and it's starting to get a little deep in here."

The waiter came back with menus and handed them each one. "Can I start you off with a glass of wine?"

She remembered the last time she'd drank alcohol and looked at Peyton. He quirked an eyebrow.

One glass and that would be her limit, and she'd dilute it by drinking her water, even though she was not, and never would be, an advocate for drinking water, no matter if it came from a bottle or the tap.

"That would be nice," she told the waiter. "Merlot."

"I'll have the same," Peyton said.

"I'll give you a few minutes to look over the menus," he said before he left.

She opened hers. Even the font that was used looked as though it was from another time period. Fancy scrolls and swirls.

"I have a feeling your classes are filled to capacity," she told him. "You're a good teacher."

"How do you know? I could be an ogre who piles on homework and gives tests every day."

She raised her gaze above the menu. "You're not a very good liar."

He opened his mouth, his expression suddenly serious, but he didn't say anything, just raised his menu. She could only wonder what he was thinking. Had he been about to ask her if she was a good liar? Then changed his mind?

He'd be right. She could slap whatever label she wanted on

it, but it all boiled down to the fact she hadn't told him the whole truth.

It wasn't as though she had a choice. Technically, maybe she did. But she wasn't ready to step into the confessional booth just yet. Still, it didn't stop her from feeling a little guilty.

The waiter came back to their table and poured them each a glass of wine. "Are you ready to order?"

She set her menu down. "I'll have the . . ." Her gaze fastened on the door.

Oh, no, she was being punished because she hadn't come clean, right? God wasn't going to wait for her to die. He'd given her hell right here on Earth—in the form of Guido.

Chapter 13

She grabbed her menu back from the waiter's hand. "I can't decide," she said as she opened it and brought it up to shield her face.

"Of course," he said, looking more than a little startled. "Would you like a few more minutes?"

"Yes! A few more minutes."

The waiter moved to a discreet distance away from their table.

How the hell could she get this unlucky? Guido had just walked inside the restaurant and was looking around, bigger than life and ugly as sin. He had some blond bimbo hanging on his arm like he was a life jacket and she was drowning in the ocean. Had no one ever told the bimbo it was dangerous to swim with sharks?

"Kaci, are you okay?" Peyton asked.

She peered over the top of the menu. "Me? Sure, I'm fine. Why wouldn't I be?"

"Because you're acting a little odd."

"I changed my mind, that's all. There are so many items to choose from." She scanned the menu. "I'd like the portabella stuffed ravioli." She glanced over the top again. "Or maybe I'll just have the three choice platter."

"And you do want to eat tonight, right?"

She made a face, but he didn't see it because she was hiding behind the menu again. "I'll have the portabella stuffed ravioli."

"You're positive?"

"Yes."

She could only hope they would seat Guido and his lady on the other side of the restaurant and she'd be safe.

When she glanced Peyton's way, he didn't look convinced there wasn't anything wrong, but he didn't say a word, only motioned for the waiter.

Deep breath. She had to pull herself together. She could get through this, although she had a feeling that kissing Peyton wouldn't work this time, and she was almost certain that having sex under the table might get them thrown out of the restaurant. Yeah, that was probably a gimmie.

Peyton gave the waiter their order, but when the waiter tried to take her menu, a tug-of-war ensued for a couple of seconds before she gave in and let go.

Please, take Guido to the other side of the restaurant, she silently chanted over and over.

Oh, Lord, it wasn't happening. Another waiter was leading Guido in their direction.

Cover her head with the napkin? No, that would only get her admitted to the state hospital.

Her purse!

She bumped it so that it fell off the table.

"Oops." She quickly ducked her head under the table. When Guido and his bimbo passed, she breathed a sigh of relief . . . until she turned and was looking directly at Peyton beneath the table.

She was pretty sure her smile came off a little sickly. "I dropped my purse."

"Is that it on the seat beside you?"

She stretched her head around until she could see it. "Oh, I guess it is. I thought it had fallen to the floor. No wonder I couldn't find it." She straightened, brushing her hair behind her ears and quickly glancing around.

Oh, no. Guido was three tables over. The alcove shielded her, but just barely, and only if she slumped down in her seat. If he saw her, she was going to be in so much trouble.

"Are you comfortable?" Peyton asked.

She jerked her attention back to him. "Yes, why wouldn't I be?"

"I don't know, maybe because you've scooted down so far in your seat that I can barely see your shoulders?"

"Sarcasm doesn't suit you. I'll have you know that I have an old back injury that flares up on occasion."

"The war?"

"No, a football injury," she said and frowned at him. His attitude really sucked.

"I suppose this is one of those times that it has flared up."

"I would think that was obvious. I must've twisted it when my purse fell off the table."

"You mean the same purse that landed on the seat beside you and not actually on the floor."

If she were on stage, she would've already won an academy award for her stellar performance. Apparently, Peyton didn't know good acting when he saw it.

Kaci raised her chin, at least as much as she could without Guido seeing her. "Are you questioning my injury? Because if you are, I can let you speak to my doctor. He knows all the details of when I fell off a ladder hanging Christmas lights. It's something I do every year—hang Christmas lights, not fall off ladders. A lot of people get enjoyment from the twinkling lights." She ended her story on a sniff.

His expression of disbelief turned to uncertainty. "You're serious?"

She hated lying to him again, but she was in a bind. If she told him Guido was out to get her and her father, he probably wouldn't believe her. Even worse, he might realize she was telling the truth and get involved. This was her problem, not his.

"Can I get you anything?" he asked.

"I just need to sit like this for a while and hope it pops back into place."

She was a damn good actress. It had just taken Peyton a little longer than most people. He wasn't quite as gullible as she'd first thought. But she had to keep telling herself she was protecting him. Besides, it wasn't actually a lie. Her back was starting to ache scrunched down in this position like she was. Maybe that was her punishment.

The waiter returned with a salad. His eyes widened as he set it and a basket of breadsticks on the table. His face quickly returned to its stoic expression, though. Good waiter. She'd slip him a little extra tip if she had more than five dollars to her name.

"She has a bad back," Peyton explained.

"Old injury," she added.

"Would you like to move to another table?" he asked. "I can find you one with more room . . ."

"No!" The hole could not possibly get any deeper. "If I don't move, then I'm sure it will improve in a bit." The last thing she wanted to do was catch Guido's attention by moving to another table.

"Of course." He took the tongs and placed some salad on her plate. "Would you like some parmesan cheese?"

"Please."

He grated the cheese over her salad, then started to turn toward Peyton. She furtively glanced toward Guido. He was standing and looking right toward her. She reached up and tugged the waiter's jacket so he blocked Guido's view of her.

"A little more cheese, please." She smiled at Peyton. "I love cheese."

She peeked around the waiter. Guido was going toward the back of the restaurant. Probably to the restroom to wash the blood of his victims off his hands before his meal arrived. She sighed with relief.

"Will that be enough, ma'am?"

She returned her attention to the waiter. Now she had a

two-inch pile of cheese on top of her salad. Great, she wasn't a big fan of cheese. She'd made the best of a bad situation, and at least she hadn't been spotted.

"Perfect," she said.

Peyton waited patiently as the waiter grated his cheese, nodding when he had enough, but as soon as the waiter left, Peyton turned his worried gaze on her.

"I think I should take you to the emergency room. They could probably give you a muscle relaxer or something."

"Really, they can do nothing for me. I just have to wait it out."

His expression became more concerned. "At least we can go home and get you into bed."

Now that had possibilities. Trouble was, Guido would see her if she hobbled out on Peyton's arm. Speak of the devil, Guido was back. She cringed.

A cell phone rang. The theme from the *Godfather*? *You have got to be kidding me,* she thought to herself.

Out of the corner of her eye, she saw Guido reach inside his pocket and pull out a cell phone. He spoke for a few minutes, then snapped it shut and said something to the bimbo. Her lips puckered into a frown as she came to her feet, throwing her napkin on the table before she made her way to the door without waiting for Guido.

"Brenda, don't be like that. I have a business to run. You know that." Guido dropped a bill on the table and hurried after her.

Relief washed over Kaci, until she realized Peyton was talking and she had no idea what he'd said.

"I'm sorry?" she asked.

"I said I thought we should at least get you home where you'll be more comfortable."

She moved her hands beneath the table and pulled on her finger at the same time she moved to the left. The knuckle popped louder than she expected. She smiled as she straightened in her seat.

"No need. It's all better. I knew my back just needed to pop." She moved her shoulders back and forth. "Perfectly fine now."

"You're sure?"

"Positive." That had been close. No matter what happened, she'd stay inside Peyton's house until she finished the job. She did not like close calls.

Their order arrived, the rich aroma wafting up to her nose. Life should be like this all the time. Not the part with Guido, but having a meal with someone whom you enjoyed being with.

"So why did you want to teach at this college?" she asked. "I mean, since you recently moved here."

"They're more innovative than any college I know." He picked out a breadstick and took a bite.

"How so?" She took a drink of her wine, letting the liquid sit in her mouth as she savored the taste before swallowing. One glass, that was all, she reminded herself.

He shrugged. "Sometimes my teaching is considered controversial."

"History?" She shook her head. "Nope, I can't see history as being a controversial subject."

He looked as though he was going to say more, then changed his mind and smiled at her.

"You're right. But I do enjoy what I teach. It's very interesting."

Had she insulted him by implying what he taught was boring? She'd have to remember how much he liked his work. History was history. She really didn't see anything controversial about it.

But it was nice being with Peyton. Her insides turned to warm mush when he looked at her like he was looking at her right now.

They finished their meal, and the waiter discreetly brought the bill. Peyton paid it and they left. The warm glow was still with her as she walked out into the evening air. She realized just how comfortable she felt in his company. That wasn't good. The guy had a PhD. He was really smart.

Kaci, on the other hand, had a high school diploma. Not that she felt inferior or anything. She was just as good as anyone. But he ran in circles that she didn't and never would—with people like stuffy Daniel. Problem was, she was starting to like Peyton way too much.

Her situation kept getting worse. She had to get rid of the ghost and get the hell out of Peyton's life. And maybe she'd find a way to go to college. She wouldn't want to take anything artsy, but she might get into a trade school. She liked the idea of fixing things.

Maybe it was fate that had sent her here. She'd needed a nudge to get out of her father's back office and explore life.

Peyton opened the door of his car, and she scooted inside. When he climbed in, she turned to him. "Thanks so much for dinner. I loved the restaurant." The only damper on her evening had been running into Guido. She'd make sure that didn't happen again.

"I enjoyed the company," he said.

She smiled as she snuggled down into the seat. Blasted warm fuzzies were like a bad rash spreading over her entire body.

The drive home wasn't long. As Peyton pulled into the garage, she was glad to see the house in one piece.

They got out and walked toward the front door, then went inside. She breathed a sigh of relief when he switched the light on and she saw that it wasn't slimed. At least, not the front part. She really didn't want to look at the study. Not after that wonderful meal.

"It's early. Let's sit a while."

She raised an eyebrow. "Don't forget that I'm here to do a job."

"I know, but I don't want the night to end. I want to know more about you. We talked about me during dinner, but I don't know anything about you."

She wasn't so sure talking about herself was a good idea, but she didn't want the night to end, either. This was so not keeping her distance.

She nodded.

"I'll get us something to drink."

"Are you trying to get me drunk?"

He looked at her as if the idea of getting her drunk had possibilities.

"I have soda," he offered half-heartedly.

"That sounds good." He looked disappointed. She rather liked the idea that he wanted to get her into bed again. He probably wouldn't have to try very hard.

"Back in a minute." He left the room.

She dropped her purse on the end table and walked to the window. Peyton lived in a quiet neighborhood. He probably knew his neighbors. She'd been here two years and only knew Sue from the library. She'd bet Peyton had a whole social life where he went to dinner parties all the time.

He broke into her musings when he returned with their drinks. "Here you go."

She took the glass. "Do you know your neighbors?" she asked as she raised her glass to her lips and took a drink.

He smiled as he looked out the window. "Mr. and Mrs. Bartlet live across the street. They're both retired. A nice couple. She makes the best raisin pie I've ever eaten." He pointed to the next house. "Kenneth lives next door. He's madly in love but hasn't got up the courage to ask his girlfriend to marry him." He chuckled.

"How long did you say you've lived here?"

"A few weeks."

"Amazing." She took her drink to the sofa and set it on a coaster on the coffee table before leaning back against the cushions.

"What about you?" he asked.

"I've lived here two years, and I have no idea who my neighbors are." He joined her on the sofa.

"Why?"

She reached for her glass, running her finger along the rim before taking a drink. "People usually shy away from ghost hunters."

"Where did you live before moving here?"

She was grateful he'd changed the subject—sort of. She didn't want to explore why she didn't know her neighbors. What if there was something wrong with her? She'd just as soon not discover she was more than antisocial. She was a firm believer in ignorance is bliss.

Okay, where had she lived? "I think I've lived all over Texas; for a time we even moved as far away as California. Dad didn't like staying in one place very long. I remember my first year of school we moved thirteen times."

"Thirteen? That must've been hard."

She shook her head. "I got to see a lot of the country."

"And your mother?"

Her hand trembled. She set her glass down and hugged one of the sofa pillows close to her. "I never really knew her. She died when I was little—pneumonia. Dad says I look a lot like her."

"She must've been beautiful."

She smiled, enjoying the compliment. She didn't get them very often. "Dad said she was the most beautiful woman he'd ever met. He fell instantly in love with her the first time he saw her."

"Do you think that's possible? That love can happen that fast?"

She shrugged. "Maybe. Who knows? I think that's why Dad moved us so often," she continued. "He was afraid the pain of losing her would catch up to him. I'm not sure he could've handled it."

"But not staying in one place made it hard for you to make friends."

"I didn't need friends. I had my father." She spoke the truth.

She hadn't really needed anyone. Her father had been fun. They'd gone to the beach a lot when she was young.

"It sounds like you love him a lot."

"I do. He's a little absentminded sometimes, but what kid can say she has a ghost-hunting father. You have to admit that's pretty cool."

He laughed, and the solemn moment eased. "True."

She uncurled from the sofa and stood. "I think I'd better change clothes and go to work."

It was getting a little too cozy, and she did want to get rid of his ghost for him.

Before she left the room, she turned back and looked at him. "I've never been comfortable around strangers. It's different with you."

She hurried out of the room before he could comment.

Chapter 14

Peyton watched Kaci leave. She was an unusual woman, and no matter what she said, he knew moving so many times had to be difficult. No wonder she found it hard to talk to people. And that was probably why she didn't know her neighbors.

But she wasn't here for him to dissect. He didn't want anyone getting hurt when they came over. Or worse, scared to death when Edward appeared.

Edward. He shook his head. It was hard to put a name to the green mist. It made it seem more—human. He wondered if the guy had been this much of a jerk in real life. Just as quickly as the thought came, he pushed it away. What did he expect? Edward had been ill. Even so, it was time for him to move on. To run toward the light.

His cell rang. He reached inside his pocket and pulled it out. Joe. His brother was probably checking up on him.

"Hey, bro, what's up," he asked as he answered the phone.

"I was checking to see if you still had your problem."

Which one? The fact that he was starting to like Kaci a little too much? Or the ghost? He decided to play it safe.

"The ghost is still here," he told him.

"I guess that means the girl is, too."

"She is."

"But she's really ugly."

He sighed. "No, she's actually pretty hot."

"Oh, man, you said she was ugly."

"No, you told me to tell you she was ugly. So I did." He couldn't believe they were even having this discussion.

"You know that's not what I meant." His sigh came over the lines. "Please tell me you haven't slept with her."

"Okay. I haven't slept with her."

Silence.

"You're lying again," Joe said.

Peyton shook his head. "No, I'm telling you what you asked me to tell you."

"Damn it, Peyton. I can still kick your ass."

Peyton grinned. Yeah, he probably could. Joe was taller and worked outside a lot. The guy definitely had muscle.

"I have everything under control."

Joe snorted. "Like the last time?"

"Kaci isn't like Sherry. The poor girl had a mental condition that no one knew about. Once she got the help she needed, everything turned out fine."

"She stalked you. It could've been worse."

"But it wasn't."

Yeah, she had stalked him to the point he'd had to call the police in on it. He'd always wondered if he could have handled the break-up a little easier. What they'd had just wasn't working. Sherry had become possessive to the point he was afraid she was going to hurt herself or someone else.

"I refuse to wonder if every female I date will be like Sherry."

"Then, damn it, be careful."

"I will."

"Okay. Call me in a few days to let me know how things are going."

"I will. You take care, too." They talked for a few more minutes about Joe's winery, and then they hung up.

Peyton came to his feet and took the glasses back to the kitchen. He started up the stairs, but had taken only a couple of steps when he remembered there was something he needed in the study.

He glanced up the stairs. Kaci was probably still changing her clothes. That was an intriguing thought. He had a ton of work to get done, though. It was always like this when a new semester started.

If he went inside the study, then came right back out, she would never even know he'd been in there. He'd be careful not to disturb her machines.

With his mind made up, he hurried to the study and opened the door, flipping on the light.

He couldn't move.

His gaze slowly swept the room. The only room in which he'd had a chance to do any remodeling. Big black splotches dotted the buttery yellow walls that he'd helped his sister paint.

He stepped closer, running his hand over one of the splotches. It had been burned.

Hell, she could've burned the house down!

His body tensed. There was no magnetic field for him to upset. The only thing upset was him. She'd played him for a fool.

"Kaci!"

Kaci stumbled to a stop on the staircase. Oops. She had a feeling Peyton had opened the door to the study. Not good. Maybe she could sneak back up the stairs and give him a few minutes to cool off.

Coward.

And not a bit ashamed to admit it.

Oh, hell, she might as well get the showdown over with. It wasn't as though it was her fault—exactly.

She hurried to the study. Just as she suspected. The door was wide open, and Peyton stood in the middle of the room. When she cleared her throat, he turned to face her. His lips were set in a grim line, and his jaw twitched. He was definitely pissed. Not that she could blame him.

"I'll paint it after the ghost is gone," she offered.

"What the hell happened?"

"The ghost was in the room the other night, and I had the chance to zap it . . . so I did."

"This is what the zapper does?" He waved toward the burned areas.

"I guess it does."

"You guess? You guess! Haven't you ever used it before?"

"Not exactly."

He ran a hand through his hair.

"I just finished putting the final touches on it when Gui—" She coughed. "I mean, when we had all these calls from people needing to get rid of ghosts. Dad went one way and I came here to help you." God, she'd almost screwed up and mentioned Guido. Damn it, Peyton was making her nervous. And his jaw still twitched.

"You just thought you'd test it on my house."

"It works." She planted her hands on her hips. Screw nervous, now he was pissing her off royally.

"I can see that it works. I can see all over the study it works. It works great burning spots all over the walls. But I still have a ghost. Do you think you could invent something that will get rid of ghosts next time rather than a giant wood-burning set?"

"You are so not funny."

"I wasn't trying to be."

Her attention shifted from Peyton to the green mist forming beside him. She quickly scanned the room while Peyton continued to berate her. Her zapper was on the window seat, about two feet away. She eased toward it as he continued to criticize her skills.

"Are you listening to me?" he asked.

"Of course, I hear every word you're saying." She reached out to the side, bending at the knees, and picked up the zapper. "I hear every word you're saying."

"What are you doing?"

"Shh . . . Edward is forming right beside you," she said, barely moving her lips. Sometimes ghosts couldn't quite make out conversations. "As soon as he's the right consistency, I'll zap him, and your problem will be solved."

"What do you mean, the right consistency?"

"A ghost has to be thick enough so that when I zap him, he'll feel the heat and be forced to go toward the light where it's cooler." At least, she hoped that would be how it worked. Her father always told her the light was cooling, beckoning.

"It's right beside me?"

She nodded as she slowly brought the zapper from her side, making sure her grip on it was tight as she looked through the sights. "Just a couple more seconds."

"Why didn't you get the ghost the last time?"

"The sights were off."

"And they're okay now?"

"Yes."

"You tested it to make sure?"

"Not exactly."

"What do you mean, not exactly?"

"I'm pretty sure they're set."

"Kaci . . ."

"Get ready. Don't move." She squeezed the trigger at the same time Peyton dove to the side. Edward immediately vanished. The zapper popped. The wall began to smoke right where the ghost had been.

"What the hell were you trying to do?" Peyton yelled as he came to his feet.

She swung the zapper toward him, glaring at him. "I could've had him! Why the hell did you move?"

"Put the gun down." His words were slow and distinct.

She tossed the zapper on the window seat. "There, are you happy?"

She grabbed up the pillow and went to the wall and pounded it against the smoking area. It didn't look as though it had done that much damage. But it felt really good to pound something. Damn it, she'd had the ghost in her sights!

"Extremely happy," Peyton said.

"Why did you move?"

"Because I'd just as soon not look like George Hamilton after he's been to a tanning booth."

"But I was dead on."

He looked toward the wall. "Maybe you were, but I'd rather not be looking down the barrel of your zapper."

"You don't trust me?"

He was thoughtful for a moment. "No, I don't. At least, not when you're holding that . . . that thing."

"Ghost zapper."

"It looks as if it came out of a sci-fi movie."

"Well, it didn't." She walked over to the machine he'd dove under. "And now look, you have my equipment all out of sync. It'll probably take me the rest of the night to get it back to the right configuration. If you don't mind, please retrieve whatever you needed from the study and let me get back to work."

"Gladly. Just don't burn the house down while I'm sleeping." He grabbed a flash drive and left.

"Good riddance," she whispered.

After all they'd shared, and he didn't trust her. So what. She didn't care. They didn't really know each other, but she'd thought they were getting there. And they'd had sex not once, but twice. Anyone would think that meant something. He could've trusted her. She wouldn't have turned him into a crispy critter or anything.

"I should've known not to let my guard down. Every time I start getting close to someone, this is what happens—they disappoint me."

She went to the instruments and began to adjust dials. The damn things were going crazy. What the hell had Peyton done when he dove between the machines?

She sniffed, wiping the back of her hand across her cheek when a tear slipped out of the corner of her eye. Damn it, she hated when she cried. It made her nose all red and stuffy, and no man was worth crying over.

Then why was she crying?

So what if Peyton didn't trust her enough to stand still while she fired her zapper. She didn't care. Not even one little bit.

She went to the chair in the corner and flopped down. Who was she trying to fool now? She sniffed again and tugged the corner of her T-shirt up to dry her eyes.

A soft melody began to play.

Great, Peyton was listening to music while she was down here suffering. A chill swept over her. And it was damn cold, too. Drafty old Victorian. She hoped when he came downstairs in the morning she would be frozen in the chair with tears glistening on her cheeks. He'd feel guilty then!

She frowned.

Except she wouldn't have the satisfaction of telling him that he'd hurt her feelings because she'd be dead. Maybe she could haunt him. Yeah, that's what she'd do—haunt his ass. And look out dinner party!

God, she was so pathetic. She didn't give a damn what Peyton thought of her. Yeah, they'd had sex—big deal.

Well, actually, it had been a big deal, but that was beside the point. It had been only sex, and it certainly didn't matter that she had started to like him a little too much.

She slumped farther down in the chair.

And it wasn't his fault, either. They hadn't made any commitments—and the other verse, they probably never would. She'd gotten caught up in the moment. No biggie. She had her head screwed on straight now.

"I don't need anyone," she said.

Now that her crying jag was over, it was time to get back to work. She wiped the back of her hand across her eyes and got up out of the chair—and was enveloped in a green mist. She held her breath as it swirled around her.

Great, her zapper was across the room on the window seat. Maybe if she eased forward until she could reach it. She took a step, silently praying Edward wouldn't slime her.

One step, two.

There was something different about the ghost. She stopped, letting him envelop her for a moment.

Sadness. She could feel his emotions.

"Edward," she said softly. "It's okay. You can go toward the light, and it will make you feel better. I promise."

The air around her grew colder. She had a feeling Edward didn't want to talk about the light or walking toward it.

His aura grew stronger as he moved over her. It was almost as though he were caressing her. What had she done when she'd let go of her emotions?

She'd seen it happen before when ghosts connected with a living person's feelings. Edward had probably been shut away in his bedroom, alienated from others. He might have heard her and Peyton talking in the parlor about when she was little. If he'd caught enough of their conversation and compared her life to his, then he might transfer his loyalty to her.

This wasn't good.

What the hell was she supposed to do now? Edward was like a puppy showing affection for its new owner. How the hell was she supposed to zap him now? Her father always warned her not to connect with ghosts.

Peyton was suddenly standing in the doorway. She blinked her eyes, hoping she'd only imagined him. Nope, he was still there.

"Go away," she mouthed.

"The mist is swirling around you," he whispered back, taking a step toward her.

"No, don't come any closer," she warned.

The temperature around her dropped by about ten degrees, and the swirling stopped immediately. Edward's anger was palpable. Oh, Lord, what was Edward thinking?

"What should I do?" Peyton asked.

"Turn around and leave," she spoke softly.

"I'm not leaving you here alone with that thing, so you'd better come up with another plan."

She shivered as the temperature dropped again. "I think Edward is trying to make a connection with me."

"I can get to the zapper."

"He's all around me. It would be too risky."

He cocked an eyebrow.

Sheesh, men! "It was different with you. He was only beside you."

"I'm still not leaving. Not until I know you're safe." He crossed his arms belligerently in front of him.

"I don't think he'll harm me, but I have a feeling he's getting angry because you're not leaving."

"Why would he be angry?"

Peyton really needed to leave. She could feel Edward growing stronger. "I think he made some kind of connection with me. Neither one of us had many friends. He probably rarely left this house, if at all."

"Are you telling me he's falling for you?"

"I think so."

"This is just great." Peyton shook his head and laughed. "Tell me that the ghost isn't in love with you. It's too farfetched."

Not good, but it was too late to warn Peyton that he really shouldn't make fun of Edward.

The green mist suddenly flew past her right toward Peyton.

Frrrrt!

"Duck!"

She covered her eyes.

Chapter 15

"Yuck!" Peyton raised his arms, green slime dripped off his hands.

Kaci peeked between her fingers. It was worse than she could've imagined. Peyton had been slimed from head to foot. Green, gooey slime.

"What the hell is this?" He slung the slime off his fingers. With a small splat, it landed on the floor.

"Edward slimed you." She grabbed the small towel that she used to wipe her hands when she was working on one of the machines.

He wiped his face and handed it back to her.

She took a step back. "You keep it."

"It feels like . . . snot."

"Ectoplasm to be precise. But, yeah, well, snot pretty much sums it up. I tried to get you to leave. Why didn't you listen to me?"

"I was trying to protect you."

"I wasn't in danger."

"He could've slimed you."

"He already has. The other day." She studied him for a moment. "Not as bad as he just got you, though. Man, you really pissed him off."

"Will he come back?"

"Doubtful. For him to slime someone this much would weaken him a lot."

"How do you get it off?"

"Shower." She kind of felt sorry for him. "Why did you come back downstairs, anyway?"

"To apologize." His gaze met hers. "I'm sorry. I got carried away, and nervous, when you pointed the zapper at me."

"I'm sorry, too. I shouldn't have taken our relationship so seriously. I thought we were becoming friends, and that doesn't happen often to me."

"But . . ."

She raised her hands when he interrupted her. She needed to say what she had to say.

"It's not your fault, I know. It's just that you're so easy to be around, and I've never enjoyed being in someone's company as much as I have yours."

Oh, Lord, had she just spilled her guts? Now he was going to think she was a sap. Her gaze dropped to her feet. She just couldn't look him directly in the eye.

"I like you, too," he told her.

Her head jerked up. "You do?"

"Yeah." He started walking toward her.

"Eghhh!" She jumped back when he reached toward her.

He grimaced. "I forgot I'm covered in snot."

She smiled. "I'll help you wash it off."

"Deal, but you'll get all wet."

"I'll take my clothes off so it won't matter."

"The night is starting to sound better and better."

"Just stay over there until the ectoplasm is all cleaned off."

"You mean it would bother you if I got some of the slime on you?

"Yes . . ." When he raised his arms and started toward her, she laughed and slipped around him and out of the study. "Don't you dare touch me!"

Kaci ran upstairs. Peyton chasing behind her all the way, growling like some kind of monster. When she glanced over her shoulder, he looked like something out of a bad B-rated horror flick. Which made her laugh even harder.

When they reached the bathroom, it took only a minute to strip and step inside the shower. The goop slid right off Peyton and down the drain.

"You still have some in your hair," she told him as she poured shampoo onto her palm. She pressed close to his front as she raised her hands and began to lather his hair. When her breasts brushed across his chest, he sucked in a deep breath. "Close your eyes. I don't want to get soap in them."

"Can I trust you?"

She grinned. "No."

He closed his eyes.

She lathered his head, massaging his scalp. His sigh was pure enjoyment.

"That's nice."

He hadn't even seen nice yet. She moved her hands to his chest, running her fingers through the wiry hairs, across his nipples. They tightened beneath her fingers. She liked knowing that he reacted so quickly to her touch. It made her feel powerful and in control.

She slid her hands downward, over the ridges of his six-pack abs, over his hips. She cupped his butt, pulling him closer so that his erection rubbed against her belly.

He cupped her bottom and pulled her closer still. She smiled, amazed he'd kept his hands off her for that long.

"I'm not through soaping you down," she said.

"I needed to touch you."

Not *wanted* to touch her, no, he'd *needed* to touch her. "I know what you mean. I can't seem to get enough of you, either." And she meant it.

When she looked up at him, he lowered his mouth to hers, just brushing his lips against her at first before his tongue delved inside her mouth and stroked her tongue. Heat flared inside her.

She could barely breathe when he ended the kiss. Holding

on to him so she didn't fall over was of the utmost importance right now. Besides the fact, the shower was slippery from all the ghost slime and shampoo.

"I want you," he said.

His words were low and husky near her ear. She almost melted into a puddle at his feet and slid right down the drain along with the ectoplasm.

"I want you, too." She moved just a fraction, and her feet began to slide. She grabbed the shower curtain. It creaked. Then the rod popped off. Peyton grabbed her waist before she ended up on her butt on the floor. Now, wasn't that just as graceful as graceful can be.

"Slippery," she said.

Heat climbed up her face. She'd just wrecked his bathroom. Great. First his study and now his shower. She was on her normal winning streak.

"I can fix it," he said. "But maybe we should pass on the shower and find a better place to make love."

His bed was soft and comfy, the kind she could sink down into, and it had worked great the last time. "Sounds good to me." She stepped out while still holding on to him and grabbed a towel.

He took it from her and quickly ran the soft terry cloth over her. She closed her eyes, but he stopped just when it was starting to feel really sensual. When she opened her eyes, she saw he was drying himself. Okay, that looked pretty darn sexy, too.

"I have an idea," he said.

She raised her gaze to his. So far, his ideas had been exciting. She was curious to see what he'd come up with this time.

"What?" she asked.

"Want to take a ride on my bike?"

She frowned. No, she wanted to have sex. Although a ride on the bike was tempting. "But I thought . . ."

He put his finger over her lips. "Hold that thought. Anticipation is half the fun."

The thought of riding his bike was pretty exciting. She'd wanted to do just that, and she had to admit, so far, Peyton hadn't disappointed her when he suggested ways to have sex. Even if after they'd had sex in the park it had gotten a little embarrassing. But before that, it was fantastic, and the memory served only to make her body that much hotter.

Her body tingled. "I'll hurry and get dressed."

"Wear a loose shirt and no bra. Do you have a skirt?"

"I think I tossed one in my suitcase." Actually, she had brought most of her clothes since she wasn't sure how long she'd be staying.

Just as she started from the room, he grabbed her arm.

"Don't wear panties, either."

Her body trembled. "What exactly do you have in mind?"

"You'll see. Oh, and wear sturdy shoes, no sandals. Tennis shoes will be fine."

Her forehead puckered.

"Trust me."

She didn't, and she wasn't sure about his requests, either, but she was intrigued just enough that she decided to give in to his instructions. Besides, two things were certain. She was going to have sex, and she was going to ride his bike. How could she refuse?

When she met him downstairs, he was wearing jeans and a black T-shirt. She almost asked him to grab his leather jacket, but decided it could wait until next time. As they started out the door, he picked up a bag off the floor.

"What's in there?"

"A surprise."

"I like surprises."

His heated gaze slowly scanned her body. "You look hot, by the way." He grabbed her hand, and they went out the front door and to the garage.

Her hands began to itch the closer she got to his bike.

"Have you ever ridden a motorcycle?"

She shook her head. "But I've always wanted to." Salivated every time she saw one going down the road, if the truth were known.

He climbed on, then motioned for her to get on behind him. She felt a little awkward, but managed to throw her leg over the seat. Oh, yeah, this was good.

"Put your feet right there." He showed her the places. "Now wrap your arms around my waist."

He turned the key, and the bike roared to life. A thrill of excitement rushed through her. She was actually sitting on his bike about to fly down the street. She laughed for the pure enjoyment of doing something she'd always wanted to do.

He eased out of the garage. She tightened her hold as a ripple of fear also made its way through her.

"I won't let any harm come to you," he told her as if she'd spoken her fears aloud.

She believed him. Besides, she'd seen him as he drove out of the garage. He looked as though he could handle the bike pretty good.

The street was devoid of traffic at eleven o'clock on a weekday. It was as if they had the town all to themselves. Except Peyton didn't turn toward downtown. Instead, he drove toward the outskirts.

Not that she cared. She was on his bike, and the wind was blowing through her hair, and she didn't feel as if she had a care in the world.

"Have you ever flown?" he yelled over the sound of the bike when they crossed the city limits.

"No," she yelled back.

"Then let's go flying."

He gave the bike more gas, and they picked up speed. She closed her eyes, reveling in the wind on her face. She almost felt as though she were flying.

All too soon, he began to slow, then turned onto a dirt road. He slowed more, until he came to a stop.

"I loved it!" She squeezed him tighter. "I've always wanted to ride a motorcycle."

"Have you ever wanted to drive one?"

Her breath caught in her throat. "You'd let me drive it?" No, she couldn't. Could she?

He turned slightly until they were looking at each other. The moon was full, so she could see he was serious.

"If you want."

"You don't think . . ."

"That you'll wreck it?" He shook his head. "No, I don't. Besides, I'll be right behind you."

It was time she started living. Doing things she'd always wanted to do but had been scared to. "Yeah, I'd love to drive it."

She slid from behind him and moved to the front, but just as she was starting to sit, he pulled her skirt out from under her so that her bare bottom was on the leather.

Her heart pounded. The leather was warm to her bare skin, and there was a slight vibration that tickled her. For a moment, she sat there, letting the sensations wash over her.

"Put this hand here," he told her and placed her hand on the handlebar. "This will give it gas."

He demonstrated by rotating the handle. The engine revved up. The vibrations increased. She could start to like this.

"Your clutch is on this side, but I'll take care of changing gears for you."

He clutched the bike and used his foot to change the gear. "Go ahead and put your feet up. We'll take it slow, so don't worry."

She nodded.

But when he let off the clutch and they began to move forward, she did begin to worry.

"Give it a little gas."

She did. His hand was on top of hers so she didn't give it too much. At first, the bike wobbled. He hadn't said it was going to be easy, and she hadn't really expected she would be driving like a pro at first.

But it didn't take her long before she was able to keep the bike going straight. And then she was relaxing. She was driving the bike. Damn! Who would've ever thought it? For someone who stayed in a back room doing books, she was pretty darn great.

"Have you got it?" he asked.

Maybe she wasn't doing that good.

"No!"

His hands were on top of hers, so it wasn't as if she was actually doing it by herself . . .

"You can do it. Have a little faith in yourself."

The blood pounded in her veins when he let go and she was driving the bike.

"You're doing fantastic," he said.

"Uh, huh, sure." But her voice wasn't very loud, and she was starting to feel sick.

"Become one with the bike."

Become one with the bike. Okay, she could do this. She took a deep breath, then let it out slowly. Calmness swept over her. Confidence began to fill her. She could do it. Peyton was right.

"Okay?"

"Better than okay," she yelled.

"Good, don't panic."

Don't panic? What did he mean, don't panic?

He moved his hands in front of her and began to unbutton her blouse. She swallowed hard. The bike wobbled, but she brought it under control.

"What are you doing?"

"I'm unbuttoning your shirt."

"Yeah, I figured that much out."

He laughed. He actually had the nerve to laugh at her!

"Don't you trust me?"

"No."

He undid the last button and fanned her shirt open. The cool night air rushed against her bare skin. She bit her bottom lip. It was erotic, it was sexy, it was decadent, and she loved how it made her feel. It was more exciting and more naughty than making love in the park.

He brought his hands up, cupped her breasts, then began

to massage them, tweaking the nipples. She moaned, but kept her eyes open as she sped down the road, even though it wasn't that easy.

His hands moved downward, rolling her skirt up and tucking it in the waistband. She might as well be naked as she flew along the road on his bike.

Please don't let me meet some old dude in a beat-up pickup truck.

He'd probably have a heart attack or something. His death would be on her conscience.

Peyton began to massage her thighs.

Screw the old dude.

She wanted to close her eyes, but that might not be practical. He slid his finger over her slit, tugging on the fleshy part of her sex, and she thought she would die. His hands were all over her, squeezing her breasts, then caressing her hips, her thighs until she couldn't stand it any longer.

"Peyton! If you don't stop this damn motorcycle, I swear I'm going to aim it for the nearest tree and put myself out of my misery."

He laughed.

Right in her ear. He didn't even try to hide his enjoyment over her frustration, but at least he slid his hands down hers and took the handles. She leaned against him.

"You loved it," he said.

She smiled. "Yes." She appreciated very much the way he made love. More than words could say, in fact. It was always different as if he knew exactly what he was doing when he aroused her to new sexual heights.

But she had her doubts when he pulled into a driveway, crossing a cattle guard. She quickly began pulling her clothes together, letting him take complete control of the bike. She really had no idea just how far he would go. A foursome with farmer John and his wife didn't appeal to her.

"It's okay. This is Kenneth's cabin, and he said I could use it anytime I wanted. I've been here before, and it's secluded."

She relaxed until another thought occurred. "He's not up here, is he?"

"I don't think so."

She coughed. He didn't think so? But as they neared the cabin, she didn't see any vehicles, and there were no lights on. Peyton slowed, but didn't stop. She looked longingly at the cabin.

Bye bed.

A couple of miles farther down what had become no more than a trail, he slowed the bike again, but this time he came to a stop and put the kickstand down before getting off.

She followed suit, noticing how her legs trembled and wondering if it was because her body still needed release or if it was from straddling the bike. She rather thought it was a little of both.

"Uh, where are we?" she asked, straightening her skirt as she looked around. She didn't bother buttoning her shirt, just loosely tied the ends together.

The moon gave enough light that she could see quite a distance, even farther if there weren't so many trees.

"You'll see."

That was all he said. Just, you'll see.

He reached inside one of the saddlebags on the motorcycle and brought out the bag from the house.

"Your bag of tricks?"

He looked at her, then pulled her into his arms and kissed her. She melted against him. Her shirt parted. He dropped the bag and cupped a bare breast, running his thumb over the nipple. It hardened.

When he pulled back, they were both breathing hard.

"I'm going to make love to you all night long," he said. "I'm going to taste every inch of your body, and I won't stop until you cry my name."

Oh, God, she almost had an orgasm just listening to him.

Chapter 16

Peyton took her hand and led her through the trees to the small rise. He wanted her so bad it was all he could do to walk. But when they crested the rise, and he saw her expression, he knew it was worth it.

There was a small lake on the other side. The moonlight made the water look like dark blue glass. There was a covered deck, and from there a dock that stretched out far enough into the water that you could dive from it—and he had. But Kaci was the first woman he'd ever had the desire to bring out here.

"It's wonderful," she breathed.

"Come on." He tugged her hand, and they made their way down to the deck. As soon as they were there, he opened the bag and spread out a blanket.

"A blanket?"

"So I can seduce you."

"Do you really think spreading a blanket will get me to spread my legs?" She slipped off her shirt and let it fall to the wooden planks.

"I was hoping." His voice was hoarse as he watched her raise her hands above her head and stretch toward the moon. Her breasts begged him to take them into his hands, stroking across the hard nipples.

When she lowered her arms, their gazes locked. "I'm not

the kind of girl that can be so easily swayed." She slipped her fingers into the waistband of her skirt and pushed it over her hips before she kicked out of it. Man, he was never so glad there was a full moon as he was tonight.

She stood before him, completely naked. She'd certainly gotten over her shyness. Not that he was complaining. His moon goddess. And she walked toward him, hips swaying, mesmerizing him.

"Too many clothes," she said and began tugging on his black T-shirt. When she raised her arms, pulling it over his head, her nipples brushed his chest. He jerked his shirt the rest of the way over his head and tossed it away from him.

"Are you hurting?" she asked with feigned sympathy. She pressed her hand against the front of his pants. He almost crumpled. "Oh, yes, I can feel that you're all swollen." She stepped closer. "Want me to kiss it and make it better?" she crooned softly.

"You've become quite the temptress."

"Do you mind?"

He slowly shook his head as he unfastened his pants, removing a condom from the pocket before he kicked out of them. "Not at all."

"I find I like being naked outside. Does that make me a closet exhibitionist?"

"It only makes you freer of your inhibitions."

"I was right. You are a good teacher."

He grabbed her hand. "Come on."

She hesitated.

"Don't you trust me?"

She frowned.

Even that looked sexy as hell, especially when that was all she wore.

"There's nowhere else to go." She looked around.

His grin was slow. "Haven't you ever made love in the water?"

"I'd never made love with the light on or in the park until

I met you. Of course I've never made love in the water. Is it cold?"

"Not at all. You don't know what you've been missing. Come on, trust me."

When she nodded, he led her to the edge of the dock. "We'll jump in on three."

"Wait a minute. There's not like snakes or fish that bite or anything, is there?" She stared down at the water.

"No. Ready?"

"Well . . . okay."

"One . . . two . . . three." He gave her a nudge forward, but he was right behind her. She came up sputtering and spitting.

"It's freezing," she gasped. "I thought you said it wasn't cold."

"It's cool," he told her, holding back his laughter. "It will be fine in a few minutes."

"You're sure nothing will bite me? I mean, you lied about it being cold."

"No."

She bounced around in a circle, looking in every direction. "But you said . . ."

He pulled her close to him, enjoying the way her breasts bobbed against him. The water was chest high, so he could stand. He nipped her on the shoulder. "I bite."

Her eyes widened; then she smiled. "Umm. I think the water is already getting warmer."

"I know I am." He lowered his mouth and ran his tongue over her lips. She captured it, sucking on it. He jerked as fire shot downward.

Her musical laughter filled the night.

He caressed her breast, tugging on the nipple, all the time watching her expression turn from amusement to passion. What was it about this woman that drove him to the edge? She had a killer body, but it was more than that. He found himself wanting to show her everything there was to the art of making love. He wanted to take her higher than she'd ever been.

Her sex nudged his erection. He almost exploded. Damn, she made him wild for her. No woman had ever done that. But he wouldn't enter her yet. He had something more he wanted to do.

"Can you float?" he asked.

"Umm, yes, but I'd rather make love."

"Soon."

He picked her up like a baby; she flung her arms around his neck and laughed.

"Now what are you planning?" she asked.

"Something you'll like. Stretch out on your back."

"You won't let me sink?"

"Trust me."

"If you push me under, you'll regret it. I don't like getting dunked."

"I wouldn't dream of dunking you."

She stretched out. His hands were beneath her until he felt she was relaxed enough to stay afloat. Then he let go. Good, it would be much easier to arouse her if she was floating rather than drowning.

Damn, she was so beautiful. For a moment, he let his gaze drift over her. From her pointed, well-rounded breasts, to her gently curving waist, to the thatch of dark wet curls at the vee of her long legs. Absolutely magnificent.

He lightly ran his hand over her body, starting at one breast and moving downward. She gasped, wobbled just a bit. He quickly braced his hands under her so she wouldn't sink.

"Shhh, you have to stay perfectly still or you'll end up dunking yourself. Inhale, then exhale. This is a lesson on focus and control."

"I don't think I have that much focus or control," she said. "I have horniness, though."

He chuckled. "You have a magnificent body, too." He moved to her ankles and lightly began to massage. "You're a good floater, too."

"Thank you—I think." She sighed. "That feels nice."

He began to spread her legs apart very slowly, just as he had the other night.

"What are you doing?"

He could feel her tensing. "Relax. I won't hurt you. I promise."

"This is embarrassing."

"You should never feel ashamed of your body. It's sexy and beautiful."

"I feel sexy when I'm with you."

He knew she'd accepted and was ready to go to the next level. "Do you feel the water lapping between your legs? It's almost as though my tongue is licking your sex."

He could feel the trembles running the length of her body. He opened her legs a little wider and began to glide her toward him, then pushing her away ever so slightly so that the water would gently splash against her.

She moaned.

He smiled, then opened her legs wider, moving between them, closer to the heart of his desires, and when he was close enough, he lowered his mouth to her sex and began to gently suck.

"I . . . I can't. Oh, God, I think I'm going to drown." She began to sink.

Peyton scooped her back out and tried not to laugh. She spit and sputtered, then glared at him.

"That was so not fair, but damn, it felt so good." She pressed her body up against his, then wrapped her legs around his waist and pulled him even closer, rubbing her sex against his erection.

His humor quickly faded. He gripped her ass, pressing against her, making the fit even tighter. This was good. "I want to bury myself deep inside you."

"Don't talk, just do it."

He reached up on the deck and grabbed the condom he'd left out and quickly slipped it on. Then he sank deep inside her. He'd held back far longer than he'd ever gone before and holding back was killing him, but still, he moved slowly, letting her become accustomed to him.

"I can't stand it any longer. I want it fast and hard." She nipped his earlobe with her teeth.

That was all the encouragement he needed. He plunged inside her again and again. The heat inside him built at a rapid pace. The water lapped against their bodies.

His butt clenched as lights seemed to explode inside his head. He vaguely heard her cry out, felt her body tremble, and then he was leaning against one of the deck pillars, trying to catch his breath.

"That was so damn good," she breathed, her head resting against his shoulder.

He liked the way she fit against him, as though they were made for each other. Peyton caught his breath, then he leaned back and looked at her. Had she fallen asleep? He nudged her.

"Do you think we can manage to get back on the deck?"

"In a minute," she mumbled.

"Is that a snake?"

She jerked her head up and looked around, then glared at him. "That was so not funny, mister."

He was still laughing as they made their way up the wooden ladder and back on the dock. Once there, Peyton reached in the bag and brought out a bottle of wine and two glasses. After he uncorked the bottle, he poured them each a glass, handing her one.

"A man after my own heart," she said as she took it, taking a long drink.

"Sustenance."

She laughed.

Until he pulled the camera out of the bag.

"What are you doing?" The look she gave him was wary.

"You're beautiful. I want to take your picture. Will you let me?"

"Can I dress first?"

"No."

She sucked in a breath. "No one has ever taken a nude picture of me."

"Then let me be the first. Trust me."

Chapter 17

Kaci figured she'd be the biggest fool in all of Texas if she let Peyton take her picture while she was naked. It was bad enough she still hadn't put her clothes back on. But it did feel fantastic sitting on the dock with just the whisper of a breeze caressing her naked skin.

But take her picture? No way, no how. Wasn't going to happen. Never in a million years. She opened her mouth to tell him exactly what she thought about his idea . . .

"Just think about it," he said. "I wouldn't want you to do it if you didn't feel comfortable."

Damn, she'd been gearing up for an argument, but he'd turned the tables. What? Wasn't her body worth fighting for? Didn't he think she'd take a decent picture?

He looked at her, his gaze slowly moving over her. "I think you're the most beautiful woman I've ever seen. Not just on the outside. Your inner beauty shines through."

Ahhh, redemption. He did know how to flirt. She wondered if he took classes in arousing women. Now, that would be an interesting class to take, and if he were the teacher, she would be first in line to sign up for it. Although it would give him an unfair advantage when it came to seducing women.

He set the camera on a corner of the blanket, then reached inside the bag again and brought out a candle.

"You thought about everything, didn't you?"

He shrugged. "I try."

She reached for the camera, picking it up and turning it over in her hand. "What if I took your picture?" She raised the camera until she looked through the lenses. "Would it bother you?"

"No."

"Why not?"

"I trust you."

Did he? Or was he just saying that so she would relax. "So you've said, but you don't know that I wouldn't blackmail you."

He held a lighter close to the candle's wick. It flared to life, the flame flickering in the light breeze. He studied her just before he raised his glass to his lips and took a drink. When he lowered it, he met her gaze. "Would you blackmail me?" His words were soft, casually spoken.

She set the camera down and lay back on the blanket. "No, I would never do that to anyone. But you don't know that. We barely know each other."

"Sometimes you can be with a person for a lifetime and not know them."

"Have you known people like that?" She stared at the sky, watching the twinkling stars.

"My father," he said.

She turned her head and looked at him. "You didn't know your father?"

"Not really." He gazed out at the water. "I thought I did. We all thought we knew him, but we didn't."

She rolled to her side, watching him. "Did he commit a crime or something?"

"What?" He shook his head. "No, it was nothing like that. My father lost his job. He was a brilliant man. He worked for a pharmaceutical company. He gave it all up."

"Why?"

"He refused to compromise his principles. They wanted him to do something unethical, and he refused."

"Is the company still in business?"

"No, he testified against them, and the government shut them down."

He looked across the water. Pity welled inside her. Poor, poor Peyton.

"Then what happened?"

"No one else would hire him. He and my mother took what savings they had and bought a few acres in the country. They grew organic vegetables and sold them on the side of the road for enough to make a decent living. What with my mother selling the beaded shawls she made and telling fortunes with her Tarot cards."

"Really?"

"No." His eyes twinkled with mischief when he looked at her.

She frowned. So not funny. "You made all that up?"

He laughed. "Yeah, but you have to admit it made for a good story. My parents are alive and well. My father is a math teacher and my mother English. They both teach at a small school in Ohio."

"That was really bad."

"I had you going, though. Admit it, you bought every word."

She sniffed with disdain. "Not the part about selling the vegetables and the beaded shawls, nor your mother telling fortunes. That part made me start to wonder."

"No, you bought into it one hundred percent."

Turnabout was fair play. "I can top that story, and this one is true."

He leaned back on one elbow, and for a moment she lost her train of thought. Damn, he was hot. The vanilla-scented candle cast shadows and light in all the right places. He looked as though he were posing for a centerfold. It might be a good idea to take his picture—a fantastic memento.

"Fire away. Top my story."

Okay, she would. "My father borrowed money from a

man they call Guido. That's why he's out of pocket. He's hiding in another state trying to get rid of a bunch of pesky ghosts so that he can pay Guido and get him off his back."

"Guido?"

"Yes."

"Italian?"

She nodded.

"As in the mafia?"

"He'd like to think he is, but he falls short of the mark. Mostly, he loans money at a high rate of interest. It costs twice as much as what a person borrows just to get him off their back."

He grinned. "Sorry, but you need to work a little on your storytelling. It's too farfetched for me to believe." He laughed. "But it was a good try."

"Don't ever say I didn't tell you the truth." She shrugged.

At least she felt better now that she'd gotten that off her chest. It wasn't her fault he didn't believe her.

"More wine?" he asked.

"Now you're trying to get me drunk so you can take naked pictures of me."

"Will it work?"

She reached her glass out to him. "I don't know. Pour me another glass and we'll see." She was getting so naughty . . . and it felt wonderful. Who knew what the rest of the night would bring. Maybe she would cast all her fears to the side.

Hell, she couldn't believe she was lying on a dock completely naked or that she'd even gone swimming nude. Since meeting Peyton, she'd come to the realization she led a very boring life.

"What are you thinking about?" he asked, running his finger up and down her arm and causing the most delicious tingles to spread over her body.

"How my life has changed since I met you."

"Are you wishing you hadn't met me?"

She laughed. "No. I don't think I was alive before I met

you. I only went through the motions of living—drifting from one day to the next. You've made me stop and think about what I want to do. I don't think I'll be working with my father as much. I'll still help him out, but I don't want to do this full-time."

"What do you love doing?"

"Building things. You know, like the ghost zapper."

"Ahh, weapons of mass destruction. I thought there was an evil side to you."

She laughed. "I enjoy working on cars, too. I like knowing how something works and when it doesn't. It's like putting a puzzle back together so that every piece fits and works together again. Who knows, maybe I'll be a mechanic."

He nodded. "A good profession. You can make a fortune, too. I know, I just got my car out of the shop." He frowned. "It looks as though I might have to take it in again." He shook his head. "I know I filled it with gas. There has to be a leak somewhere."

Major guilt trip.

He was going to spend his hard-earned money to have someone take a look at his car when she knew that she was the reason it had been nearly empty. She couldn't, in good conscience, let him do that.

"I'm pretty good. Before you take it in, let me look at it. It could just be a loose ignition screw." But she wasn't stupid enough to tell him the truth, either.

"Huh?"

"After you have your car worked on, sometimes they forget to tighten the ignition screw. It's no biggie."

"You would do that?"

"I won't even charge you."

"Then, yeah, I'd appreciate it."

"What are friends for?" She hoped he wouldn't look up ignition screw. As far as she knew, one didn't exist. But she couldn't very well tell him she'd stolen his gas. No, not stolen, only borrowed. She had every intention of returning it—someday.

She could feel his gaze on her. It was like a heated caress. All thoughts about working on cars immediately vanished, and she had an incredible urge to open her legs. Lord, she was becoming such an exhibitionist. She swallowed the rest of her wine and realized she was a little tipsy. She reached her glass toward him.

"More."

He raised an eyebrow. "Are you sure?"

She nodded. "Maybe I'm looking for courage."

His expression turned serious. "You don't have to pose for me. It won't change anything between us. I shouldn't have even brought the stupid camera. I thought it might bring an edge of eroticism."

"And maybe I want the same thing. I just need to be a little more relaxed."

He filled her glass.

Peyton watched her, knowing she had come a long way in just a few days. He wanted to capture on film what he saw: a sultry, vibrant woman. Kaci was like a caged bird that had suddenly been set free.

And there was a way he could take the pictures that might make her feel less exposed.

"I want to paint you," he told her.

When she sat up, there was a bounce in her breasts. Damned if he didn't want her again.

"You're an artist, too?"

He reached into the bag and brought out a paintbrush. "Not exactly." He had a jar of creamy chocolate fudge sauce and another one of raspberry jelly that he retrieved, then tossed the empty bag out of the way. "Your body will be the canvas."

Desire flared in her eyes. "You want to paint the fudge and jelly on me?"

He nodded, wondering if she would let him. He found that he wanted to show her just how far one could go when heightening desire during lovemaking.

"Can I paint you, too?"

His smile widened. He loved that she was eager to try new things. "We'll take turns."

She scooted to her knees. He followed suit until they faced each other. She watched as he opened each jar and set them down between them, but she looked startled when he handed her the brush. He was letting her go first. Cool.

"Just dip it inside and paint it on?" she asked.

"Exactly."

Her lips slowly turned up as she dipped into the chocolate first, then painted across one nipple. He sucked in a breath when she leaned forward and licked it off. Laughter bubbled out of her.

"The smell of chocolate got to me." She licked the corner of her mouth where there was a smudge. "I have a weakness for chocolate."

"So that's why my chocolate milk has been disappearing. You've been drinking it. I thought maybe the ghost was doing something."

"That, and your peanut butter and jelly."

"Then I'm lucky I bought more the day before."

She dipped in the jelly and smeared the deep red across his other nipple. A ripple of pleasure ran through him.

"Do you like that?" she teased.

"You tell me." He took the brush from her and dipped it into the chocolate. First, he painted her face. Across her forehead and over her cheeks.

"I feel like I'm at a spa getting a decadent treatment. I like it."

"Then you'll love this."

He ran the bristles down one breast. The nipple was already hard in anticipation. She closed her eyes and bit her bottom lip as he slowly drew the brush over her nipple, then flicked it back and forth.

"So, does it feel good?"

"Oh, yeah."

He leaned forward, taking her breast in his mouth, tasting the chocolate, tasting Kaci. He rolled the nipple around with his tongue. She grabbed his head, pulling him closer, moaning.

They had just started, though, and he wanted to draw their play out as long as he could. He pulled back.

"Don't stop," she said.

"First we paint."

"This is a form of torture, isn't it? Because I drank your chocolate milk."

He laughed. God, he loved her sense of humor.

He dipped the brush again, painting the other breast with chocolate, then replaced the chocolate he'd sucked off the other.

She thrust her chest out. He moved to the jelly next and painted it across her abdomen, coming close to the top of her mound, but careful not to paint that area—not yet.

"Enough," she said, grabbing the brush from him.

"Is there something wrong?" he asked with all the innocence he could muster. From the look on her face, he didn't think he was very convincing.

"My turn."

She went for the chocolate, painting his abdomen and down each thigh, then frowning. "Stand up."

He obliged, enjoying watching her really getting into the sex play.

"Spread your legs wider."

He glanced down at her. She smiled back, not looking any more innocent than he probably had.

"Trust me."

He spread his legs apart. "Just know that I've never cared for soprano."

She let her breath out. It brushed lightly over his dick. He drew in a sharp breath.

"Oh, don't worry, baby, I won't do a thing to harm such a magnificent erection."

She took the brush and painted jelly up the inside of one leg. It tickled, but in a good way. The jelly had been in the refrigerator, and it was still cool. But then she dipped the brush in the chocolate and ran it up his length. He grabbed the deck post, his body tightening. If he was going to last much longer, he had to steal the brush back.

But when he looked at her, it was all he could do to reach down and take it from her hand. She looked so enraptured painting him.

"I was creating a masterpiece," she told him, but he heard the laughter in her voice.

"My turn. Stand."

"Is that an order?"

"Yeah, but you'll get plenty of enjoyment out of it when I finish painting you."

"Just one taste, then."

He almost lost it when she sucked him deep inside her mouth. He couldn't breathe, he couldn't think. Hell, he didn't want to think.

She came to her feet moments later. "There, all clean." Her eyes twinkled.

Maybe he *would* spank her, later. He dropped to his knees, wanting to see what he was about to cover. It was almost a shame, but he wanted her to experience this to the fullest.

"Lean against the rail," he told her.

She did.

"Now spread your legs apart."

There was just a moment's hesitation before she spread her legs. He dipped the brush in the jelly, smearing it in a vee down each leg, the point stopping at her knees. Then he dipped into the chocolate and brushed down the insides of her thighs.

He dipped into the chocolate again.

She sucked in her breath as he scraped the bristles over her mound, over the fleshy part of her sex. Then he stood back, admiring his work. She looked as though she wore a body suit of chocolate and deep red jelly.

"I want to take your picture," he spoke softly. He wanted to free every last one of her inhibitions.

"But . . ."

"But what? You're covered."

She glanced down. "So I am." She looked back up. "Go ahead."

"Don't move." He grabbed the camera off the floor and snapped her picture. "Keep leaning against the post. Now look out over the water and put your hands behind your back." Her breasts were thrust forward, the nipples hard. He snapped another picture. Beautiful and sexy. Naked, but not.

"Turnabout is fair play, you know."

"Of course."

"And no glossy eight-by-tens, please."

"Never."

She smiled. There was a dreamy expression on her face.

"What are you thinking?"

"That I enjoy the freedom you've given me."

"I'm just getting started."

Chapter 18

"Now face me," Peyton told her.

She did, feeling sexier than she'd ever felt in her life.

"Spread your legs and raise your arms high above your head. Pretend you're reaching for the sky."

She heard the whirring of the camera and saw the flash bouncing off the water as he snapped picture after picture. Then he had her move to the blanket and stretch out.

"You remind me of a panther," he said. "Sleek and sensuous. The flickering candle is creating mysterious shadows."

"Meow," she purred. "Better be careful, I might scratch."

"I don't think I'd mind if you left your mark on me."

He moved the camera away and stared at her. His look was appreciative. Peyton had a way of making her feel wicked and wild. It was so different from the way she'd been before meeting him.

He raised the camera again. "Now move your arm back toward your leg. Ah, nice. Very nice."

"My turn," she said. She itched to look at his magnificent body through the viewfinder.

"Just a few more." He walked toward her.

She stood, wondering what he planned to do now, and admitted to herself that he excited her. She knew whatever he did, she would derive enjoyment from it.

When they faced each other, he met her gaze head-on. "I

want to take your picture but without all the chocolate. He set the camera down and lowered his head to her breast.

Kaci drew in a deep breath as he licked first one nipple, then the next. His tongue scraped over her breasts until the areolas were both free of chocolate. Then he stepped away and raised the camera, snapping her picture.

When he set the camera down once again, she had to bite her bottom lip. The anticipation of knowing what he would do next was almost more than she could bear.

"Did I ever tell you I have this thing for chocolate, too?" he asked as he knelt in front of her.

She couldn't take her eyes off the top of his head as he moved closer to her.

"And I especially love the fact you're covered in it." He licked up her clit before sucking her inside his mouth.

A hard tremble rippled through her body. She grasped his shoulders for support as he sucked hard, nibbling on her.

"I need . . . I need . . ."

As if he could read her mind, Peyton helped her to lie down on the blanket. Then he was parting her legs; but then he picked up the camera.

"Think about me kissing you down there, licking you, sucking you into my mouth."

She moaned, her body arching toward him.

"Touch yourself," he said, his words hoarse with emotion.

Tentatively, she touched her breasts.

"Squeeze your nipples."

As if her body were on automatic, obeying his softly urged commands, she did as he asked, and all the time she heard the clicking of the camera, but she didn't care. She was too caught up in the moment, a moment she never wanted to end.

He took one of her hands and moved it between her legs. Her body jerked when her fingers touched her most sensitive area. More clicking.

Peyton lay down beside her after quickly slipping on a

condom. "You're so damn hot," he said just before he entered her.

When she would've moved her hand from between them, he stopped her.

"No, I want you to pleasure yourself."

She met his gaze, looked deep into his eyes, and saw only honesty and something else she didn't understand.

"Remember what I said about making love. It should be about whatever gives you pleasure—nothing held back and nothing to ever be ashamed of."

She nodded, unable to speak.

He sank deep inside her, then pulled out. Her fingers worked a magic of their own as he continued the motion. Her body felt as if it would explode into a ball of fire; her breathing became ragged as she strained toward release.

Just when she thought she wouldn't be able to last another second, her body tightened, and release hit her full force. Her body quivered. She grasped his shoulders, looked into his eyes as he came, and saw the excitement and joy that she was giving him. She was doing this to him. Giving as well as receiving pleasure. The woman who'd made love only in the dark.

His body jerked; he groaned, collapsing on top of her, then rolling to the side, taking her with him, holding her tight, as though he were afraid to let her go.

"Perfection," she whispered.

"As close as anyone can get."

She laughed for the pure enjoyment of it.

"I don't think I can move," he told her on a groan.

"We have to. I think my body is cracking. At least, the chocolate part of it."

He came to his feet and held his hand out for her. "Then off to the lake we go."

She took his hand, and they went to the edge of the dock, jumping into the water together, laughing like children.

It was cold and refreshing all at the same time. She ducked her head underwater and scrubbed the chocolate off her face.

They'd been so naughty smearing the gooey mess all over each other. Who would've thought naughty would be so much fun.

She pushed with her feet and surged upward. She took a deep breath, looking around for Peyton, but it was as though he'd disappeared. For just a second, she felt a moment of panic, then something grabbed her leg. She screamed and jerked away. Peyton popped up in front of her, laughing.

"You scared the hell out of me! I thought jaws was attacking or something."

"No sharks here. Just me."

"Hmm, a piranha."

He pulled her close. "Yeah, one who enjoys nibbling on you." To prove his point, he nipped her shoulder.

A tingle of pleasure swept over her. God, she couldn't want him again. They'd just had the most incredible sex ever. Besides the fact that she was starting to get a little sore.

She pushed away, laughing. "Oh, no, you're not tempting me again. I need rest."

His grin was slow. "Is that what I do? Tempt you?"

"I think you know exactly what you do to me. I'm supposed to be getting rid of your ghost, remember?" Not falling in love. Oh, crap, where had that come from? She was so not falling in love. She barely knew Peyton.

But he made her smile and laugh, and he'd shown her more in the last few days than she'd experienced her whole life. And he gave her the warm fuzzies. When Peyton's ghost was gone, they would probably part ways, never to see each other again. He ran in different circles. Hell, she didn't even have a circle to run in. No, it wouldn't work.

But that didn't mean she couldn't have fun while it lasted.

She swam to the dock and climbed back up.

"Hey, where are you going?" he asked. "Don't you want to play in the water?"

The expression on his face said they would probably end up doing more than playing. Yes, he was very tempting.

"It's my turn," she said.

"Your turn for what?"

She walked over and picked up the camera, then brought it up, snapping his picture. "To capture you on film."

"Ah, you're trying to steal my soul."

She smiled. If only she could steal another part of him—like his heart. Instead, she said, "Pose for me."

He struck a pose. If you wanted to call it that. He brought his hands above his head. He looked more like a ballerina with hair on his chest. She snickered. He brought his arms down and frowned at her.

"You dare to snicker at my pose," he said.

"I wasn't laughing at you. I was laughing with you." She bit the insides of her cheeks. His frown looked comical.

"I was only trying to do what you asked. Is it my fault I'm not any good at posing?"

"You need to relax. Be more natural. Try going under the water and pushing to the surface with your feet."

"The water's getting cold."

"Poor baby."

When he went under, though, she brought the camera to her face. He exploded out of the water. She took the picture. This was great. She snapped another picture as he came back down, slinging water from his face, droplets flying away from him.

He wiped his hand across his face. "Good enough?"

"Oh, yeah."

"I'm getting out. The water is starting to get cold."

"And your point is?"

He raised an eyebrow as he climbed the ladder and was once again on the dock. He didn't say anything as he came toward her in all his glory. She aimed and shot. Water glistened off his body, droplets falling with each step he took. She snapped picture after picture until he stood in front of her.

"Damn, you're beautiful," she said, then felt her face heat when she realized she'd spoken the words aloud.

"Beauty is in the eye of the beholder," he said, laughter in his voice.

"And I'm certainly beholding to you."

He took the camera from her and set it down and tugged her into his arms, swaying back and forth as he held her close. "I have a class in the morning."

"I think it is morning." She didn't want this night to end. It had been magical. But all good things had to come to an end eventually. "We'd better start back so you can get some sleep."

"I'd rather stay here and watch the sun come up with you."

"Another time, maybe?"

He brushed his lips across the top of her head. "I'll hold you to that."

She stepped out of his arms and grabbed her skirt and top, almost hating to put her clothes back on. Sheesh, the next thing she knew, she'd be joining a nudist colony.

What she wouldn't give for a blow-dryer right now. She wrung the water out of her hair as best she could and hoped she wouldn't catch cold on the ride back. Just as she straightened, Peyton began to briskly dry her hair with the blanket.

"Remind me to bring towels next time."

She hoped there would be a next time.

They walked back to where they'd left the motorcycle. All she wanted to do was snuggle down in bed and sleep for the next ten hours. She felt as though she'd run a marathon. Ah, but she also felt as though she'd won the race.

The ride back to the house was nice. She wrapped her arms around Peyton's middle and rested her head against his back. Before she knew it, they'd arrived.

Back to reality.

She still had a job to do, and she still disliked ghosts. How did she find herself in these situations?

As they walked inside, she warily looked around. If Edward had transferred his affections to her, that would make

Peyton fair game. She could have compounded his problems rather than eliminated them. Some ghost hunter she was.

He flipped on the light switch. "All clear," he whispered close to her ear.

His breath tickled, causing shivers of pleasure to run up and down her spine.

"Shall we make a run for the bedroom?" she said, then realized how her words must've sounded. Heat climbed up her face. "I mean, because I'm really tired after . . . uh . . . all that swimming." Damn, she could say some of the dumbest things.

"The sex wasn't bad, either."

She lightly punched him on the arm. "Don't tease."

"Come on." He grabbed her hand, and they went up the staircase, then down the hall to his room. "Stay with me. It's lonely when you're not beside me."

She nodded. "I'll just need a gown." Okay, her face was probably going to be a permanent shade of red.

"I'll keep you warm." He pulled her inside his bedroom. But he didn't have to pull very hard. There was little resistance.

She sighed. He did have a way with words. She took off her top, then her skirt, letting them lie where they fell, and crawled beneath the cover. He snuggled in beside her, pulling her close.

"Sweet dreams."

"They won't even come close to comparing to reality." She glanced at the clock on the bedside table. Three. She yawned and closed her eyes.

If Kaci dreamed, she couldn't say what they were about. All she knew was that when she awoke, she felt rested and very satiated. She stretched, and her arm connected with a piece of paper, but when she brought it to her face, she couldn't read it.

She sat up in bed, wiping the sleep from her eyes and pushing her hair out of her face. For a moment, she only stared at the two words.

You Snore.

She frowned. No she didn't. At least, she didn't think she did. She turned the paper over.

But I like you anyway.
Gone to class. See you this afternoon.
Peyton

A smile formed. He was so sweet. Her smile quickly disappeared. He hadn't signed it "Love, Peyton," or "Hugs, Peyton." Just "Peyton" scrawled across the bottom.

Get over it!

What did she expect? Declarations of undying love? Wasn't going to happen. Sure, they had good times together and the sex was like nothing she'd ever experienced, but this was a short-term affair. Equally satisfying but nothing more.

Then why did the thought of leaving him make her feel sad? *Pffft,* because they were becoming friends. Besides, who said they never had to see each other again? They lived in the same town. It was more than likely they would run into each other.

She only hoped he wouldn't have another woman hanging on his arm when she did see him.

Bad thoughts for first thing in the morning. She pushed the cover aside and climbed out of bed. Coffee, that's what she needed. But then she glanced down. Okay, clothes first, then coffee.

After throwing on sweats and a baggy top, she trotted down the stairs to the kitchen. As she waited for the coffee to finish, the phone rang. She warily eyed it, but finally picked it up. After all, it might be Peyton.

" 'Ello, govna." She'd at least play it safe, even though if it were Daniel, he'd probably wonder how Peyton could afford a housekeeper every day of the week.

"I love when you do that fake English accent," Peyton said.

"I was protecting your reputation." She smiled.

"Too late. I think everyone knows I'm an unrepentant sinner."

"I think you were that long before I ever met you."

"You might be right."

She poured coffee into her cup, then cradled the phone between her ear and shoulder as she added sugar and powdered creamer, then stirred.

"What are you doing?" he asked.

"I'm having my first cup of coffee. One more and I'll be ready to start the day."

"Be careful." His voice changed, had become more serious. "I don't like leaving you there alone with a ghost."

"I actually think you're the one who has to be more careful. Once there's a transference of affection, the ghost can become rather belligerent toward the person they once attached themselves to."

"You're saying Edward liked me? I'd hate to see what he would do to someone he hated."

"I think he was trying to get your attention, but you basically rejected him when you brought me into the picture."

"So why does he want to befriend you if you're trying to zap him toward the light?"

"Who knows? Maybe he thinks I won't zap him if I get all sentimental."

"But you won't, right? Get sentimental, I mean."

"*Pffft,* of course not. Although my father once told me a story about a man who fell in love with a female spirit. He ended up buying the old house she was haunting and living his days out there. Just him and the ghost. Never married, never had guests." A shiver ran down her spine.

"Maybe I should come home."

"Don't worry, I'm firmly grounded in the real world. If you should have any doubts that I might not be, just remember last night."

"Then Edward isn't any competition?"

She raised her cup, taking a drink.

"Kaci?"

She almost choked, then decided it might be better to set the cup of hot coffee on the counter. "Sorry, I was taking a drink of coffee." She chuckled.

"I don't see anything funny about it."

"I think I like the idea that you'd be jealous."

"Well, I don't."

"Then I'll tell you that you're the only man in my life right now besides my father." Well, and Guido, but she really didn't count him since he wanted to do her father, and possibly her, bodily harm.

"Good."

They talked a few more minutes before Peyton had to leave for class, but when she hung up the phone, she was smiling. The man was definitely addictive.

Chapter 19

Peyton closed his cell phone and dropped it into his pocket, but didn't move, only stared out the window of the teachers' lounge.

"You look like a man in love," Daniel said as he went to the coffeepot and poured himself a cup.

His day had been going so well. "Good morning, Daniel."

Daniel stirred sugar and creamer into his coffee, then took a drink, grimacing. "This coffee is horrible. You would think the people who take care of the lounge would know to keep a fresh pot at all times."

"Everything you need to make one is below in the cabinet. It's really not that difficult."

Daniel cocked an eyebrow. "That's not the point, old chap. It's not that I can't fix a fresh pot. It's not my job."

"Of course. How come I didn't see that?"

"No apology is necessary."

"But then, I wasn't apologizing." He went to the pot and refilled his cup. The coffee was fine, and it hadn't been there that long. In fact, he'd been in the room when Mary fixed it. Daniel just wanted something to complain about. Hell, he'd probably complain if he were going to be hung with a brand-new rope.

"So, who's the lucky lady?" Daniel asked, apparently choosing to ignore his other remark.

"No one you know."

"Not one of the other professors?"

"No." Peyton raised his cup and took a drink.

"Please tell me you're not dallying with one of the students. I wouldn't let the dean find out if I were you. It might jeopardize the grant that you want so badly."

"Would that be the same grant you would give your eyeteeth to have awarded to you?"

"Of course I want it. That's why I'm not about to risk losing it by foolishly toying with one of the students. It was a friendly warning."

Sure. "Well, don't lose any sleep over it because it's not one of the students, either."

Daniel took a drink of his coffee, apparently forgetting that he wasn't supposed to like it. Peyton hoped he would drop the matter.

"It's that maid, isn't it?" Daniel asked, his eyes growing wide. "It is, isn't it?"

So much for hoping. "I refuse to discuss my love life with anyone."

"Of course, I perfectly understand. Not gentlemanly to let anyone know you're sleeping with the help."

"You know, Daniel, you really need to get a life." He dropped his empty cup in the wastebasket and headed toward the door.

"Did I offend you, old chap? I apologize if I did. It certainly wasn't my intention to do so. Just remember whom you're dealing with when you take someone in her position to bed. Women try to trap men into marriage, especially someone in our position."

He didn't even bother to answer. Daniel was in his own little world. So rather than punch the guy in the face, he walked out the door.

He hadn't gotten very far when he heard his name called. He stopped and turned, a smile forming. He enjoyed the dean's company. The man had a wicked sense of humor. He still wondered exactly who it was that had told him the dean was stodgy. Hmm, Daniel? The more he was around him, the less he thought that was true.

"Dean Adams, how are you, sir?"

"Fine, fine. I haven't had a chance to talk to you, let's walk." The dean made his way toward the doors that led outside. "I don't get a chance to go outdoors often enough. My poor wife says I'm starting to look like a ghost."

Peyton really didn't want to talk about ghosts.

Kaci crossed her arms in front of her and stared at her thong as it floated up the stairs. "That is so not funny, Edward."

She really didn't like ghosts. Their idea of something humorous was often not funny at all. Like right now. She'd just as soon her underclothes didn't fly about the house. Especially her good black lace thong.

Not that she liked the damn thing. It chafed her. Once she'd used medicated powder because she figured if it was medicated it should make the raw area heal faster. She should've read the directions first.

Her butt had been on fire. Up came both lids on the toilet and down she went, and she'd never been so glad she'd just cleaned the toilet, too. But she should've gotten rid of the thong, no matter how sexy she looked in it.

Just because she didn't like the thong, it didn't mean she wanted the damn thing flying through the house, either.

She grabbed it when it came within reach and stuffed it in her pocket. Too bad Edward didn't materialize. Of course he wouldn't. She had her zapper slung over one shoulder. That would be way too easy.

Her cell phone rang. Probably her father. Since he was the only one who called it, she figured that would be a pretty good guess. She flipped it open. Yep, it was Pop.

"Hi, Dad."

"Where were you last night? I tried calling." He sounded very disgruntled.

Busted.

"I must've left my cell phone in the guest room." That sounded good.

"Where were you sleeping if you weren't there with it?"

Darn, he was good.

"Downstairs." One little lie wouldn't matter. *Pffft,* not when you figured in all the other ones. Besides, his death would be on her shoulders if she told him the truth. She certainly didn't want to live with that guilt for the rest of her life.

"Oh." He cleared his throat. "How's it going?" He sounded relieved.

He might be good, but she was better. She slipped the zapper's strap off her shoulder and set it down, then wandered out to the patio. Peyton had mentioned he was sure it was safe out there.

"I think the ghost did a transference number on me." She heard his indrawn breath as she pulled a chair from the table and sat in it.

"You know you're not supposed to let them get that close. Remember that time you let the ghost use your body. It changed you after that. You didn't want to have anything to do with the business."

"First off, I didn't let it use my body. The ghost saw an opportunity and took it. I'm not nearly so vulnerable as I used to be."

"Okay, explain how the transference happened, then."

"I don't see that it matters after the fact."

"It matters to me."

"I think he heard one of mine and Peyton's conversations and sort of connected with me." She crossed, then uncrossed her legs, not at all liking her father's probing questions.

"How did it connect?"

Sometimes her father was like a dog with a juicy bone—he just wouldn't turn it loose. "I might have mentioned that I don't get out very often. You have to admit I'm pretty much of a loner." She could almost hear her father deflating, and a rush of guilt went through her. This was exactly why she hadn't wanted to tell him.

"I haven't done well by you. I realize that now. We've moved too damn many times for you to make any real friends. You should've been dressed in frilly pink do-dads and going to little girl parties instead of me dragging you halfway around the country."

"Dad, it's okay. I'd have much rather been with you." She smiled. "You're a lot better than some old party."

"And now you've had to deal with that scumbag Guido," he said as if she hadn't said a word.

"Dad . . . Dad!"

"Sorry, did you say something, dear?" Her father was like that, always losing himself in his thoughts.

"I said it's okay."

"No, it isn't. You don't even like ghosts. I shouldn't have forced you into the business. As soon as I get all this straightened out, I want you to do what you want to do. I won't be satisfied until you're happy."

That was her dad. Forever trying to make life better.

"What exactly are you interested in doing?" he asked, sounding a little confused.

"I've been thinking about it, too. I like tinkering with stuff, and I know a little about cars and stuff. Maybe I'll get certified as a mechanic."

"You always saved me a bundle on repairs. Just make sure it's something you're passionate about. The passion has to be there."

She immediately pictured Peyton, but quickly blocked the mental vision of him rising from the water and stepping onto the deck. She wasn't even going to think about that kind of passion while talking to her father.

"I think working on cars would be something I would enjoy," she said instead.

"Good, good. We'll look into it as soon as this Guido mess is taken care of. Now, tell me what's been happening with the ghost."

"My undergarments flying through the air, for one. This ghost can be very irritating."

"Flying clothes won't kill anyone, though."

"He slimed Peyton."

"Not good. Damned stuff is like snot."

"You don't have to tell me anything I don't know."

"Is that it?"

"For now."

"Then just be careful. If the ghost has transferred to you, then it might get pissed off at Peyton, especially if you two have spent any time together. Not that I can see you having anything in common with a stuffy history professor." His chuckle echoed over the phone.

"Of course I wouldn't. What would we have in common?" She shifted in her chair.

"Yeah, you're probably right. Okay, just be careful and call if you need me."

"I will—oh, how's it going on your end?"

"Making progress. Slowly but surely."

"I miss you."

"Me, too. Be good and I'll see you soon."

She closed her phone and dropped it into her pocket. Her father truly did mean well. At least he understood she wasn't happy working at his ghost-exterminating business.

Maybe she could work part-time and go to school the rest of the time. Lots of people did that. It was an idea. She really hated the thought of leaving her father on his own, though. She didn't even want to think about what trouble he could get into if left to his own devices. Look what had happened with Guido when she wasn't paying attention.

She picked up her zapper and went to the study to check

the machines. The first one was spiking all over the place. Her heart began to pound. Stay calm, she told herself.

Warily, she brought the zapper up, finger on the trigger. "I know you're here, Edward. The machines don't lie."

Her gaze slowly scanned the room. Nothing.

"You feel some sort of connection to me because we're both outsiders. You were forced to become a recluse because of your illness. I understand, truly, but I'm not the answer. I'm alive, and well, you aren't."

A cold chill swept over her, and she knew it was Edward trying to connect.

"I'm not a psychic, Edward. I don't have that kind of gift. But if I were, then I'd say the same thing: go toward the light." She bit her bottom lip. His spirit was becoming stronger, even though he hadn't formed. The sadness emanated from him. "I promise, it'll be okay."

"Kaci, I'm home," Peyton called out.

The cold quickly darted away from her. She did a quick survey of the room. Except for an initial buzz when Peyton called out, there was nothing. Edward had left.

Frrrrrttttt!

"Damn it!" Peyton cursed.

Oh, no. What had Edward done now? She ran to the hallway, her feet skidding to a halt.

"This is not funny!" Peyton said. "What if he does this during my dinner?"

Peyton had been slimed . . . again. He dripped green goo from head to feet.

"Edward, that wasn't nice. I'm really mad at you." She slapped her hands on her hips and glared at . . . at thin air. Wherever he was, though, she hoped he knew she was really pissed.

"You're mad at him? Think how I feel and multiply it by ten."

"Go shower. I'll clean this up. Then I have an idea what we can do."

"If it'll get rid of the ghost, I'll try anything." He stomped off toward the stairs.

She hadn't added that he might not like what she was going to suggest.

Bleh, cleaning up green globs of goo was starting to become a habit. She went to the closet in the kitchen and grabbed a plastic trash bag and the broom, along with a roll of paper towels.

"This is so gross, Edward," she said as she started cleaning the mess. "Do you really think this is going to endear me to you?"

A faint sound of laughter echoed in the room. She stuck her tongue out. Oh, yeah, that was a good way to get even. That had probably really hurt his feelings.

She had the mess all cleaned, including the tracks Peyton left as he made his way up the stairs, and was just pouring them each a glass of wine as he came into the kitchen.

"Thanks," he said. "You don't have to clean up after the ghost, you know. I could've done that."

"No problem."

"I appreciate it."

"Let's go to the patio." Before he could say anything, she headed out the French doors and sat down at the table.

"Okay, tell me your plan." He took a chair across from her.

"Move out."

He raised his eyebrows.

"Not forever or anything. What I'm proposing is for you to leave for a few nights. Let me see what I can do on my own. Right now, he's not only focusing on me, but you as well. If he only has me to focus on, then I might get the chance to zap him toward the light."

"No."

Stubborn man. "I told you, I know what I'm doing."

"No."

She let out an exasperated sigh, but before she could say more, he continued.

"I don't like the idea of you alone in the house with a ghost that has transferred his . . . his affections to you." He jumped to his feet and began to pace across the tiles. "What if he hurts you or something? How will I know?"

"We can keep in touch by phone."

"You're scared of ghosts."

"But not so much Edward." Wow, she was actually telling the truth. She wasn't as afraid as she had been in the beginning.

He stopped, and turned to look at her with a grimace. "I don't like it."

"Let me do my job. You're in my way."

He shook his head. "No, I don't like it."

"Like I said before, this isn't my first rodeo, cowboy."

She knew he was struggling, and she knew he'd give in. She relaxed for the first time since coming up with her plan and had one obstacle out of her way. If the truth were known, she didn't like the idea of Peyton not being close at hand if something went wrong, but she felt obligated to finish the job.

"Not until tomorrow. I won't leave until then," he said.

She shook her head. "It's best if you leave as soon as possible." Had she actually uttered those words? She was giving up lying in his arms tonight for the chance to get slimed by Edward.

"Are you sure?"

Of course she wasn't. "Yes. You can probably come back in a few days."

He didn't say anything for a minute, then looked at her with a tender smile. "You sure you won't burn the house down while I'm gone?"

She relaxed. "Absolutely not." That wasn't a lie. At least, she hoped it wasn't. She gave him her cell phone number just in case he might need it, then watched as he went upstairs to pack a few things.

It didn't take him as long as she expected. She knew if she

said one word about regretting her decision, he'd toss his bag and probably carry her upstairs where they'd make mad passionate love.

This dinner meant a lot to Peyton, though. As much as ridding himself of the ghost. So she bit back the words that would make him stay and followed him to the door.

"You'll call me if you need anything . . . anything at all, right?"

She nodded. "I'll be fine. Remember, I'm experienced. My dad is the best in the business, and he taught me everything I know. Now go."

He pulled her into his arms and gave her a swift kiss before going down the stairs. She watched until he roared down the street on his bike and was out of sight.

"I'm such an idiot," she said.

When she turned back around, she wore a fierce expression. This was war now. The battle lines had been drawn. She would not be defeated.

At least, she hoped she wouldn't be.

Chapter 20

Five days gone. Zip. Nothing.

Kaci, on the other hand, was quickly becoming addicted to coffee. She'd drunk so much caffeine that her hands trembled worse than an addict looking for his next fix.

And what was Edward doing? Toying with her.

Not this time.

She glanced at the machines. They were going crazy. She'd get him this go-around. She had to. There wasn't much left of Peyton's study. He was going to freakin' kill her when he saw it. Especially if Edward was still around. She'd scorched practically everything in the room, and the ghost was still here. She was tired of playing cat and mouse.

"I know you're here!" she called out, turning in a full circle. He would not get the better of her this time. Never again!

Her eyes narrowed. Edward was not going to make a laughingstock out of her again.

She froze when she saw the green mist forming.

"Edward," she breathed. Okay, get a little denser and I'll zap you to kingdom come!

Emotions began to swirl around her. Oh, no, she was starting to feel his sorrow. Not good! It happened more each time the spirit formed. A hazard of the business. She hated feeling their emotions. It always created a sense of guilt that she was sending them somewhere they didn't want to go, even though she knew it was a better place.

"This is for your own good." She closed her eyes and pulled the trigger.

Pop! Sizzle!

When she opened her eyes, the machines had stopped going crazy. Emptiness filled her. She looked around the room. Everything was quiet.

That was it, then.

He was gone. She'd gotten rid of the spirit.

"I'm sorry, Edward." It didn't matter that she talked to an empty room. She sucked in a sob as she tossed the zapper to the window seat. "You'll be much happier there than here. I hope you're with your family . . ."

Ffffrrrrt!

Splat!

Slime plopped down on top of her head from somewhere above. She closed her eyes and pressed her lips together as it ran down the sides of her face, oozing over her body.

Eeeyuck!

"That wasn't nice, Edward!"

Damn, she hadn't used enough heat. Edward was still here. She hadn't wanted to hurt the ghost, just send him off toward the light. She'd underestimated how much voltage she should use.

This was just great.

Bleh! She stomped out of the study and up the stairs. She really hated ghosts. She hated getting slimed even more.

Once inside her bathroom, she stripped and stepped under the soothing spray of the shower. A shiver of revulsion ran down her. It followed the ectoplasm as it slid down the drain.

It wasn't fair. Edward should be long gone by now. She really sucked at getting rid of ghosts. She wanted her life back. She wanted . . .

Peyton.

There, she'd admitted the main reason for her frustration. He'd called her every day, but it wasn't enough. She wanted to see him. She wanted him to pull her close against his body. She wanted to feel his naked body against hers. She wanted him to make sweet love to her all night long.

God, she was so pathetic.

She sucked it up and turned off the shower. The way to get Peyton back in her life was to get Edward out of it. She knew what she had to do, and she would just have to live with the guilt. It wasn't as though she was sending him to a bad place.

After drying off and dressing, she grabbed her tools and went downstairs. The instruments in the study were quiet.

Of course they were. Edward had spent all his energy sliming her. She hoped he felt really bad. Could a ghost feel bad? She didn't know. They probably just faded away until they'd powered up and were ready to go again.

She grabbed the zapper and set about tweaking it. Two turns of the screw, an adjustment of the inner workings, and she was done.

This time she would test it. Peyton probably wouldn't have anything to do with her ever again if she did burn down his house. She had a feeling he liked the Victorian.

The patio should give her enough privacy from prying neighbors. But when she stepped out the French doors, she wasn't quite sure what to aim at. She didn't want to take a chance she might destroy something he was partial to.

The grill was probably out. Besides the fact, he cooked a mean steak.

There was a row of bushes. The one on the end looked kind of frazzled. Some of the branches didn't have leaves, so part of it was obviously dying anyway.

The end bush, it was. She aimed the zapper, looking down the sights. Slowly she squeezed the trigger.

Pop!
Sizzle!
Got it!

She grinned. The plant was smoking. The zapper had packed a punch strong enough that she was positive it would get rid of the ghost. Just let Edward start to form and she'd . . .

The bush burst into flames.

Oh, crap.

She set the zapper on the patio table and grabbed the water hose, turning the faucet wide open. She ran with the hose toward the bush, but was jerked backward when the hose tangled. The water stopped coming out the nozzle. No, no, no! This was not happening!

"Come on," she growled as she yanked on it as hard as she could.

Time moved in slow motion. The bush was burning the one beside it.

Oh, Lord, she was going to burn Peyton's house down, and he was going to be so mad at her.

She jerked on the hose, popping it up and down. The kink came out, nearly causing her to fall. Water sprayed out of the end of the hose. She whirled around, pointing the nozzle at the fire.

The flames fizzled and began to die as she doused them with the water. She breathed a sigh of relief when the last spark was gone.

Her heart slowed to a more normal rate as she twisted the nozzle to stop the flow of water and plopped down on the patio tiles.

This was so not her day.

A little fire extinguisher was what she needed. Maybe she would leave the house long enough to buy one. She'd feel awfully bad if she burned Peyton's house to the ground.

She turned off the water and rolled the hose up. As she straightened, her gaze went to the zapper.

It worked even better than it had before. She couldn't stop a feeling of pride. Not that there was a big market for ghost zappers. Her father would be excited, though.

She went to it and picked it up and went back inside just as the phone rang. She hurried to answer it.

"Hello?"

"What, no English accent?" Peyton asked.

She smiled. "I forgot."

"I miss you."

"Same here."

"I take it Edward is still there."

"I almost got him today. Not enough power in the zapper. I tweaked it, though. One more time and he shouldn't cause you any more problems." She nibbled her bottom lip. "By the way, do you have insurance on your house?"

Silence.

"Peyton?"

"Why do you need to know if I have insurance? What happened?"

"Oh, nothing. I'm sorry, I didn't mean to alarm you. I just wanted to know . . . just in case. Believe me, I'm being extra careful."

"But you said you'd tweaked the zapper. What did you mean?"

Darn, now she'd opened a can of worms. "I had to add a little more power. Not too much. When I zapped him this morning, it wasn't enough jolts to send him toward the light. I swear, I'll be really careful." And she would definitely buy that extinguisher.

"The dinner party is in a few days."

"He'll be gone before then. I promise." God, she hoped he would be.

She heard his sigh and felt terrible.

"If he's not gone soon, I'm coming back to the house anyway," he told her.

"I'll get rid of him—promise." She needed to talk about anything besides Edward.

"I have to teach a class or I think I'd be on the way home right now. I want to see you, and hold you in my arms."

Her laugh was shaky. "Then we'd better hang up so you

can go fill everyone's head with history." *I want you, too,* her mind screamed.

"Actually, there's something I've been meaning to tell you . . . We'll talk later."

"Later," she agreed and closed her phone.

What had he wanted to tell her? He'd said if he hadn't had a class, he would be on his way home to her, so she really doubted he wanted to end their relationship. She shrugged. It must not have been that important.

Kaci started back to the study when she heard a car door slam. She walked to the window and glanced out.

Great. Daniel was coming up the sidewalk.

He looked up, their gazes met, one eyebrow rose. So much for hiding until he gave up and left. She went to the front door and opened it.

"It be the man from me lovely England. The prof is at the college teaching his classes. 'Fraid you missed him."

He opened the door and walked inside as if he owned the place. "Yes, I know."

His words were even more nasally than the last time. The guy was really creepy. And he had a greater-than-thou attitude that totally sucked.

"Then can ah be askin' your business here, govna?" And what it would take to get rid of him.

He looked down his nose at her. "You can drop the accent, and I know you're not a cleaning woman, either." His nose wrinkled. "You wouldn't make a very good one apparently, either. There's a distinct odor in this house. Quite unpleasant."

Ghost farts.

He was right about that. There was a lingering odor, but it had diminished more than she thought it would.

That was beside the point right now, though. Peyton hadn't mentioned anything about Daniel knowing who she was or he would've told her when they talked on the phone. Was

Daniel guessing? Peyton said they were in the running for a grant.

She decided to play dumb. "Ah don't know what ye be talking about, govna. Ah come in a couple of days a week and straighten up a bit."

He laughed. "Your accent is atrocious."

Her eyes narrowed. No one laughed at her. She planted her hands on her hips. She was a damn good actress. "And you think yours is any better?" she asked, dropping any pretense of being from England.

"As I said," Daniel spoke with stilted words. "You're not a cleaning woman, and you're certainly not from England."

"Okay, so what's your point?"

"None, really." He flicked an imaginary piece of dust off his jacket. "I just think it's silly that you would hide your relationship with Peyton. We are adults, after all. If he wants to use you to further his career, then, although I think it's a little underhanded, I can give credit where credit is due."

"What the hell are you talking about?" Not only did he have a bad accent, but the guy was crazy to boot. Great, and here he was in the house alone with her . . . well, except for the ghost, but Edward didn't really count.

"Why, I thought it was obvious. I know you're helping Peyton with his research so he'll be awarded the grant rather than me."

"Yeah, right, I'm helping him research history." That was a joke.

"History? No, of course not history. What use could he possibly have with you in that department?"

She drew in a deep breath, then slowly exhaled as she tried to keep calm. Silently counting to ten didn't help, either. "Explain what you're talking about, then," she told him.

"Research in sexual arousal."

"Huh?"

"Oh, I do beg your pardon. I thought you were sleeping with him."

"Whoa, go back to the sexual arousal part."

"Didn't Peyton tell you that he's also doing research on different behavior during sexual arousal? It's part of the psychology course he teaches. At least, that's the technical name he used to apply for the grant. We all know better on campus, and I must say, it is a popular class." He was smirking when he looked at her.

She opened her mouth, but no words came out. Peyton had been using her? She couldn't get rid of the ghost, so he decided to use her for research?

No, of course he wouldn't do that. It was crazy to even think it. Daniel was pulling her chain.

Then why hadn't Peyton mentioned the other class?

"Oh, I am sorry," Daniel said, drawing her attention back to the conversation. "I see that he didn't mention his other class. I could, of course, be wrong in my assumption. I certainly don't want to cause a problem between the two of you."

She glared at Daniel. "I think you probably take it upon yourself to assume a great many things." She looked him up and down. "No, I'm not his cleaning woman. What he hired me for is his business, and if you want to know more, then you'd better discuss it with him. But just for the record, he did not hire me for sex. Now, if you don't mind, I have work to do."

It was all she could do to keep her temper in check as she strode to the door and opened it, then waited for him to leave. It was so tempting to slam the door behind him, but she didn't. She had a hell of a lot more class than that.

Daniel was trying to start something between her and Peyton. Daniel wanted the grant and would do anything to get it. His ploy wouldn't work.

She turned on her heel and stomped through the house and out the French doors.

There was probably a perfectly good explanation why he hadn't told her about that other class. One reason could be . . .

could be that she might not understand the complexities of this . . . this sex course.

And another reason might be that he was using her for research.

No! She wouldn't even think like that. She . . .

Why should she even believe Daniel? He would love to do something that would cause Peyton to drop out of the running for the grant money.

She marched to the phone and got the number of the university. One call, that's all it would take for her to find out the truth.

The operator gave her the number, and she quickly punched it in. A woman answered.

"Yes, I need to get in touch with Professor Peyton Cache. I don't think he's in his history class. It's the other one, I believe."

"The Psychology of Sexual Arousal. Hmm . . . No, he teaches that class on Wednesday and Thursday. If you'd like I can . . ."

"No, that's fine. It wasn't that important. Thanks so much for your time."

She replaced the phone in the cradle.

Daniel had been right. Peyton had used her as a case study. She hugged her middle. But look at everything they'd done together. The ways he'd brought her to the brink of sexual pleasure over and over, each time different, then bringing her to fulfillment.

She sat down heavy on the patio chair.

"Oh, God, he's been using me like a guinea pig. One of those little mice that run through the maze." The only difference was his maze had been sexual arousal and gratification.

Had she performed the way he'd wanted? Jumped through as many hoops as he'd hoped?

Damn, she was such a fool. Trust me, he'd said. And she had done exactly that, and then some.

Oh, God, the pictures!

She couldn't leave without them. Her hands began to shake. What if he'd taken them to class—show-and-tell? Oh, God, she'd die. Absolutely die!

It wouldn't take long to find out.

She hurried upstairs and into his room. The camera was on the dresser. She grabbed it and went back downstairs to the study.

Time moved at a snail's pace as she hunted for the cord to hook into the camera so she could download the pictures. Finally, they started to come up.

Her face grew warm as she stared at each and every picture. She looked . . . sensuous, sultry. Peyton had been right; there was nothing that she should be ashamed of. Hell, she looked pretty damn hot.

Her gaze scanned the one of Peyton exploding out of the water. Magnificent. She couldn't delete the ones she'd taken of him. That would be a sin.

But she could the ones that he'd taken of her.

She clicked delete every time a picture of her appeared on the screen until they were gone. Then turned off the computer.

Warmth swirled around her as Edward enveloped her in heat.

Oh, Lord, he'd probably seen every picture. Not good. She was so out of here!

Chapter 21

Kaci had her bags packed and loaded in the car. Peyton could do the rest of his research alone—and he could go screw himself! Let him use that in his research.

She sniffed back a sob. Damn, she was so pathetic.

She took one last look at the house. It didn't appear nearly as scary as it had that first day. It seemed like forever ago. So much had changed. About her, about her life. She only wished . . .

No, it wasn't going to happen.

And it was time to go.

She climbed in the car, fastened her seat belt, and turned the ignition.

Uggggg . . . ugggg.

"No, don't do this to me. I left a note and everything. How can I make a dramatic exit if you won't start?" She turned the key again.

Uggggg . . . ugggg.

This was the sum of all her life? A dead battery, no life to speak of, a ghost exterminator who couldn't get rid of one measly ghost, who disliked ghosts tremendously . . .

Her life was zip. The only good thing that had ever really happened was when she almost got the lead in a stupid play . . . and the day she met Peyton.

And he'd lied to her.

Pathetic. Just pathetic.

She sniffed, but it didn't do any good as tears slid silently down her cheeks.

A car pulled in behind hers.

Oh, hell, she couldn't let anyone see her like this. She scrubbed at her face with the back of her hand, then blew her nose on a crumpled Sonic napkin that was on the seat. She'd known there was a good reason not to clean out her car.

Someone tapped on her window. She jumped. *Please don't let it be Peyton,* she silently begged, then looked out the window.

"Oh, double crap."

She closed her eyes.

Okay, I'd rather face Peyton. Can you just exchange the two?

But when she opened her eyes and looked out the window again, her father was still there. What the hell was he doing here?

She opened the car door and stepped out. "Dad, I didn't expect you. What are you doing here? I thought you'd still be getting rid of ghosts." She smiled as if she were the happiest woman in the world.

"They're gone. I would've come anyway, though." He looked down at his feet, then back at her. "I was getting worried about you. And I'd say from the looks of your watery eyes and red nose, maybe it was a good thing I did show up. Now, you want to tell me exactly what's going on?"

She should've known she couldn't fool him. But she wasn't ready to give up. "Nothing." She sucked in her trembling lower lip.

"It doesn't look like nothing to me." He nodded toward the suitcases in the backseat. "Did you get rid of the ghost?"

She shook her head.

"Did the professor hurt you?"

She nodded. Her father opened his arms, and she went into them, sobbing against his chest. "Is that why your eye looks a little bruised?" His hands curled into fists. "I may not be young, but I still know a little about fighting."

"No, no, that was an accident."

"What did he do, then?" he asked in a tight voice. "And no lies. I want the truth."

"He made me fall in . . ." She sniffed. "He made me like him a lot, but I think he was just using me for research so he can get this grant, and I thought he liked me too and . . ."

"Whoa, go back to the first part."

"He made me like him?"

"Not that far back. Something about you think he was using you for research?"

She nodded.

"What kind of research?" His eyes narrowed dangerously.

Oops. Now what was she going to tell him?

"He's a history professor."

She stepped back, looking at his face. He seemed to be thinking it over. His forehead wrinkled in thought.

"It's not that big of a deal, but he didn't trust me enough to tell me," she hurried it on, hoping he would go into information overload and forget about the liking him part.

"Ahh, now I see."

She breathed a sigh of relief.

"But that means you don't know for sure that he doesn't like you, too."

So he hadn't forgotten that part. And her father was right. It didn't mean that Peyton didn't like her, too. She sniffed. It didn't change anything about him not trusting her enough to tell her about that other class, either.

"Why don't we go into the house and you tell me the whole story. It's not good for me to hang around out in the open too long."

"You didn't spend the money that you were supposed to pay Guido, did you?"

He frowned. "Of course not. I just don't have all the money I need."

"How much more?"

"What this job will bring in."

Great, she couldn't even do a disappearing act. She'd wanted Peyton to feel bad that his test subject had walked out on him.

"Help me take my cases back inside, then, since I can't run away."

"We'll leave if that's what you want," her father said. "Just until I can earn enough money to pay Guido, then we'll come back."

"And where would we go? What would we do? You don't have another job lined up." She shook her head. "We can stay here, get rid of the ghost, and then have enough money to pay him. That's the best solution and you know it."

He didn't say anything for a moment, but she knew he'd give in. They didn't have another choice.

"You're right," he finally said. "I just wish I had thought before I borrowed money from someone like him."

"It'll be okay."

They each grabbed two cases and started toward the house. It took them a good half hour to put everything back the way she'd had it.

"No activity," her father said as he studied the graph. He sniffed, then grimaced. "Ghost farts. Not as bad as some, but still noxious. Is this the room with the most activity?"

"Yeah." She slowly scanned the study.

Her father walked over to the wall and ran his hand along the burned areas. "Odd markings."

She cringed. "My zapper."

He nodded. "He's a tricky one. I can feel it."

"I bet he knows we're here, too."

"You can count on it." He cleared his throat. "Now that we have everything set up again, don't you think you should tell me a little about this professor?"

She really hadn't thought he'd let the matter drop. "Okay, but not here. Let's go to the patio. That seems to be the safest place to talk."

After they settled around the patio table, Kaci still found it hard to discuss her affair with Peyton, especially with her father, but she knew it would be better to come clean with him. Besides, she was tired of . . . of acting. The part she played was getting tiresome.

Besides, she knew she could tell her father anything. They didn't have the normal father-daughter relationship. They were more like friends, buddies.

Kaci propped her feet on the rail under the table. She didn't meet her father's gaze. "I . . . we . . . well, actually, it was more me than him . . ."

"I'd never be ashamed of anything you did," he said, leaning forward and taking her hand in his.

She sighed. "I know."

"On the other hand, if he forced you to do something you didn't want to, I'll castrate him." He spoke calmly, and a few seconds passed before his words sank into her brain.

"No!" She could feel the heat rise up her face. "What I mean is that I got scared—the ghost frightened me and I ran to Peyton's room. Things sort of escalated from there. Dad, I swear, I'm not a . . . a loose woman. I don't go around sleeping with men I barely know. Except for that night, I guess."

She pulled her hand from his and pushed her hair behind her ears. Damn, she was making a mess of everything. They might be close, but it was difficult to admit to her father that she wasn't perfect.

"I know about raging hormones. You're young." He didn't meet her gaze, and his face had taken on a rosy hue. "We're none of us perfect, and I'm just about the least perfect person I know. I don't have any right to judge you."

"I was running away," she quietly told him.

"Running away only makes things worse. Believe me, I know about running away. The first few years after your mother passed, that's all I did. I was afraid if I stopped, I'd have to face the fact she was gone."

"I'm sorry." She couldn't even imagine what it would be like to lose the one you loved. She'd known Peyton only a few days, but when she'd made the decision to leave, the pain had ripped through her.

Her father reached into his pocket and pulled out a handkerchief, then wiped it across his eyes, sniffing loudly.

"Your mother was a good woman. The best thing that ever happened to me. I still miss her, but in a different way. I guess we all go through stages."

This was the first time she'd heard him talk about what it had been like for him after her mother died. Before, he'd always shied away from her questions. Maybe he was finally healing.

He drew in a deep breath. "So, tell me about this professor. Do you love him?"

"I like him a lot, but I think it would be a little premature to call it love." So why did her heart beat faster when she thought about him?

"The first time I laid eyes on your mother, I knew she was the one for me. Sometimes it happens in the blink of an eye, and sometimes it takes years. Love is like that—unpredictable. That's how it should be. Now, what made you want to run away, Little Missy?"

She told him what happened when Daniel came over and she found out that Peyton taught a class in sexual arousal as well as being a history professor.

Best buddies or not, he was still her father. Her face felt as though it were on fire the whole time, and she didn't even mention when they went out to the pond. Some things just had to be left unspoken.

"Okay," her father began. "You're saying that they're both in the running to get research money. Why would you believe anything this Daniel guy had to say?"

"I called the university. Daniel was right about the other class. I guess we've both been unlucky trusting people. With you it was Guido, and with me it was Peyton."

"Then we'll get rid of the ghost and get out of here. You won't ever have to see him again."

So this was it. With her dad here, the ghost wouldn't be around much longer. She might be gone by tomorrow. Maybe even today. Why didn't that make her feel better?

At least she wasn't so alone now that her father was here.

"I'm glad you're here, Dad."

"Me, too." He patted her hand. "Tell me about the zapper."

Finally, something that would take her mind off her personal problems. She leaned forward. "Dad, it's so cool! You're going to be amazed when you see what it can do." She could barely contain herself.

"It's that good?"

Some of her excitement diminished when she thought about all the burned areas in Peyton's study, but really, that was such a little price to pay.

"The first time I used it, the ghost invaded my dream. When I woke up, I started firing at random. I don't think I ever hit him, and I really destroyed Peyton's study."

"The burned areas. That's not good."

"Yeah, I know. You've told me about staying alert, and I didn't."

"So why is he still hanging around. Why haven't you zapped it toward the light?"

"If my calculations are correct, he has to be a certain density before I can force him toward it."

"And he hasn't gotten to that stage since the first time?"

"He has, but I didn't have the zapper juiced up enough. It didn't faze him."

Her father's forehead wrinkled. "But if you increase the power, won't that be a . . . a little dangerous?"

"I'll just have to make sure I have him in my sights."

"You've tested it, I hope."

She glanced around at the partially burned up bush and grimaced. "Yeah. It might be a good idea if we buy a small fire extinguisher."

"I'll see to it today."

* * *

Peyton finished his last class, gathered the papers he needed to grade, and left the classroom. He missed Kaci. A lot. More than he thought possible. He could run in, check on her, then run out. Five minutes tops.

He could also call like he had been doing.

He frowned. Not liking that idea at all.

What would it hurt if he just stopped by the house? He needed to check to make sure everything was ready for the dinner, anyway.

He'd hired a service to come in and clean the downstairs, and he had a lock for the study door just in case all the equipment was still in there. That, and he didn't want to try to explain the burned patches on the wall.

The caterer would arrive the day of the dinner to start setting up. Everything was taken care of except one detail.

The ghost had to be gone by then.

Peyton wasn't quite sure how he would explain Edward's presence if the spirit decided to make an appearance.

"You look deep in thought, old chap. Not worried about your dinner party, are you?" Daniel said as he began walking with Peyton down the hallway.

What was Daniel doing? Stalking him? Sheesh, he'd had enough of that in his lifetime.

"Long day." Maybe that would be enough to send Daniel in another direction.

"I stopped by your place today."

Peyton froze, then turned to look at Daniel. "And?"

Daniel covertly scanned the area. "Don't worry, old chap, your secret is safe with me. Kaci let it out of the bag that you two are having an affair. I would offer a word of advice once more. Although she seems rather nice, people of her station are usually trying to better themselves when they seduce someone of our standing."

Peyton started laughing. He couldn't help it. "You're joking, right? We're professors at a college, not royalty. And I don't know about you, but I put my pants on one leg at a time like everyone else."

"Yes, but our pants are a higher quality than most." He cocked an eyebrow.

"But then, I've never judged a man by what is on the outside. I judge him by who he is on the inside."

Daniel bristled. "Yes, you would think like that."

"Yes, I do, and if you upset Kaci in any way, form, or fashion, you'll have me to answer to. Do I make myself clear?"

Daniel took a step back. "Of course I didn't say anything to your girlfriend. Not intentionally, anyway."

Great. Peyton knew damn well whatever Daniel did would have been intentional. He silently counted to five.

"And if it was unintentional, what exactly did you do?"

"Well, she seemed rather put out when I just happened to mention the other class you teach, as well as do research. I didn't know she wasn't aware of it and didn't realize you were keeping it secret."

He wanted nothing more than to flatten Daniel, but he didn't have time. He had to get home so he could talk to Kaci and explain. If Daniel had told her about the other class, then he'd probably explained it in the worst possible way.

He had a feeling Kaci was really pissed at him.

Chapter 22

"Come out, come out, wherever you are," Kaci whispered. She'd slung the strap of the zapper over one shoulder and grasped the gun tightly. She was ready. Now all she needed was a ghost to blow to smithereens.

She cringed. Okay, maybe not smithereens, but at least toward the blasted light. Yeah, much better way to think about Edward leaving this world.

The front door opened. Man, she must've really been lost in her work not to hear her father pull up.

She glanced at her watch. Ten minutes. It hadn't taken her father long to go to the store and back. But then, she was pretty sure he didn't want to take a chance of running into Guido.

She heard footsteps coming down the hall. They didn't sound like her father's. She glanced toward the open doorway.

Not her father.

Her hands began to tingle.

Peyton.

No, she would not zap him and fry his ass to a crisp. Damn, what was he doing here? "I thought we'd agreed that you wouldn't return until Edward was out of the picture." Her treacherous heart began to pound.

"We did," he said.

She raised her eyebrows. "And?"

"I saw Daniel. He mentioned that he came by and told you about the other class I teach."

"And you wanted to know how pissed I am at you?"

"I was going to tell you that night at the pond, but I got caught up in the moment. My teaching the other class has nothing to do with us."

She laughed. "Us? Peyton, there is no us. Sure, we have fun together, but it doesn't mean anything—right? You're a good time, but as soon as Edward is gone, then so am I."

Yeah, that sounded good. A big lie, but it sounded good. She refused to let him see how much he'd hurt her. She would've been a superb actress.

Good, he looked unsure of himself. But he wasn't leaving. *Please go,* she silently pleaded. She wanted to toss down the zapper and throw herself in his arms. If he'd lied to her, then so be it.

"We're more than that and you know it," he quietly told her.

No, she would not let herself be taken in by his words. She would stay strong. But did it have to hurt so much?

"Did you get plenty of information from our relationship? You were good, I must say, on sexually arousing me, that is. I hope it helps you get the grant money you want so much. I'm sorry that I won't be able to . . . help you out anymore, though. I hope you understand."

His expression turned grim. "I teach as well as research the sexual habits of people. I can help men and women who are sexually dysfunctional. But it goes deeper than that. I study high-risk sexual behavior. My research can also help in the study of AIDS and other sexually transmitted diseases. Some people like to lessen the importance of my research, but believe me when I say, it's very important."

"Then why keep it a secret. I'd say you were being noble." She could feel herself wavering, but damn it, it had hurt when he hadn't told her.

"I was afraid you'd jump to the wrong conclusion—which you did."

"In other words, you didn't trust me." She shook her head. "All that time at the pond you asked me to trust you, and yet, you didn't trust me. A shame."

"Damn it, Kaci . . ."

The front door slammed. Peyton whirled around.

"Who the hell are you?" Peyton asked.

"Kaci's father and I'd just as soon you not talk to my daughter like that."

Great, now her father decides to show up. Peyton could feel himself start to sweat.

"I was trying to explain something to her."

"Like why you hurt her?"

"I didn't mean to."

"Don't tell me, tell her."

"I'm trying to, sir."

The older man looked at his daughter. "I don't think you were doing a very good job. She still looks irritated."

"Then I'll keep trying to convince her."

And he would. He left and went outside, grabbing the suitcase that was strapped to the back of his bike, and going inside.

"What are you doing?" Kaci asked, stepping into the hall as he came inside again.

"I'm moving back in."

"But Edward is still here."

"As well as your father. One more person won't make that much difference."

"Fine." She glared at him. "Just stay out of our way."

"I'll make sure of it." He walked past her, barely looking at her, but he caught her scent. She smelled nice.

The ghost odor was nearly gone. He almost wished it was still as strong so he wouldn't be so tempted.

On the other hand, the sultry scent Kaci wore tugged at his

senses. He wanted to pull her into his arms and kiss her, feel her lips against his.

But he didn't do any of those things. He just kept walking.

Peyton thought seeing her again had gone pretty well. She hadn't thrown anything at him, she hadn't zapped him—thank goodness—and she was still here. If she stayed, he was almost positive that he could convince her that he did trust her.

Damn it, he should've told her about the other class. It made him look bad.

No one ever understood the importance of his research and what he was teaching. He was definitely going to see if he could get the name changed.

He suddenly grinned.

His psychology of sexual arousal class was always the first class to fill up. The students might come in with preconceived notions about what they would learn, but when they finished the semester, they had an entirely different outlook.

He went up the stairs and down to his room, then unpacked his things. When he went back downstairs, he could hear Kaci and her father talking in the study.

Kaci had warned him to stay out of their way. He could do that.

Maybe.

Probably.

It shouldn't be that difficult with her father in the house.

Peyton grabbed a soda and closed the refrigerator door.

Her father walked inside the kitchen, stopping when he saw Peyton.

Speak of the devil.

They stared at each other a moment. Peyton held up his can of soda. "Want something to drink."

"Got something with a little more bite?"

Peyton opened the refrigerator and grabbed a beer, then held it up. "Will this do?"

"That'll do just fine." He took the beer and twisted the cap off, then took a long drink. "Ice cold. Good."

Kaci's father studied him for a few seconds. Peyton kept his gaze steady, even though he felt like the boy caught with his hand in the cookie jar.

"We didn't really get much of a chance to talk," her father finally said, breaking the tense moment. "I figured what needed to be said, needed to be said to my daughter and not me. Besides, you looked as though you wanted some alone time with her to explain. She's pretty pissed at you."

"I know. She has every right to be, Mr. Melton."

"You can call me Paul. I don't normally stand on ceremony. Besides, if a man hires me, I figure he can call me by my first name."

"Paul it is."

"Do you really teach a class on sexual arousal?"

"Yes." *Here it comes,* he thought.

"And they pay you to teach it?"

"Yes."

Paul took another drink of his beer. When he lowered the bottle, he shook his head. "If I'd known they had classes like that in college, I might have gone. Just can't believe you can actually make a living teaching that."

"And yet, you're a ghost exterminator?"

"Yeah, but that doesn't mean I make a living at it. Sometimes I think we just scrape by, but there's a need for my services, and it gives me a good feeling to know I'm helping people cross over toward the light."

"And do people laugh at the line of work you're in?"

Paul leaned against the counter, resting one elbow on it. "All the time. They have no idea what I actually do. Sometimes I think that people imagine I'll walk into their house with a can of spray. A couple of squirts and the ghost is gone. But there's a lot more to it."

That hit a little bit too close to home. He remembered he'd

thought that very same thing when Kaci first came inside the house.

He was thoughtful as he raised the soda to his lips and took a drink. When he lowered it, his gaze met and held Paul's. "I feel the same way about my work. I guess we're in the same boat."

Paul looked momentarily confused; then Peyton saw the lightbulb go off.

"Maybe we might have judged without knowing all the facts. Damn, I hate when people do that to me, and here I go and do the same thing." He held out his hand. "I'm sorry."

The older man's handshake was firm.

"I accept your apology. Now if I can just get Kaci to accept mine."

"You like my daughter a lot."

He slowly nodded, realizing just how much he did like Kaci. "I do."

"I think she must like you a lot, too."

"She has a hell of a way of showing it."

"Don't give up on her. Kaci had a harder life than most. Her mother died when she was just a kid."

He stared down into his bottle. For a moment, Peyton wondered if he was going to continue. Then he looked up. His eyes were sad.

"I wished for a long time I would've been the one who'd died. What did I know about raising a kid? Not one damn thing. I don't know how it happened, but Kaci turned out pretty good in spite of the way she was brought up. She's not one to trust easily, though."

He drained the bottle, set it on the counter, then looked straight at Peyton.

"I think Kaci trusted you. That doesn't happen very often. Not telling her about that other class was just a small thing when you think about it, but sometimes the small stuff can mean just as much."

"I'm discovering that."

"My Betsy could get mad at some of the oddest things." He shook his head, then grinned. "She was a firecracker, though. Damn, I still miss her."

"Kaci takes after her, then," Peyton said before he thought. "I meant that she . . . uh . . . she's passionate. Not passionate in the sense that . . . I mean that she . . ."

"Kaci has something inside her that's been waiting a while to come out. A passion for life. I'm glad you opened the door for her, even if it means that I'll probably lose the best accountant I've ever had."

Peyton sighed with relief.

"Hey, what kind of road does a ghost like best?" Paul asked.

Peyton shook his head. "I don't know."

"A dead end! Get it? Dead end?"

Peyton chuckled. "Yeah, I get it." If there was any tension left between them, it wasn't there anymore.

"I have lots of those jokes. Got to when you're in my line of work."

"Are you going to be able to get rid of the ghost?"

"All we have to do is get him to show himself and all your troubles will be gone."

That's what Kaci had been telling him for almost two weeks now, and the ghost was still here, and his study looked like a battle zone.

"Hey, did you hear about the ghost that went on vacation?"

Kaci squatted down beside the device her father fondly called the screamer. It was a high frequency projector—similar to a dog whistle. Except something had jiggled loose when he moved it from the last job, and now she was trying to fix it.

"What have you done this time, Pop?" She raised some wires and shined the flashlight inside the machine.

If she could get it into working order, the frequency might

be enough to force Edward to materialize so that she could zap him.

She tugged on one of the wires, but stopped when she heard laughter. Kaci cocked her head to the side and listened. Edward? Was the ghost laughing at her? No, unless there was more than one of them. Oh, Lord, she didn't even want to think about that.

No, that sounded like her father and . . . Peyton?

Had her father crossed enemy lines? She stood, slapping the wrench down on top of the machine. It was her father laughing. More laughter. And that was Peyton. Her father was consorting with the enemy.

She marched to the kitchen and stood watching them as they sat at the table drinking beer and talking and laughing as if they'd known each other for years. They hadn't noticed her yet.

How could her father do this to her? Peyton happened to look up, laughing at one of her father's corny jokes, and noticed her standing in the doorway. He choked on his chuckle.

"Hello, Kaci."

She cast a heated glare that should've burned him to a crisp. Her father looked up; his face turned a rosy shade of red. And so he should be embarrassed at getting caught.

"Paul was just telling me some of his ghost jokes."

She raised an eyebrow. He'd won her father over listening to his dumb jokes. Her father had sold her out pretty cheap.

"I just thought I'd take a break," her father told her. "It's not as though I can help you fix the screamer or anything." He brightened as if he'd just realized what he was doing was okay. "I would only get in the way. I thought it was better if I let you work in peace."

"I'm trying to get the machine fixed that you broke," she told her father. "And you're in here drinking beer with . . . with him."

"Do you want me to come back in there with you?" her father asked.

"No, you'd just get in my way. I hope Edward slimes you both." She turned around and stomped toward the study.

"I think she's pissed at both of us now," she heard her father say.

"I heard that," she yelled over her shoulder. "And yes, I'm pissed at you both now."

How could her father even talk to Peyton after what he'd done to her? It wasn't fair.

She squatted back down in front of the machine, her lips clamped shut as she forced herself not to lose her temper, but all she wanted to do was kick something—preferably Peyton.

The sooner she got the equipment fixed, the sooner she'd get rid of Edward, and then she was outta there!

Chapter 23

Peyton went to the kitchen sink and poured the rest of his beer out. He hadn't wanted it in the first place. It was a dumb attempt at being friendly and joining Kaci's father in drinking a beer.

Dumb idea.

He glanced out the window, soaking in the peacefulness of his backyard. The inviting patio with the terra-cotta tiles. The comfortable chairs. His grill. The trees casting shadows and light. The burned bush.

His forehead wrinkled. One of the bushes looked as though it might have caught fire.

The burning bush?

Doubtful. He was too much of a sinner.

Nope, the only thing religiously burning at his house was Kaci's smoldering temper. Now she was even angrier with him. She probably thought he'd manipulated her father into joining ranks with the enemy. She might be a little right, but not entirely. He'd actually enjoyed Paul's company. The guy was kind of funny.

He tossed the empty bottle in the trash. He had a feeling Kaci was behind his half-burned bush, and he planned to find out what role she'd played.

But when he turned around, he saw a man dressed in a

white suit sneaking around on his patio. Where the hell had he come from?

He didn't look like a ghost. No, Peyton was positive it wasn't another ghost. He ducked back when the man leaned toward the French doors and peered past the glass.

Who the hell was this guy? He didn't look like your run-of-the-mill burglar. He wore a suit. As far as Peyton knew, he didn't think anyone would wear a suit to rob a house. The guy was short and squat—laughable.

But when the stranger reached inside his pocket and pulled out a gun, Peyton was no longer amused. He eased toward the doorway, and when the guy turned and looked behind him, Peyton hurried to the study, and Kaci.

"There's a man trying to break into the house," he said as he burst inside the study. He quickly brought out his cell and dialed 911. "Get out the front—hurry."

Kaci's father grabbed her arm, and they started for the door.

"Yes, operator, there's a man trying to break into my house. Yes. White suit and he's armed."

Kaci and her father stopped in their tracks and looked at each other. What the hell were they doing?

Go, he mouthed, then gave his address to the dispatcher. He hung up and hurried them both toward the door.

"Guido?" Kaci grimaced. "He must have followed you from the store."

"He has a gun." Peyton pushed them both toward the door. "Can you just move it? We can talk about who he is once he's under arrest."

They ran out into the hallway.

"Leaving?" a man asked. "But I just got here. How rude."

Peyton turned around. The guy was pointing his gun at them. Peyton tried to shield Kaci as much as possible. "I suggest you turn around and leave the way you came, and nothing will happen to you."

The man laughed, raising the gun and wiggling it. "But I'm the one with the gun. It won't be me who gets hurt."

"I have your money, Guido," Kaci's father quickly said.

Guido? They had to be joking. He looked at each one of them. They didn't look like they were. Guido? Where had he heard that name?

"All of it?" Guido asked.

"Almost. As soon as we finish this job, we'll have the rest." He reached into his pocket and brought out a wad of bills. "Here, take it."

Guido motioned for Kaci's father to lay it on the hall table. When he did, Guido looked at it, then stuck it into his pocket.

"Maybe I'll stick around until you get the rest." Guido grinned, showing yellowed teeth.

"I wouldn't if I were you. The cops are on the way," Peyton said.

Guido's eyes narrowed to mere slits. "That wasn't smart. Especially when I know where you live. And a jail won't hold me. I have a lawyer on retainer. He'll have me out by the end of the day—that is, if I even go to jail."

"You're a real slime bucket, you know," Kaci snarled.

Peyton wanted to clamp a hand over her mouth.

Guido turned his focus on her, then pointed the gun at her. Peyton's blood ran cold. "Leave her alone."

Guido looked at Peyton. "So that's the way it is. And I thought she was saving herself for me," he said, leering at Kaci.

Peyton could see Kaci's temper was about to explode full force. "How much do they owe you?" he quickly spoke up.

"What this job would bring in," her father said.

Peyton reached in his pocket and counted out the amount. "There. Now leave them alone."

"All I wanted was my money," Guido said, but his gaze strayed to Kaci one last time as cars pulled up and doors slammed shut. Guido slipped the gun in his pocket. "If you know what's good for you, then you'll tell them your call was all a mistake."

Peyton went to the front door, but before he opened it, he glanced over his shoulder. Guido was already gone.

"I'm sorry officers, it was all a mistake," he said as he stepped to the front porch. "I was just about to call and cancel."

The cop looked around. "We had a report about a guy in a white suit. You said he had a gun?"

"It was only a salesman, and it was a screwdriver. He was selling tools."

The other cop's eyes narrowed. "Don't I know you?"

Peyton looked at him, then realized it was the cop from the park. "I don't believe so."

He squinted his eyes as he looked past Peyton and right at Kaci, who'd joined him on the porch. "Yeah, you're the couple from the other night. The one who said you were being chased by that gang." He looked back at Peyton. "You seem to be getting a lot of stuff wrong. You can get into trouble calling in a false report."

"That's why I would never do that," Peyton said.

He looked at Peyton, then Kaci. "We'll be watching you." His radio crackled. The cop pushed the mic button on his shoulder. "Yeah?"

"We have a report of a suspicious man in a white suit in that same area. Ran behind one of the houses and got into a cream-colored car. The caller said the man knocked over one of her flowerpots and she wants to file a formal complaint."

He keyed the mic again. "We'll check it out." His eyes narrowed on Peyton. "Salesman, huh?"

"He must've taken a shortcut," Peyton said. "You know salesmen, always trying to make a fast dollar."

"Just keep your nose clean."

They turned and left. Peyton breathed a sigh of relief, then looked at Kaci. "It would seem neither one of us knows how to trust. Guido?"

Kaci cringed. "I did tell you about Guido." She knew exactly how this looked, but she had told him—sort of.

"No, you didn't . . ."

"At the pond, remember?" She glanced out the corner of her eye at her father. She could feel her face warming. "You told me the story about your father—the one you made up." She looked down at her feet. "That's when I told you that Guido was after my father because he owed him money and we were sort of in hiding. So, see, I did tell you about him."

"But I thought you made that up!"

"I didn't."

"Yeah, I see that now."

What was he getting so angry about? She had told him. Was it her fault that he hadn't believed her? But she couldn't stop the twinge of guilt that swept through her.

"What I want to know," her father began, "is what a gang was doing chasing you through the park."

She looked at Peyton, who shrugged as if to say he didn't care what she told her father. Apparently, he thought she wasn't so bad at telling stories now.

"That's when I saw Guido. Remember, I told you about being in the park and seeing him talking to the man who works for him."

Peyton frowned. "You saw Guido while we were at the park?"

Oh, yeah, she hadn't mentioned that to him, had she? "Yeah. I didn't want to pull you into a family mess."

He raised his eyebrows.

"And I didn't this time, either. Guido must've followed Dad home from the store."

"But what about the gang?" her father asked.

Sheesh, what was this with the third degree? "It wasn't a gang. Just a couple of teenagers."

"And they were chasing you?" His forehead puckered in concentration.

"No, they weren't chasing us, Dad. They were shooting off

fireworks, and the loud noises startled us." At least that was partially true.

"I see."

He didn't look as though he did, but she certainly wasn't going into more of an explanation.

"Does anyone have anything else they'd like to ask? If not, we do have a job to do, and I'd like to get back to work." Kaci hoped she could get back to work. All the questions were making her feel very uncomfortable.

"Just one more," Peyton said.

She crossed her arms in front of her. "And what would that be?"

"Do you have any idea who burned up my bush in the backyard?"

"I have to get the screamer working." She hurried back into the study, knowing she probably should've come clean about the bush, but she really didn't want to tell him how she'd sort of tweaked the zapper to mega power. After all, he did want to get rid of the ghost.

She looked up when her father walked into the room. Odd that she would feel disappointed because Peyton wasn't with him. Not that she wasn't still mad at Peyton for not trusting her enough to tell her about his stupid sex class. Except now that didn't hold water because when it came down to it, she hadn't trusted him either.

"You like him that much?" her father asked.

"He's okay." She reached inside the back of the machine with her wire strippers and stripped one that had a bare spot. It was a wonder her father hadn't shorted out the machine and caused major damage.

"Just okay?" her father prodded.

She stuck her head around the side of the machine and gave him her I-don't want-to-talk-about-it look. "Yeah, just okay." She grabbed the electrical tape and, after twisting the two wires together, taped them.

"I think it's more than okay for him."

She tightened a loose screw. "What's okay for him?"

"You. I think you're more than okay to him."

She grabbed the back and screwed it on. "That's his problem," she said as she came to her feet. "Can we talk about something else?"

"Is it going to work?" He nodded toward the screamer.

"I guess we'll see." She turned the dial all the way up. At least windows weren't busting out. That had happened once when she'd boosted the power on the device a little too much.

Peyton walked into the room. "Is that thing going to force the ghost out of hiding?"

"It usually takes twenty-four to forty-eight hours to work. I guess that's how long it takes to drive a ghost batty," her father said.

"My dinner party is tomorrow."

"Then you'd better hope this one gets tired of it really fast," Kaci said in a voice that almost dripped honey.

"And if it doesn't?"

"Then I guess you'll have three uninvited guests at your party tomorrow. Me, Dad, and the ghost. It should prove interesting."

"That's what I'm afraid of."

So was she, but she was going to keep that tidbit of information to herself.

Chapter 24

"I'll take over," Kaci's father spoke from behind her.

She jumped. Her heart pounded inside her chest. "You scared me."

"Sorry. I wasn't trying to be quiet. Figured you heard me."

"I was lost in thought."

"Unfamiliar territory?"

She raised an eyebrow. "That was so not funny."

He chuckled. "Yes, it was." Just as quickly, he sobered. "Anything from the ghost?"

She shook her head. "Not a thing. I wish there were some way of knowing if the machine was working."

"It is." He wore a self-satisfied smile.

She scanned the room, wondering what he was detecting that she hadn't. She still didn't see anything out of the ordinary. "How can you be certain?"

"I can feel it."

She should've known. "And that's why you're so good at what you do. You have a natural instinct that I don't. Not that I'm complaining. I'm very proud of you. I always have been."

"You have your own special gifts. You can fix the machines and I can't. It's your natural ability. Everyone has at least one."

"Sometimes it takes a long time to find it."

He kissed the top of her head. "And when this job is finished, I want you to pursue your dreams. You don't need to stand in the shadow of mine. It's time you lived your own life."

"Have I mentioned how much I love you?"

He smiled as he stepped back. "A time or two."

She stifled a yawn.

"Off to bed with you. I'll take over now."

She nodded as she slipped the strap off her shoulder and handed the zapper to her father. "Here you go." She started to turn away, but remembered something else at the last minute. "You'll need this, too." She had fastened a clip to the handheld fire extinguisher and hooked it on her belt loop. She smiled when she remembered how Peyton had eyed it with more than a touch of concern.

Her father took the fire extinguisher from her. "Do you think I'll need this?"

"If you use the zapper, you'll need it."

He nodded. She left the room and climbed the stairs to the guest room. It was three in the morning and she was done for. Why the hell couldn't Edward show so she could send him on his way? He was being really stubborn.

Edward didn't know her father, though. Pop had more tricks up his sleeve than a magician, and he'd use every one of them. She hadn't been lying when she'd said her dad was a natural. He had a gut instinct that she had never been able to grasp.

She paused outside Peyton's door. For a moment, she closed her eyes, running her hand over the wood frame. It would take only one turn of the doorknob and a few steps for her to be in bed with him, to feel his naked body pressed against hers.

It wasn't going to happen. They'd had a good time, but it was over. Neither one had trusted the other, so what did that say about the future of any relationship they might have? Not a whole hell of a lot.

She continued until she got to her room and silently opened the door. It felt cold, and she didn't think it was the ghost.

It was a good thing exhaustion seeped from every pore. That's probably why she was thinking so much about Peyton, but it would also help her to fall asleep faster. Once she had a little sleep, she'd have her emotions under control.

She quickly stripped out of her clothes, pulled on a thin nightie, and crawled beneath the cover.

Sleep, wonderfully blissful sleep. That was all she needed.

Fatigue overtook her. She didn't even try to keep her eyes open. And maybe, just maybe, she wouldn't dream about Peyton. Damn, she was sleepy. . . .

Peyton walked out of the darkness toward her. This so wasn't good, and yet it was exactly what she needed. Damn, she'd missed him.

No, she was dreaming. Oh, man, not again. Wake up! Edward was messing with her head. Drag your eyelids open!

It wasn't happening. She couldn't even raise her hand to push her eyelids open. Just too tired.

"You're not Peyton," she mumbled.

"I can be. If that's what you want. It is what you want, isn't it?"

"No, I'm mad at him."

"Why? Because he didn't tell you about a silly class?"

Peyton changed, and in his place was a wiry young man. He was pale, as though he'd been sick for a long time, and there were dark circles beneath his eyes. And he looked sad.

"Edward?"

He bowed. "At your service."

"You need to go toward the light. There's family waiting for you on the other side."

"No."

"Why do you linger? There's nothing for you here."

"You're here." He downed his head. "I want to stay with

you. You're the only one who knows what I went through. We're lonely souls, the two of us."

"I have a great life," she defended herself.

"No, you don't. I heard you talking with your father."

"I'm going to change—go back to school."

"It won't be any better than it is now."

"What do you know? You've never left this house, I bet."

He walked closer to her. He wasn't as pale as a moment ago. He looked almost handsome. What was he trying to do? This didn't feel right. She needed to wake up.

But when she tried to force her eyes open, she felt a warm breeze wash over her and a gentle rocking motion to lull her back to sleep. It was nice. She gave up the struggle to awaken.

"I could make your life better," Edward told her.

"How can you? You're a ghost."

"Join me. Look, it's beautiful where I am." He waved his arm slowly in front of him.

The darkness that had previously surrounded him disappeared, and in its place was a wonderful garden with huge flowers that would make a gardener green with envy. And there were trees that one could sit beneath and daydream forever.

"It's beautiful," she told him.

"And it can all be yours. Yours and mine."

Her forehead puckered. "How would that be possible? I'm not dead."

"It wouldn't be hard. There's a bottle of pills in your suitcase."

"They're just over-the-counter."

"If you take enough, your death will be painless. We'll be together forever. Join me, my love." He held out his hand toward her.

She only had to take the pills. One right after another and all her worries would be gone. She could do that. But sitting up on the side of the bed took a lot of effort.

"Tomorrow," she told Edward. "I'll take them tomorrow. First thing."

"No!" His eyes blazed with fury. Just as suddenly his anger was gone and his features calm. "You have to take them now. Don't you want to be with me?"

She looked at him. Odd, how much Edward looked like Peyton. They could almost be twins.

"Come, be with me."

Of course she wanted to be with Peyton. She'd been angry with him earlier, and angry with herself, too. They each should've trusted the other.

"Kaci, come to me."

"Yes, Peyton."

She pushed to a sitting position. Damn, she was so tired. She sat on the side of the bed, trying to come awake enough to do what she was supposed to do.

What was she supposed to do?

Pills. Yes, that was it. She had to take the pills.

"Kaci, you're so close. You have only a little more to do. Don't you want to be with me? I thought we were so perfect for each other."

"We are." She stood, going to her suitcase, feeling around, and then opening it. The pills were in the top zippered part. She brought them out, then shut the case and stood there. If she didn't have to open her eyes, then she didn't have to wake up, and she didn't want to wake up. It had been such a long day, and she was so very tired.

She started back to the bed.

"Where are you going, Kaci?"

"Back to bed."

"But you can't."

She tried to raise her arm to show Peyton the pills, but it was too heavy. "I have the pills. Just as you asked. I just need to go back to bed for a little while."

"No!"

Her bottom lip puckered. "Why are you mad at me? Is it because I didn't trust you, either?"

"Not at all. I love you."

"You do?"

"Of course. Why else would I ask you to be with me? Now open the bottle and take the pills. For me. For us."

She twisted the top. Nothing happened. "Can't open them."

"You're not trying!"

She sniffed. "Why are you yelling at me?"

"I'm not."

"Yes, you are."

"Just try again."

Maybe if she just sat on the side of the bed, she could get the bottle open. She sat down. Damn, she was so tired.

"No, you can't go back to sleep. You have to take the pills so we can be together forever."

"As soon as I rest for just a little bit, then I'll take them."

Peyton seemed to be fading.

"Where are you going?"

But he didn't answer, and suddenly Peyton wasn't Peyton. He became Edward, and the ghost didn't look at all happy. She'd deal with it in the morning. Right now she was going back to sleep.

Kaci stretched, slowly opening her eyes. Lord, she felt like death warmed over. No, it was too damn early to think about death and ghosts. She needed coffee.

But rather than getting up, she just lay there thinking about her dream. It was actually more like a nightmare. Except for the parts with Peyton. It had been nice when he'd said he loved her.

But then Peyton was Edward and vice versa. Edward had wanted her to take a bunch of pills and kill herself so she could join him in ghostland forever where they would live hauntingly ever after.

Pffft, like that would ever happen.

She would be so glad when they were rid of the ghost and she could get her life back to normal.

But right now, she would settle for coffee.

She rolled over, coming to rest on something hard. *Owwww.* She pushed up on her elbow and stared down at the bottle of pills.

Chapter 25

Okay, this wasn't good. Not good at all.

Kaci jumped out of bed, grabbing her robe. After a quick wash, she hurried downstairs. Her father was already in the kitchen, drinking a cup of coffee.

"I just made another pot so it's fresh," he said, looking over the rim of his cup.

His eyes were puffy and he looked tired. It suddenly struck her that he was getting old, and a tremble of fear went through her. She quickly shook it off, blaming last night for her morbid thoughts.

"You don't look like you got much sleep," he said. "I was up most of the time. The machines were going crazy, but the ghost never showed himself. He was lurking around, though."

She poured a cup of coffee, added cream and sugar, then took it back to the table. "There was so much activity because my room is directly above the study."

His eyes narrowed. "What are you saying?"

"That Edward was with me most of the night."

He sighed. "I should've known he was up to something. The needle on the graph was all over the place. I never thought that he might not be in the main area that he usually visits. Ghosts pretty much stay in a place they're familiar with or like." He studied her. "He visited your dream, didn't he?"

She nodded, cupping the coffee, letting the warmth seep into

her cold hands. "His attachment to me has grown stronger."
She raised her cup and took a drink.

"How strong?"

"Where's Peyton?" She glanced down the hall, then toward the patio, but she didn't see him anywhere.

"Said he had an early class. Took off about an hour ago.
What happened?"

The last thing she wanted was Peyton to overhear, so she
breathed a sigh of relief knowing he was gone. "The ghost
tried to get me to join him," she blurted.

Her father's face lost some of its color, and she wished
she'd eased him into it a little better.

"He came to me in a dream. At first, I thought he was Peyton, but he couldn't keep up the pretense for very long." She
took another drink, then set her cup on the table, moving her
hands under the table so her father wouldn't see how badly
they were shaking.

"How did he expect you to join him? You couldn't unless . . ." He slowly set his cup on the table and clasped his
hands together. "Tell me everything."

"I'm still here, so his plot didn't work. There's no reason
to go into any detail."

"I need to know."

She hesitated. He was going to be upset, but Kaci didn't
think it could be helped. If her father was going to get rid of
Edward, he had to know just how far the ghost would go.

"He kept switching back from Peyton to Edward," she
said. "I was in such a deep sleep that I couldn't wake up. And
when he told me to get the pills out of my suitcase and take
them, it was as though I were sleepwalking."

"You didn't take any, did you?"

She shook her head. "Thank goodness for child proof caps
or I don't know what would've happened. As it was, I fell
back asleep. I remember Edward was furious."

"And you're sure this actually happened and you didn't
just dream it?"

"When I rolled over this morning, the bottle of pills was in bed with me."

"I want you out of the house right now," Peyton spoke from the doorway.

They both jumped at the same time. Damn, he'd almost accomplished what the ghost had tried last night, except instead of pills, Peyton nearly scared her to death.

"Do you think next time you might announce yourself rather than barking orders?" she said, frowning at him.

"I won't have you in danger," he said. His jaw twitched, as though he barely held his temper in check.

"It's a little late for that," she said.

"Not if you leave."

"She can't," her father said. "The ghost has attached itself to her. It would only follow her wherever she went."

Peyton's expression was more than a little annoyed. "Then why hasn't it left the house before now?"

Her father shrugged. "Who knows? He probably attached himself to each owner and never felt the need to leave. But now he's formed an attachment to Kaci. Wherever she goes, so will the ghost. She's just as well off here."

"So he can get her to take the bottle of pills next time?" Peyton asked. "I don't think so."

Oh, he'd been there for a while, Kaci thought to herself. She should've heard him walk down the hall. How did people move so quietly? She weighed only one hundred and twenty pounds but had never been quiet on her feet. Must be the shoes she wore. Okay, no more combat boots. It was tennis shoes from here on out.

"We'll keep her safe," her father said.

"You look like you're about to fall over," Peyton pointed out. "And in case you've forgotten, my dinner is tonight."

"The more people, the easier it will be to protect her. You'll have to stay with her until I've caught up on my sleep, but after that, I can take over. It won't be long now before she won't need protecting."

"I can take care of myself," she said. They talked as though she weren't even in the room. "And how do you figure it won't be much longer?" she asked.

"Because he was desperate last night," her father said. "Enough that he wanted you to join him. I'd say the screamer is working."

"Why doesn't he just leave and come back later?" Peyton asked.

"Because he doesn't want to take a chance of losing his connection with Kaci," her father explained.

"So, what do we do now?" She wasn't so sure she liked the idea of Peyton babysitting her all day, even though the thought of being in his company made her body tingle to awareness.

Not that they could do anything with her father in the house. Besides the fact, she was still irritated he hadn't told her about the other class, and the fact that Daniel had smirked. She really disliked people who smirked.

Her father stood. "I'm going to bed for a while." He looked at Peyton. "What time did you say that dinner was?"

"Seven. The caterers will start arriving at five-thirty, and I have some people who will be here"—he glanced at his watch—"anytime now to clean the house."

"We'll have to hope the ghost gets tired of the screamer before then."

"If not?"

"Then we'll blend in. You won't even know we're here."

That would be a first! They'd never blended in anywhere, but when Peyton looked to her for confirmation, she nodded as though they did it all the time. Peyton still didn't look convinced.

Her father kissed the top of her head. "If the ghost gives you any trouble, wake me up. Together, we'll get him."

" 'Night, Dad."

Peyton was still standing in the doorway watching her. For some reason, he was making her awfully nervous.

"There's coffee," she finally told him.

Without saying a word, he walked to the cabinet and took down a cup, then poured coffee into it. When he turned around, he leaned against the counter.

"What?" she finally asked.

"I was trying to decide if you were still angry with me for not telling you about the other class I teach."

She arched an eyebrow. "I am." She raised her cup, finishing the last drop and stood.

He straightened. "Where are you going?"

She turned at the doorway and looked at him. "To get dressed. Do you mind?"

He didn't seem a bit put out because of her sarcasm.

"No, but maybe I should come with you—for protection." His gaze drifted over her, touching and caressing.

Her body immediately responded. She drew in a sharp breath. "I think when my father asked you to keep an eye on me, he didn't realize he would be sending a fox to guard the hen-house."

"The class wasn't that big of a deal."

"I know. But the lack of trust between us is." She left the room. He didn't follow.

Peyton watched her leave, then took a drink of his coffee. She was right; he hadn't trusted her, but then neither had she trusted him. Maybe by the end of the day they would be able to resolve the issue.

There was a knock on the front door. As he walked down the hallway, he could see the cleaning people had arrived. He opened the door for them, showed them where to clean, and made sure they stayed away from the study.

By the time he was finished, Kaci was already hard at work. He quietly stepped inside, shutting the door behind him. She was deep in thought as she checked the stats on the machines. He knew she hadn't even heard him come in.

For a moment, he just stood there, staring. She was so damn beautiful it made him ache. Made him remember what it was like to hold her, to kiss her, to make love to her.

She raised a hand and brushed her hair behind her ear, and even that simple move was seductive.

He apparently made a noise, or maybe she just sensed a presence, because she looked up. For a second, their gazes locked. Then she looked away.

"The ghost must've drained his energy last night when he came to me. I think father is right; he won't be able to last much longer."

"This grant means a lot to me."

"For sex research, right?" She cleared her throat, straightening from the machine. "I'm sorry. I didn't mean that."

"If you hadn't meant it, then you wouldn't have said it," he told her. He'd hurt her by not telling her about the class, and now her pain was killing him.

"In high school, there was a group of girls. Everyone wanted to be in their little group. I think there were ten of them. I trusted them—really dumb of me."

She moved to one of the instruments and checked the dials. He had a feeling he knew where she was going with this story, but he also knew she needed to talk. Hell, they still had the cliques in college, except now the unpopular kids learned to form their own. It made things a little more even.

"They invited me to join. I was flattered. I knew everyone was aware that my father chased ghosts, and I knew most everyone thought he was crazy. But I fell very neatly into their trap. They made me the laughingstock of the school."

"I'm sorry."

She looked at him. "I got over it, but it taught me a good lesson about trusting people."

"I miss you."

"I miss you, too, and it's really okay how everything turned out between us." Her laugh was short, almost bitter. "And it's not just you. It's me, too. I don't trust you any more than you do me." She shrugged. "A two-way street."

"It takes time to trust someone completely."

"You're right. I imagined our relationship was more than what it was. Crazy, I know."

Damn it, she was twisting everything he said. He ran a hand through his hair. "Then we'll take all the time we need. I like you a lot. I don't want what we have to end like this. I'll wait for you. I won't give up."

"Would you wait for me forever?"

He watched her face. "No." Some days it didn't pay to be honest.

She chuckled. "I don't blame you. I don't think I'd wait for anyone forever, either."

"A relationship has to grow. You have to give us time. Maybe we could start right here, right now, being honest with each other. Trusting."

"I siphoned your gas," she told him. "There wasn't anything wrong with your car."

"You stole my gas?"

She frowned. "I'd rather think that I just borrowed it. I was going to repay you after you paid me for getting rid of the ghost." She grimaced. "Except you paid Guido, and I can't pay you for the gas."

"I don't care about the gas."

"I drank the rest of your chocolate milk, too. I was going to tell you it soured."

"I don't care about that."

She sighed. "Someday you would get tired of it. But by then, I would have fallen in love with you. I'd be so devastated when you walked out, I might even kill myself, and then I'd probably be stuck with Edward for the rest of my . . . death. I figure we're much better apart than we are together."

It took a full minute for him to digest everything she'd just told him. "You're breaking us up before we ever really get together?"

Her expression turned thoughtful. "Yeah, it would look that way."

He started to say something, but there was a discreet

knock on the study door. He opened it just wide enough to peer out at the cleaning woman.

"Do you happen to have an extension cord we can use?"

"One moment." He shut the door and turned back to Kaci. "This conversation is far from over. When I get back, we're going to continue to talk about our relationship."

"We don't have a relationship."

"Yes, we do. You might have given up on us, but I haven't." He opened the door and walked out of the room. "Stubborn, crazy . . ."

"Sir?"

He looked at the young maid. "Nothing. I was talking to myself.

"Yes, sir."

But the look she gave him said she thought he might be a little off upstairs. He didn't care. The only thing he did care about was getting Kaci to trust him.

And he'd do it even if it killed him and he had to haunt her the rest of her life.

Chapter 26

Kaci stared at her reflection. Not bad. Long black dress, heels, dangling earrings. She cleaned up pretty good. What would Peyton think when he saw her?

Get over it! God, she was so pathetic. She'd vowed a long time ago not to be ruled by someone else's opinion of her. She wasn't about to start caring now.

But she couldn't stop the traitorous tingle of excitement when she thought about his reaction. She was so doomed.

There was a tap on her door. Her pulse quickened. She was shameless and she knew it. He was going to hurt her—she knew that, too. He didn't trust her.

But Peyton was like a delicious treat she knew was going to make her sick, but she just couldn't stop herself from taking one more bite.

She turned in a way that would show off her figure to its best advantage and brought her hair to lie over one shoulder, near the deep vee of her dress, right at the curve of her breast. She could be such a slut sometimes. That, and she'd probably regret what she was about to do, but damn it, she did miss him.

"Come in?" Her voice was low, husky, and, she knew, incredibly sexy.

Her father opened the door. "You okay? You sound a little hoarse."

So much for sexy and sultry. No wonder her dates had all been duds in the past.

She sighed with regret. It was probably for the best. Really, when she thought about it, she and Peyton had nothing in common. He was a professor and she was—hell, she didn't even know what she was. She'd just been drifting aimlessly through life without direction. Like a boat bobbing up and down on the ocean waves.

She squared her shoulders. But she would find her direction as soon as this job was over. Peyton had made her realize there was more to life than working in a small, cramped office. Something good had come out of their relationship.

"You look nice, Dad."

He looked down at the only suit he owned, then smiled at her as he walked over to the mirror and stood beside her. He brushed his hands across the sleeves, then beamed at her.

"We both look nice," he said. "Maybe you a little more than me."

She smiled as she studied their reflection and for the first time realized her father wasn't that old. He looked pretty good now that he'd rested.

"Why haven't you ever dated?" she suddenly asked.

He shrugged. "I had a child to raise, then got caught up with the business. I had your mother's memory. That was always enough for me."

"You should get out more. Start dating."

He shook his head. "And tell women what? That I hunt ghosts for a living. It wouldn't work. They'd either laugh in my face or run off screaming."

"I'm sure they would understand."

"Like you did with Peyton's other class? You going to hold that one mistake against him for the rest of his life?"

"I don't know yet."

"Maybe there are things we both need to change in our lives. I guess we can thank Peyton for that."

She smoothed a hand down her dress, straightening imaginary wrinkles and not meeting her father's eyes. "Why would you say that?"

"He's the one who got you thinking about your life and where you were going, didn't he?"

"I was already thinking about it." She met his skepticism head-on. "But maybe he nudged me along a bit," she conceded.

"He's a good man. I think you've gotten upset over nothing. That class was such a little thing to raise a fuss over."

"It was more than the class, Dad. It was about not trusting each other. You need to trust the one you're with." She sighed. "We're just so different, Pop. It would never work."

"I think you're afraid."

She should've known her father would see past her shields. "You're right. I am. But I can't help that, either." She glanced at her watch. "We'd better get downstairs."

"What do you think about Peyton telling everyone the truth about us?"

Her insides clenched when she thought about what he'd told them earlier. It was a mistake. "I think we'll be ridiculed. It's a bad plan. We'll be great entertainment, though, won't we?" Peyton didn't understand how cruel people could be.

He took her hand. "Never be ashamed of who you are."

She held her head high. "I'm not. I just don't want to be taken advantage of, and I'm afraid that's what will happen."

"Peyton's a good man." He patted her hand. "He won't let that happen."

She wasn't quite as positive as her father. Paul Melton was gullible. Look at the transaction he'd made with Guido. That should tell her his judgment of people was off target by a mile.

They walked out the door of her room and started down the stairs. A warm burst of air lightly kissed her. She stopped, her hand on the rail, and looked around. Had she imagined it? No, she didn't think so.

"What?" her father asked.

"Edward is here. I just felt him. It was like a warm breeze." She looked at her father. "Did you feel it?"

He shook his head. "But that doesn't mean he isn't here. Where's the zapper?"

"Downstairs. I put it in the dining room so I'd have easy access. If he shows before then, I'll just have to hope I can get to it."

"So, you think he'll make an appearance tonight, too?"

She nodded. "Gut feeling." She looked at her father and smiled. "Either that or I'm hungry."

"I think you have more of this ghost hunting in your blood than even you know."

"They still scare me," she admitted.

He snorted. "They scare the hell out of me, too."

"Really?"

"What, you thought I wasn't frightened?"

"Well, yeah." He'd never once let on that he was afraid. Her whole way of thinking was being turned upside down. What the hell was happening?

They were almost at the bottom of the stairs when Peyton walked past. He glanced up, then stopped, staring at her.

"My God, you're beautiful."

She could feel the heat rise up her face. It was just words, she told herself, but she couldn't stop her smile. She could get used to compliments.

"You look nice yourself." Okay, now, that was a bald-faced lie. He looked a lot better than nice. He looked very edible, and she *had* said she was hungry.

Her father glanced between them. "I think I'll just get something to drink."

Traitor, she thought.

"Do you think the ghost will make an appearance?" Peyton asked.

Odd, but she had a feeling when he opened his mouth he'd been going to say something else, but then changed his mind at the last minute.

"It will make great conversation in case your party gets dull."

"What's that supposed to mean?"

Before she could answer, the doorbell rang.

"Your guests are here."

He studied her for a moment, then went to answer the door. Her palms began to sweat. She didn't like parties—never went to them, in fact.

Once, her father had given her a birthday party when she was ten. She'd been so excited and helped him address all the invitations, but only one little girl had shown up. Maybe it was a good thing. Fate or something. They'd become friends. At least until the school year ended and once again they'd moved.

Cheryl. That had been her name. She hoped Cheryl was doing well and had a wonderful husband and maybe kids. She'd been nice.

A cold chill of dread washed over her. Kaci had a feeling this party would be even worse. All Peyton's friends and colleagues would be there. They'd laugh at her and her father. She was strong, she could take it, but she'd zap anyone's butt who said one cross word to her father.

She went down the rest of the stairs, flinching when she heard Daniel's voice and another man's. He would have to be the first to arrive.

Okay, up shield. The one that protected her from the barbs of people who thought they knew better how she should conduct herself. The correct words she should speak . . . all the rules of society that she cared nothing about.

But she could act. She was damn good at that. In fact, she had her role down perfectly.

"Oh," Daniel said when he saw her. "I didn't realize you would be here."

She stepped forward. "Hello, Daniel." She smiled warmly and reached her hand out so that he had no choice but to take hers. *Yuck!* It was like shaking hands with a fish.

Act the part.

"It's so nice to see you again." She nodded to the older gentleman who had come in with Daniel. He bowed his head slightly, smiling. She liked the twinkle in his eye. How the hell had Daniel ended up in this man's company?

"So, you're living here?" He looked toward Peyton.

"She's working here," he explained.

Daniel dropped her hand as if his touching her was something distasteful. "Oh, I see."

La-di-da. Too good to associate with the help. He didn't even bother to introduce her to his friend.

"And I'm Albert Johnson," the man said, apparently not a bit concerned with social status.

"She's the help, Albert," Daniel said, sniffing.

"No," Peyton said. "I don't think you understand."

Peyton took her hand. His touch made her body ache for more. This wasn't good. If that was all it took to have her crying uncle and falling into his arms, then she was doomed to suffer a lot of heartache.

"Then please enlighten us." Daniel raised a condescending eyebrow.

"Kaci is a paranormal specialist."

Daniel looked between them, then burst out laughing. He crossed his arms in front of him. "When she's not being a maid, right? I wasn't born yesterday, old chap."

"I didn't think Peyton would want me to tell people what I really do, so I pretended to be a maid," Kaci explained.

Albert glanced around. "Is this house haunted?"

"Oh, please, Albert." Daniel pursed his lips. "Tell me you don't really believe in that nonsense?"

Albert frowned. "Yes, I do. I'm not so naïve to think this is all there is." He waved his hand. "I'd be thrilled to learn more about it."

Her father chose that moment to step out from the kitchen.

"Yes, the house has a ghost. If you want to learn about paranormal activity," she said, holding her hand out toward her dad, "this is my father, and he knows a lot more than I do."

She introduced the two, not bothering to mention Daniel to her father. They immediately headed into the study so her father could show him the machines. Kaci's dad was in his element talking about his business and ghosts. Her heart warmed that Albert was so interested and didn't seem a bit concerned with her father's lack of social graces.

"If this is another ploy to get the grant money, then it won't work," Daniel said. "Albert might have been fooled by your so-called ghost hunter, but I'm not, and I really doubt the dean will be, either."

She wondered if smacking him would help him to understand. It was a nice thought.

"Careful, *old chap*, your true colors are coming through," Peyton warned.

Daniel's cheeks reminded her of a puffer fish as he struggled for words. Kaci doubted very many people stood up to the professor.

"I don't know what you're talking about. I only meant my words as a little friendly advice. After all, I've been at this university much longer, and I'd hate to see you embarrassed . . . or fired."

"I'm sure you would."

The doorbell rang again before Peyton could say more. Kaci slipped away in search of her father and Albert. The other professor might be into the paranormal, but she wasn't so sure about the rest of Peyton's associates. She'd just as soon stay in the background. If they saw the study, they might just think he'd lost his mind.

She didn't see much of Peyton after he let the other guests in. Everyone seemed to arrive at once.

"Anything?" her father asked as he came to stand beside her.

She'd chosen an area of the room away from the crowd

and nursed a drink. She'd nodded and smiled, but she wasn't the type to mingle.

She shook her head. "I've felt him a few times, but I haven't seen anything out of the ordinary."

"Nice party, huh?"

She shrugged. "I suppose." She didn't want to tell him that the only thing that would make it better was if she weren't here.

"Have you met the dean and his wife?"

Couldn't he see? It was as though he'd tuned out how Peyton's friends were treating them. Like they were some kind of oddity. "I've tried to stay away from everyone."

He shook his head. "They're staring because you're so beautiful. Other than Albert and that other fella—don't care for him at all—I don't think they even know about the ghost. Peyton hasn't exactly shouted out what we do, but he isn't shying away, either."

Her gullible father. He'd always been immune to what people thought. Maybe they didn't know now, but when the guests discovered she and her father were ghost exterminators, her father might change his opinion.

"No one has said anything out of the way to you, have they?" he suddenly asked.

"No, everyone has been very polite, Dad."

"Well, if anyone does, you tell me, and I'll box them up beside their head. That'll teach them."

She laughed. God, she loved him so much.

"If everyone would like to go into the dining room, dinner is ready to be served," Peyton announced. His gaze met and held hers; then he smiled.

Why was he always doing that to her? Making her feel things she didn't want to feel. She could see now that she was so much better off in her own little world where she didn't have to worry about making a mistake.

The sooner this was over, the better.

Chapter 27

There were place cards where everyone would sit. Thankfully, she noticed Daniel was seated at the other end of the table.

Albert was next to her father, so she wouldn't have to worry about him, either. There were twenty other guests. She shouldn't be expected to do more than carry on polite conversation. She could do that.

Peyton had introduced her to everyone else as a friend, so she had a feeling they didn't know what she and her father did for a living. Albert was in deep conversation with her father, and she didn't think either one of them had said much to anyone else. She was fine with that, and as long as the ghost didn't make an appearance, everything might continue without a hitch.

Except for Daniel. She didn't trust him. He'd been casting sly glances in her direction all evening. She didn't think he'd said anything to the rest of the guests. She wasn't sure why. But, no, she didn't trust him.

She went around the table and found her seat. Peyton had put her beside him. She raised an eyebrow and looked at him. He shrugged. Damn it, she'd dumped him. Why couldn't he leave well enough alone rather than trying to win her back?

He leaned toward her, and for a second she wondered if he

was going to kiss her. A flutter of excitement swept over her. His warm, minty breath fanned her face.

"The zapper is on the rails under your chair in case Edward shows himself," he whispered near her ear.

So much for the kiss.

He pulled out her chair.

She sat down, dropped her napkin, and felt beneath her chair. Once she knew where her zapper was, she straightened, and then laid her napkin across her lap.

"This is very nice, Peyton," the dean said. The dean was a short, squatty man with a thick head of white hair. His wife sat beside him. She was on the thin side, and Kaci noticed she didn't say a whole lot. She just stood in her husband's shadow. Even her name, Dorothy, was rather bland.

"Yes," Daniel drawled. "It's a splendid gathering."

Kaci wondered if he realized his English accent had slipped. Not that she was about to tell him.

"And he even has local celebrities," Daniel continued with a smirk.

Her heart started to pound. *Oh, hell, here it comes,* she thought to herself. No, she could get through this. She would ignore the barbs, the sly innuendos that were sure to come. She took a deep breath and made sure her shields were clearly in place. No one could hurt her now.

"Oh, really," Dorothy exclaimed, her attention shifting to Kaci.

Then again, she could get the zapper. One shot. That's all it would take to end Daniel's miserable life. He could join Edward, and they could live unhappily ever after.

Peyton reached over and squeezed her hand.

No, she silently prayed, don't be nice or the shield will crack. She glanced at Peyton. His eyes told her that he would stay right beside her; he wasn't going anywhere.

Rather than crumble, her invisible shield seemed to gain strength. She knew she wouldn't have to face his friends alone. Peyton would be there with her.

"We have . . ."—Daniel looked around the table, his eyes sparkling with malicious glee—"ghost hunters at the table."

When Daniel looked straight at Kaci, she could feel the evil oozing from him as if he'd thrown a dagger at her. And he had in a way. Verbal daggers could be just as painful as the sharp edge of a knife.

"Ghost hunters?" The dean's wife looked at her husband.

Great, here it comes. Peyton wouldn't get his grant, and Kaci and her father would be laughed out of town.

"Really?" the dean said.

"How interesting!" Dorothy scanned the room. "Is there a ghost here? I mean now?"

Kaci looked around at the other guests, then shifted in her seat. "I've felt him, yes."

"A haunted house," Dorothy breathed. She leaned forward to look at a woman just down the table. "Did you hear that, Cindy? A real ghost! How exciting."

Cindy, who Kaci had earlier learned taught at the college, smiled at Kaci.

"If we had known you were a ghost hunter, we would've mobbed you for information. Dorothy and I are fascinated with the paranormal."

"And this is Kaci's father. He owns Ghost Be Gone, right here in town," Peyton added.

"Really? Oh, you should advertise more. I wondered about that little store," Dorothy said.

"You must do a lecture at the college," the dean put in. "Fascinating subject. I would definitely listen in. My wife and I have gone on a few ghost hunts. Up around North Carolina."

"Oh, really, this is ridiculous!" Daniel threw down his napkin. "There are no such things as ghosts. If there's a ghost in this house, then why don't I see it? This . . . this woman and her father are frauds!"

Pfffrrrrt!

Oh, no.

Daniel came to his feet at the same time a glob of green slime hit him on top of the head. The two sitting next to him quickly moved out of the way.

"What . . . what . . . ," Daniel said as the slime began to slide down the sides of his face.

"Ectoplasm," Kaci said as she reached beneath her chair and slowly brought the zapper to her lap.

"What is it?" the dean asked.

"The ghost," her father said. "He slimed him."

"It's here? With us right now?" Dorothy breathed.

" 'Fraid so."

"You can't have her, Edward," Peyton said.

"What are you doing?" she frantically whispered.

Peyton looked her in the eye. "I'm trusting you." He came to his feet, backing away from the people in the room to stand in the corner. "She'll never be yours, Edward. She loves me, and I won't let you have her."

A green mist began to form near Peyton. Kaci held her breath.

There was a collective gasp from the others around the table.

"You can't do anything except maybe toss a little slime my way. Do you think that will actually stop me from taking Kaci away from you? Why don't you show yourself and fight like a real man instead of some sniveling coward?"

The green fog began to grow thicker.

"Do it," Peyton said, looking at her.

"I can't. It isn't safe. You're too close. What if I miss?" Fear ran through her.

He looked right at her. "I said I trusted you, and I do."

Yeah, but she wasn't so sure she trusted herself. She would never forgive herself if she missed.

"Take the shot," her father whispered. "You can do it."

The green fog grew denser. She could almost make out a head. They were right. This was the best shot she would ever have.

She raised the zapper, aimed, and pulled the trigger. There was a pop; then billowing green smoke fogged the area.

Peyton made a choking sound.

The blood drained from her face. Had she hit him? Oh, no, she'd aimed for the ghost. Finally, someone had given her complete trust, and she'd disintegrated him. She hadn't meant to . . .

"I think the wall is on fire," Peyton yelled.

She breathed a sigh of relief. No, he was fine. And Edward was off toward the light. At least, she hoped he was.

"Got the fire covered," her father said as he jumped to his feet. He whipped open his jacket and brought out the handheld fire extinguisher, pulled the pin, and sprayed the wall.

The guests began to cough as fumes filled the area. They began moving to the other room.

"Will someone get this stuff off me?" Daniel whined.

The dean frowned. "Oh, go stick your head in the . . . sink, old chap!" He turned to Kaci and her father. "That was absolutely the most amazing thing I've ever seen. I was going to see if you wouldn't mind being a guest lecturer for one of the summer classes, but I really think we need to expand it. That is, if you're willing. We would give you a salary, of course. You and your daughter."

"My dad is the ghost hunter. It's him you need to talk to."

Her father stood tall, taller than she'd ever seen him. "I'd be honored."

"I could show you around the campus," Cindy said.

"As long as your husband wouldn't mind," her father said.

"No worries." She smiled warmly. "I'm not married."

As they started toward the other room, Peyton grabbed her arm and pulled her out of the dining room and behind the stairs.

"And what exactly are you planning to do with me here?" She raised her eyebrows.

"This." He pulled her into his arms and lowered his mouth.

His tongue caressed hers, and she could feel her body melting against his.

He ended the kiss all too soon, but he didn't let go of her. She was rather glad he didn't because this was exactly where she wanted to be.

"What you did was dangerous," she said.

"Because I might have ended up like the burned bush?"

"I was going to tell you about that. I figured you could handle only so many confessions in one day."

He chuckled, but just as quickly sobered. "Don't ever be afraid to trust me. I'll always be there for you."

"I know." And deep in her heart, she did. "But I'm not like your friends. I never went to college or anything."

"I don't care."

"I enjoy tinkering with motors and inventing machines like the zapper."

"As long as you don't take apart my motorcycle, I don't care."

"I'm just not sure a relationship will work between us."

"I'd wait forever for you."

She studied his face. She had a feeling he would. Maybe they would have a future together.

"Oh, there is one other little thing that I didn't mention. I sort of deleted the pictures of me that you took at the pond."

He frowned. "Those were fantastic pictures."

She sighed. "Yeah, I thought they were pretty good, too."

"I guess we'll just have to take more." He grinned, then nuzzled her neck.

Now, that sounded good. Very good.

DISCLAIMER:
No ghosts were harmed during the writing of this book.

Like this book? You'll love
DARING THE MOON by Sherrill Quinn,
out this month from Brava. . . .

"Look, Ms. Gibson . . . Taite." He sat next to her, angling his body so that their knees touched. When she shifted slightly, pulling back from him, he wasn't surprised. What *did* surprise him was the sense of hurt he felt at the movement. But it was no more than he deserved. "I know I've been . . . less than hospitable," he went on. "I'd like to apologize."

She did look at him then, her gaze solemn. She sighed and rubbed her fingers across her forehead. "Mr. Merrick—"

"Ryder. Please." He stretched his arm along the back of the sofa and leaned in toward her, just slightly, to gauge her reaction. She stayed put, though her pupils dilated and her lips parted.

After a moment, she broke his gaze and looked down at the book, one hand coming up to push a thick strand of hair behind her ear. "Ryder." Her voice was huskier than it had been.

His name on her lips sizzled like lightning through him. He wanted nothing more than to take her in his arms and protect her from the big bad wolf she was so afraid of.

But then who would protect her from *him?*

Meeting his gaze once more, she said, "I understand, really I do. We've descended upon you without notice and, from what I understand, against your wishes. And then we tell you this incredible story. . . ." She sighed and played with her hair, twirling a strand around and around her index finger.

"Still, it's no excuse for my poor behavior." He took her hand in his, and they both went still. He heard her breath catch and felt the thrumming of her pulse under his fingers. Rubbing his thumb over the back of her hand, he tried to remember what he'd been about to say.

She leaned forward, her gaze fastened on his mouth, and all thought fled his mind like water sliding down a drain. He couldn't ignore his need any longer. He had to get a taste of her. Setting his lips on hers, gently, Ryder sipped at her sweetness, taking her sigh into his mouth and returning his own.

When she moaned, he pulled her fully into his arms and leaned back, drawing her over the top of him. Dimly he heard the thud of the book as it fell to the floor and the flutter of paper as the tablet followed it, but his entire focus remained on the woman in his embrace.

Ryder slid his tongue over her bottom lip then sucked on it, eliciting another moan from her. He nipped her lightly and then slanted his mouth over hers once more.

Her softness settled over his erection and, when she shimmied against him, he groaned and moved his hands to her hips to hold her in place. God, she felt so good, so right. Forcing himself to slow down, he moved his lips to her jaw, then down her throat to the curve where her neck met her shoulder. Sliding his mouth over her skin, he rested his lips against the pulse pounding there.

Well, he thought with self-deprecating humor, *this sort of behavior is certainly what one should expect from a host.* But then the heat and smell of her drew his mind back to more carnal thoughts.

Life thrummed beneath his tongue. Lust roared through him, tightening his body all over, drawing his beast closer to the surface. With a low growl, he twisted, sliding her under him, rocking his erection against the cleft of her body.

"Ryder." Her voice was a rasp in his ear, her hands gripping his shoulders with fierceness.

He took her mouth again, nipping and licking and sucking until she cried out and clasped his head, holding his face to hers. Her tongue twisted around his, surging into his mouth when he retreated. He sucked on it, drawing her deeper, making them both groan.

Her nipples pressed like hard diamonds against his chest, branding him through their layers of clothing. His entire body was taut, something dark and primal inside him urging him to strip her naked and mount her then and there. Make her his. Savage possessiveness surged through his blood. His hands tightened, holding her still, and he crushed his mouth to hers, needing—demanding—a response.

Taite was springtime in his hands—fresh and light, bringing him such a sense of renewal, he felt it deep in his bones. She was everything he wasn't—soft, giving. Not wanting to scare her with his passion, to lose her before they'd even begun, he tempered his response, gentled his touch.

Drawing slowly back, he rested his forehead against hers. "I've wanted to do that from the moment you walked through my front door. What you do to me . . ."

"Is no more than what you do to me." She rolled her forehead back and forth on his, then turned her face to one side. "I can't do this."

"Can't do what?" When she pushed at his shoulders, trying to lever him off her, he settled his weight more completely on top of her. "Can't do what?" he asked again.

She made a vague gesture with her hand, indicating him, then her. "This." She pushed at him again, frowning when he wouldn't budge. "I've got enough trouble without adding to it."

Somehow, hearing her put his own feelings into words irritated him. "So, you think I'm trouble?"

Giving him a look that suggested not only was he trouble but he was also a bit on the slow side, she shoved against his chest. This time he moved, sitting in the place where she'd been.

She bent over and retrieved the book and tablet. He heard

her deep breath as she sat up, saw the trembling in her hands. Her arousal was a sweet musk in his nostrils, and he started to reach for her.

One slender hand came up, palm outward, warding him off. "Don't." She fisted her hand and let it fall to her thigh. "Just . . . don't. Not now."

Ryder sat back and ran his hand through his hair. She was right. Of course she was right. He had to share what knowledge he could and then send them on their way. No matter how much he wanted to lose himself in her sweet warmth, it wasn't meant to be.

And don't miss Lucy Monroe's latest,
THE SPY WHO WANTS ME,
available now. . . .

"That is one sweet ride," Beau said as he got out of the passenger side of Elle's Spider.

"I like it."

"It's easy to see why."

They'd pulled up in front of a sprawling Mission-style home, an hour east of L.A. in the desert. The neighboring houses were far enough away to ensure real privacy. Used to the cramped and crowded conditions, even in their smaller community out of Los Angeles city proper, Beau took a deep breath, enjoying the sense of space. "Nice."

"It was a good place tog row up."

"It reminds me of home."

"Where is that?"

"East Texas."

"So, that's where that sexy drawl comes from"

"You think my drawl is sexy?" he asked, purposefully stretching his syllables with a Texan twang.

She grinned. "It's sexier when you aren't doing a Keith Urban impersonation."

"Bite your tongue. That good ol' boy is from Down Under. Not the sacred state of Texas. His drawl ain't anything like mine."

"I didn't know there was such a thing as a sacred state." She rolled her eyes for emphasis.

He leaned forward until he was whispering right next to her ear. "That's because you weren't' raised in Texas."

"Oh," she whispered back. "So, it's some kind of secret, huh?"

He moved even closer until he was as close to her super-model body as he could get without actually touching. Then he leaned in so his lips actually did touch the shell of her ear. "I'll share my secrets with you if you share yours with me."

Her while body shuddered, and if that didn't send him zero to sixty from one breath to the next. His cock ached and pressed insistently against the fly of his good jeans.

He flicked his tongue out and tasted the sensitive skin just under her earlobe. "What do you say? You ready to share your secrets with me?"

Damn if she didn't turn just so and lean her forehead against his shoulder. She didn't say anything, but he could feel tension emanating off of her.

He nuzzled into her neck, still whispering. "You got a lot of secrets, princess?"

"Who doesn't?" Her voice was quiet and muffled against his body.

He didn't know why he did it, but he rubbed her back in comfort. Just right then, the beautiful government agent who was lying to him and pretending to be nothing more than a security consultant seemed vulnerable. And he wanted to protect her. Take al her cares away.

What a sap.

Vulnerable. Right.

It was probably part of her act. Her cover. Only he felt like there was something growing between them. Something real and inescapable.

Dumb.

She was just doing her job and pretending to be something she wasn't to get information her agency wanted about his company.

He *had* to remember that.

If only he could convince his body to listen. Never mind the heart he was smart enough not to risk for a woman who was living a lie.

Be sure to catch
INSTANT ATTRACTION,
the first in a new series from Jill Shalvis,
coming next month from Brava. . . .

She'd been working for Wilder Adventures for a week now, the best week in recent memory. Up until right this second when a shadowy outline of a man appeared in her room. Like the newly brave woman she was, she threw the covers over her head and hoped he hadn't seen her.

"Hey," he said, blowing that hope all to hell.

His voice was low and husky, sounding just as surprised as she. With a deep breath she lurched upright to a seated position on the bed and reached out for her handy-dandy baseball bat before remembering she hadn't brought it with her. Instead, her hands connected with her glasses and they went flying.

Which might just have been a blessing in disguise, because now she wouldn't be able to witness her own death.

But then the tall shadow bent and scooped up her glasses and . . .

Handed them to her.

A considerate bad guy?

She jammed the frames on her face and focused in the dim light coming from the living room lamp. He stood at the foot of the bed frowning right back at her, hands on his hips.

Huh.

He didn't look like an ax murderer, which was good, very good, but at over six feet of impressive, rangy, solid-looking muscle, he didn't exactly look like a harmless tooth fairy either.

"Why are you in my bed?" he asked warily, as if maybe he'd put her there but couldn't quite remember.

He had a black duffel bag slung over a shoulder. Light brown hair stuck out from the edges of his knit ski cap to curl around his neck. Sharp green eyes were leveled on hers, steady and calm but irritated as he opened his denim jacket.

If he was an ax murderer, he was quite possibly the most attractive one she'd ever seen, which didn't do a thing for her frustration level. She'd been finally sleeping.

Sleeping!

He could have no idea what a welcome miracle that had been, damn it.

"Earth to Goldilocks." He waved a gloved hand until she dragged her gaze back up to his face. "Yeah, hi. My bed. Want to tell me why you're in it?"

"I've been sleeping here for a week." Granted, she'd had a hard time of it lately, but she definitely would have noticed *him* in bed with her.

"Who told you to sleep here?"

"My boss, Stone Wilder. Well, technically, Annie, the chef, but—" She broke off when he reached toward her, clutching the comforter to her chin as if the down feathers could protect her, really wishing for that handy-dandy bat.

But instead of killing her, he hit the switch to the lamp on the nightstand and more fully illuminated the room as he dropped his duffel bag.

While Katie tried to slow her heart rate, he pulled off his jacket and gloves, and tossed them territorially to the chest at the foot of the bed.

His clothes seemed normal enough. Beneath the jacket he wore a fleece-lined sweatshirt opened over a long-sleeved brown Henley, half untucked over faded Levi's. The jeans were loose and low on his hips, baggy over unlaced Sorrels, the entire ensemble revealing that he was in prime condition.

"My name is Katie Kramer," she told him, hoping he'd return the favor. "Wilder Adventures's new office temp." She paused, but he didn't even attempt to fill the awkward silence. "So that leaves you . . ."

"What happened to Riley?"

"Who?"

"The current office manager."

"I think she's on maternity leave."

"That must be news to his wife."

She met his cool gaze. "Okay, obviously I'm new. I don't know all the details since I've only been here a week."

"Here, being my cabin, of course."

"Stone told me that the person who used to live here had left."

"Ah." His eyes were the deepest, most solid green she'd ever seen as they regarded her. "I did leave. I also just came back."

She winced, clutching the covers a little tighter to her chest. "So this cabin . . . Does it belong to an ax murderer?"

That tugged a rusty-sounding laugh from him. "Haven't sunk that low. Yet." Pulling off his cap, he shoved his fingers through his hair. With those sleepy-lidded eyes, disheveled hair, and at least two days' growth on his jaw, he looked big and bad and edgy—and quite disturbingly sexy with it. "I need sleep." He dropped his long, tough self to the chair by the bed, as if so weary he could no longer stand. He set first one and then the other booted foot on the mattress, grimacing as if he were hurting, though she didn't see any reason for that on his body as he settled back, lightly linking his hands together low on his flat abs. Then he let out a long, shuddering sigh.

She stared at more than six feet of raw power and testosterone in disbelief. "You still haven't said who you are."

"Too Exhausted To Go Away."

She did some more staring at him, but he didn't appear to care. "Hello?" she said after a full moment of stunned silence. "You can't just—"

"Can. And am." And with that, he closed his eyes. " 'Night, Goldilocks."